Homeward Trails  Book Two

THE
CORPORAL'S
Codebook

Susan Page Davis

Scrivenings PRESS
Quench your thirst for story.
www.ScriveningsPress.com

©2021 Susan Page Davis

Published by Scrivenings Press LLC
15 Lucky Lane
Morrilton, Arkansas 72110
https://ScriveningsPress.com

Printed in the United States of America

Paperback ISBN 978-1-64917-163-4

eBook ISBN 978-1-64917-164-1

Library of Congress Control Number: 2021948006

Cover by www.bookmarketinggraphics.com.

All scriptures are taken from the KING JAMES VERSION (KJV): KING JAMES VERSION, public domain.

All characters are fictional, and any resemblance to real people, either factual or historical, is purely coincidental.

1

August 1845
Albany, New York

"I'm sorry we came all this way for nothing." Charles Miller took his sister Amy's arm. "Are you ready to go?"

Amy sighed and looked around at the room full of hopeful boys and stern-faced adults. "It's all right, Charles. You didn't know they wouldn't have any girls. But I know Daniel wouldn't like it if I came home with a boy. Especially not a half-grown boy who looks tough." She shivered, surveying the candidates for adoption.

"I should have inquired further," he said.

"No, you were busy with Papa's funeral and the estate."

He followed her gaze to a boy in trousers that were too short and a coarse cotton shirt two sizes too big. When he sensed them looking at him, the boy straightened and stared pleadingly into Amy's eyes.

"That little boy looks different."

Charles noted a fading bruise on the child's left cheekbone. Their eyes met, and Charles pulled in a deep breath.

"Why don't you get some tea? Let me have a few words with him."

"I can't take a boy." Amy's voice rose in a warning.

Charles patted her shoulder. "I know. But everyone's ignoring him, and he looks as though he could use some attention."

"Fine, then." Amy glided away, and Charles ambled over to the boy.

"Hello, young fella."

"Hello."

"What's your name?"

"Elijah, sir." The boy swallowed hard. "But I'm willing to answer to another name."

That struck Charles's heart like a dart. "Come sit down, Elijah." He led the boy to a bench near the wall. "How do you like it here?"

Elijah's eyes flickered, but he said nothing.

"It's all right to tell me," Charles said. Still nothing. "I see you've got a bruise on your face. How did that happen?"

"I'm not from here," the boy said quickly.

"Oh?"

He nodded. "They brought me here from White Plains. I don't even know where we are."

"We're in Albany, son."

Elijah blinked. "That's the capital."

"Right." Charles couldn't help smiling. "How old are you?"

"I think I'm six, sir. My birthday's August first. Have we passed it?"

"Yes, a couple of weeks ago."

Elijah nodded soberly. "I thought so, it being so hot for a while."

He was very well-spoken for his age, Charles thought. "Why did they bring you here, son?"

"Nobody wanted me at the other orphanage. They brought a bunch of us boys up here so different people could look at us."

"I see." The advertisement had said boys suitable for farm

work. He'd been visiting his sister, and they'd thought they would chance it, since Amy hoped so badly for a girl. Charles looked the boy over. He was a bit small for his age, but he seemed bright and able to speak well for himself. "So, why were you in that other orphanage?"

Elijah pulled in a ragged breath then another.

"It's all right," Charles said gently. "You don't have to tell me."

"Please take me, sir."

His heart lurched and he looked around quickly, spotting Amy with a cup of tea in her hands, talking to a well-dressed couple near the refreshment table.

"Son, I can't do that. I'm sorry I got your hopes up. I brought my sister here—Mrs. Wells over there, in the black dress. She was hoping to find a baby girl here."

"They didn't bring any girls," Elijah said, his voice on the verge of cracking. "I had a baby sister, but they took her already. In White Plains."

"Who took her?" Charles could sense the boy's despair, and it squeezed his own heart.

"A man and a woman. I don't know their names. Mr. Cresswick said they'd take good care of her, but they wouldn't let me and Zeph say good-bye."

"Who's Zeph?"

"My brother. A man came wanting a boy that could work hard on a farm. Zeph tried to get him to take me too, but he said he could only feed one, and anyway, I was too small."

Charles sighed. "I'm sorry that happened to you. Do they take good care of you?"

Elijah's blue eyes darkened. "I can't speak about how things are here—unless it is to lie and say that all is well. Please, sir. I'm all alone now. And the other boys—" He gave a little sob.

The orphanage director strolled over and stood before them. "Well, Mr. Miller, find a boy you like the looks of?"

"Perhaps," Charles said. "I understand this boy hasn't been living here, but he's from White Plains."

The man shrugged. "From time to time we make a combined effort to find new homes for the children. It gets them in front of a new set of prospects."

And helps you unload some of the troublemakers no one has cottoned to yet, Charles thought.

"We're getting acquainted," he said, as pleasantly as he could manage.

"Then I'll leave you to it."

As the administrator nodded and moved away, Charles noted that Elijah exhaled, as though he'd been holding his breath.

"Elijah," he said softly, "this is very important to me, and I want you to be honest. Do the staff members ever punish you?"

The boy's eyes widened. "Every day, sir, if we do something wrong. If we are late for lessons or a meal, or if we don't finish a chore on time."

"I see. And how is this punishment administered?"

Elijah shuddered. "Most times with a stick. Or a strap. It depends. Mr. Cresswick favors a belt."

"Mm." Charles leaned close and saw that the bruise extended around the side of the boy's cheek and up toward his eye. "Did you get that here, or in White Plains?"

"On the way, sir. I took a few oats from the horses' pail." He ducked his head and stared at the floor.

"Why?" Charles asked.

"They hadn't fed us, sir."

"You were hungry enough to swipe a handful of the horses' feed?"

Elijah nodded, not looking at him.

"How long were you kept unfed?"

"All day, sir. The driver and the man they sent along with us had a lunch, but we boys had nothin'."

Charles leaped to his feet, and Elijah cringed back against the wall.

"I'm sorry," Charles said. "I didn't mean to frighten you.

Please wait here. I'll be back, but I must talk to the director for a moment."

The boy gazed up at him, fear in his glistening eyes. "Am I in trouble?"

Charles could barely hear the words.

"No, son. Not a bit of it. I am going to ask what it would take to adopt you. What do you say?"

Elijah's lower lip trembled. "I say thank you, sir! Even if he won't let you, thank you. I'll always remember your kindness."

Charles had a word with the director, who was eager to hustle him into his office to sign documents. He paused to speak to his sister.

"Don't let that boy out of your sight, Amy. He's going with us."

"What? Oh, no, Charles! I told you—"

"It's all right. If you and Daniel can't take him, I will. This shouldn't take long." He glanced at the sandwiches and tea cakes on the long table. All of the boys were avoiding the food, and he was sure they'd been told not to even think of going near it. "Do me a favor. Load up a plate and go share it with him while I take care of business."

She stared at him. "You're serious. All right, then. I hope Frances is more receptive than Daniel would be."

"HOW COULD YOU DO THIS?"

The woman's face contorted, and Elijah edged back against the closed door.

"Charles, we already have four children."

"Now, Fran, take it easy." Mr. Miller stepped forward and touched the woman's shoulder. "I couldn't leave him there. If you'd been in my place, you'd have done the same thing."

"I highly doubt it."

"It was awful, Frances." Mr. Miller had lowered his voice, but

Elijah could still hear him. "Those boys, they were desperate, all of them."

Mrs. Miller pulled in a ragged breath and looked Elijah up and down. He tried not to shrink from her gaze.

"Couldn't you at least have got a healthy one?"

"Believe me, this one's the pick of the litter." Mr. Miller turned to face Elijah and slipped his arm around his wife's waist. "Some of them looked sick. One of them had his arm in a sling. Most of them had bruises."

Elijah blinked, and the puffy skin around his left eye hurt. Exhausted, he leaned back against the hard door to keep from swaying on his feet.

"Mama?" A little girl with long, flowing hair tiptoed into the room. Her flannel nightgown brushed the floor as she moved. "Who's that?" She stabbed a plump little finger toward him.

Her mother opened her mouth, but Mr. Miller was quicker.

"That's your new brother, Jack."

His wife glared at him.

"I have a new brother?" The little girl sounded babyish. She stepped toward him in her bare feet, her eyes wide.

"Caroline, go back to bed," Mrs. Miller said.

"I want to see Papa and Jack."

"Jack." The woman's frown deepened, making deep grooves in her cheeks on either side of her mouth. "Is that why you picked him? Because he had the same name as my poor, dead brother?"

"No, but ..." Mr. Miller and stooped and plucked the little girl up into his arms. "I thought we could call him Jack, in your Jack's memory. I asked the kid, and he said it's all right."

Elijah would have agreed to anything if it meant getting away from the orphanage for good, and Jack sounded like a manly name. One that other boys would make less fun of than Elijah.

In some ways, he wanted to scream and kick and run away. If Mr. Miller gave him a new name, wouldn't that make it harder for Zeph to find him, if he was able to try? On the way, he'd toyed with the idea of escaping from the train and setting out on his own to find Zeph. The couple who took his brother away lived in Tarrytown, he knew that.

He might be able to get away from Mr. Miller when they got to the city and had to leave the train. He could somehow make his way to Tarrytown. He had an idea it wasn't too far from New York.

But Mr. Miller seemed like a kind person. He kept buying food at nearly every train stop and plying Elijah with sandwiches and fruit. If he ran away, he could be much worse off. When they stopped in New York and changed trains, Elijah didn't leave his side.

"Jack Miller," the man had said with a smile. "Sounds pretty good, doesn't it?"

"Yes, sir."

Now Mrs. Miller was objecting to the name. Would she refuse to keep him because her husband had given him her dead brother's name? Elijah hoped not. He liked Mr. Miller. The house, what he'd seen of it, wasn't fancy, but it was as good as the one he'd grown up in. And the kitchen smelled good.

Mrs. Miller stood simmering for a long moment. Elijah could almost feel the heat peeling off her. Finally she reached for Caroline and shifted her onto her hip. "I'm going to put her back to bed. I don't know where he'll sleep."

She left the room, and Elijah darted a glance at Mr. Miller.

"Don't worry, son. You'll have a place to sleep." He looked around. "It may be on the floor near the stove for tonight, but I'll make sure you have a bed tomorrow. Stay here and I'll bring you a blanket and a pillow."

She doesn't want me, Elijah wanted to say, but he swallowed the words.

2

June 20, 1849
Emmaus, Pennsylvania

Jack knocked smartly on the door to the girls' bedroom.

"What?" came Caroline's voice.

He pushed open the door and saluted. "Afternoon, Miss Miller." He nodded toward her doll, which sat in a small wooden chair their father had crafted. "Miss Juliet."

"What do you want?"

"I have a telegram for Miss Juliet."

Caroline blinked at him. "My dolly got a telegram?"

"That's right." Jack held out a folded piece of paper.

Caroline took it and opened it. "No fair. It's in Morse."

"So."

"Telegraph people are supposed to change it into regular words before they deliver it."

Jack sighed. "I did it to help you practice code. You can read it."

Her lips waggled back and forth as she frowned over the message he'd penciled. Caroline was only seven, and she was still learning to read well, but she was quick. Jack had started

9

teaching her Morse Code soon after their father introduced him to it. Pa now made a good wage as a telegraph operator at a desk in the local post office.

The children saw it as somewhat of a game, but the older girls, Jenny and Elizabeth, had soon tired of it. Jack was eager to find a partner who would practice with him. Ned was too young, and the youngest boy, Silas, was barely toddling about.

"It doesn't make sense," his sister whined. A moment later, Caroline's frown vanished in a flash, and she wriggled. "Meet at the swing?"

Jack grinned. "Told you!" He dashed down the stairs and through to the back door. In the back yard, a swing hung from a low branch on a big maple tree. Pushing Caro for a few minutes would be her reward for solving his message.

He didn't have to wait long. Caroline came out the back door holding Miss Juliet tightly against her pinafore.

"You have to swing us," she said.

"Of course."

"For an hour."

Jack wrinkled up his face. "That's crazy. Ten minutes."

"Fifteen."

"Only if you write a message back to me."

She pushed her lips into her signature pout. "I'll think about it."

"Well, climb aboard, and let me push you while you think."

Soon Caroline and Miss Juliet were flying toward the sky. The little girl's feet went higher than the clothesline, and she squealed in delight.

The ten minutes were nearly up, Jack judged, when he heard his name called. Ma Miller stood on the back stoop, watching them and holding a lard pail.

Jack grabbed the swing's seat board and slowed Caroline to a halt.

"More," she roared.

"No, I've got to take Pa his dinner pail."

Caroline jumped down and flounced into the house.

Ma smiled wearily. "I don't suppose you'd take Ned with you?"

"Sure." Ned, at five, was quite a handful, and Jack tried to entertain him whenever he could. It grew tiresome, but he loved his brother. The Miller home was a pretty good place to have landed, and he tried to do his part with the little ones. Chasing them around tired their mother out worse than doing laundry for the growing family, especially in summer, between school terms.

Ned was in the kitchen, polishing off an apple Ma had no doubt given him to distract him.

"You go with Jack," she told the younger boy. "And stay with him, you hear me?"

The warning was not given without reason. Since he first began to walk, Ned loved to run and explore.

"I'll watch him, Ma." Jack took the lunch pail. "Come on, Ned. Let's go."

Jack walked briskly, but Ned ran loops, dashing ahead and circling back.

"Watch it," Jack yelled when a wagon came toward them down the street.

Ned darted back to his side, but as soon as the wagon passed, he was off again.

"Race you!"

They were within sight of the post office, so Jack let him go.

Pa was talking to a man when he stepped inside the post office, speaking through a metal grille where folks handed in their messages for him to send. Ned had slipped inside the cubicle and was cuddled against his father's knee, fiddling with Pa's pencil. Jack hung back and waited until the other man left.

"Got your lunch, Pa." He stepped forward and held out the bucket.

"Thanks. I hoped I'd get home this noon, but we've been busy."

Whenever he didn't show up for lunch, Ma packed his lard pail and either sent one of the children to deliver it or took it herself. Since Silas's birth just over a year ago, she depended more and more on Jack and the two older girls.

Pa laughed and chatted with them for a few minutes, until a customer came in to give him a message to transmit.

"Best take Ned home," he said to Jack.

The second they were out the door, Ned raced off toward home.

"Come back," Jack yelled. Several people looked at him, and his face grew hot. He began to run. There was no controlling Ned when he got bored.

Jack jogged along, keeping sight of Ned's gray shirt farther up the block. The rambunctious boy ran at full tilt—until he slammed into a man coming out of a shop. Jack could hear the man's protests clear down the street, and he quickened his pace. Ned had toppled into a water trough at the edge of the street and was now sitting up, spluttering.

"You're nothing but a rapscallion," the man ranted at Ned.

Jack arrived panting. "I'm sorry, sir. He's my brother. I'll take him home."

"I should hope so." The man turned and stalked away without so much as another glance at Ned, who was now sitting miserably in the water trough.

"I didn't mean to." His face scrunched up like a withered apple.

"Of course you didn't." Jack extended a hand to help him clamber out of the trough. "You never mean to. Yet somehow you always do."

Ned climbed out and stood still for once, with water pouring off him and dripping from his clothes.

"Ma won't be pleased," Jack noted.

"Maybe I can sneak in the back."

"No, if you don't go in with me, she'll want to know where you are. You've got to take your lumps, Ned."

Water continued to trickle down the younger boy's face, but Jack couldn't tell if it was from his dunking or tears.

He sighed and reached for Ned's hand. "Come on. If Ma's in the kitchen, you can duck into our room and get changed. Drop your wet things out the back window, and I'll throw them over the clothesline. But if Ma sees them, you've got to fess up."

"All right." Ned hung his head. His feet dragged the rest of the way home.

Ma sat at the kitchen table peeling potatoes when Jack reported to her.

"Pa says he'll try to be on time for supper, and thanks very much for the dinner pail."

"That's fine, Jack. Where's Ned?"

"He went in our room." Jack chatted a minute longer, then slipped out the back door. There were Ned's soaked trousers, shirt, drawers, and socks, lying in a heap under the window, his bedraggled shoes lay jumbled nearby. Jack hadn't thought about the shoes. He would have to oil them tonight if they didn't want their parents to find out.

He sighed and scooped up the soggy clothing, hoping someday Ned would learn to take care of himself.

3

July 3, 1855
Emmaus, Pennsylvania

Jack's pulse raced as he followed his father into the post office on a hot Tuesday morning. They walked over to the booth that held the telegraph station, where Pa worked ten hours a day, five days a week. His supervisor, Mr. Bane, sat behind the grille looking harried and worn out, with dark smudges beneath his watery gray eyes.

"Morning, Mr. Bane," Pa said.

"Miller. You have no idea how glad I am to see you."

"Busy night?"

"More so than usual. Tomorrow's Independence Day, you know, and there's been some holdup on getting the fireworks in hand. Even the mayor's involved. I think it's straightened out now, and we'll have our display on time, but ..." Bane shuddered. "If this receiver starts up, it's all yours."

"I wanted to ask you something," Pa said quickly, knowing he'd lose his audience in a flash. "I know we've been shorthanded since Douglas left."

"You wouldn't see me sitting up all night here if we had a

replacement," Bane said sourly. "But I might have a lead on a new fellow." He glanced hopefully up at Charles. "I don't suppose you'd take off early, say three o'clock, and come back at midnight?"

"Well ..." Pa glanced over his shoulder at Jack. "Maybe. But there might be another solution."

"I'm open to anything. Do you know someone?"

"My son, Jack, here—"

"He's only a boy."

"He's sixteen, or nearly, and he's very good at code. He could give you a demonstration."

Bane frowned, looking him over. Jack tried to stand as tall as possible, his shoulders straight, with a neutral expression on his face. How he'd love to get a job and be able to help Ma and Pa.

Raising eight children took money, no two ways about it. And they'd taken Jack in when he had no one. It pained him to think the other children would have more if he wasn't there, to the point where he often refused seconds at mealtime.

"I don't know."

At Bane's doubtful tone, Pa said hastily, "He's almost as good as me, Mr. Bane. I wouldn't stretch the truth on that. Give the boy a chance."

"Well ... we couldn't let him work alone here."

"Let me keep him with me today and tomorrow. You can go home and rest. Come in later today, or tomorrow morning, and see him in action."

Bane rose and walked stiffly to a cupboard on the far wall of the little office. He lifted a metal item and brought it to the window. Jack recognized it as a telegraph key, but it wasn't attached to a receiver or the wires that went through the wall.

"This is an old piece of equipment," Bane said, looking at Jack. "We don't use it anymore, but you can tap out a message on it."

"Yes, sir," Jack said.

Pa stepped aside, allowing Jack to move in close to the window.

"What do you want it to say, sir?" Jack asked.

Bane thought for a moment. "Send this: If you can send and receive accurately on the first try, you've got a job."

Jack grinned and put his hand to the key, tapping out the code for each word swiftly but carefully. He ended the message with R BANE, EMMAUS PA.

He looked up at Mr. Bane. The supervisor lifted his chin slightly, looking down his nose at Jack with an enigmatic stare. After a moment he said, "All right, now tell me what message is coming in."

Pa stood beside Jack with his eyes closed. Jack fancied he was praying the real telegraph—the one that was wired up and working—wouldn't start clicking while this interview continued.

Mr. Bane placed his first two fingers on the key Jack had used and started depressing it in a distinctive pattern. Jack listened for perhaps fifteen seconds, until Bane stopped.

"You heard?" Mr. Bane said.

"When we are planning for posterity, we ought to remember that virtue is not hereditary." Jack smiled. "Sent from yourself, sir, but I believe from Thomas Paine originally."

Bane looked at Pa. "Well. Though virtue is not hereditary, it seems intelligence and keen wit are."

Charles laughed. "You forget, Jack is not my natural son."

"That's right. I applaud you, Miller. You seem to have cultivated this lad's sharp mind and a good deal of diligence. Keep him here today. Tomorrow I'll stay when I come off duty and watch him take a real message or two. Meanwhile, fill him in on procedure, delivery, all that."

"With pleasure." Pa beamed at Jack.

As Mr. Bane emerged from the booth, the apparatus began to receive.

"That one's all yours, Miller," Bane nodded at Jack and headed for the door.

Jack edged into the small office and stood at Pa's elbow while he transcribed the incoming message. Jack didn't dare speak aloud while Pa concentrated. He couldn't help translating the code in his head.

At the final stop, Pa sighed and looked up at him. "You heard?"

"Yes. Mrs. Kane's mother died. She's to go at once."

Charles nodded soberly. "We get a lot of those. Can you keep from absorbing other people's woe, Jack?"

"I ... think so."

"Well, we need Benny Jackson to deliver it."

"I could deliver it, Pa."

"No, you'd be taking Benny's work from him. Besides, you need to stay here and learn the rest of the job, beyond just the code."

"Right."

That afternoon, Pa sent Jack home at three o'clock. "Days are long here, son, and you need to come with me tomorrow morning rested and ready to work."

When he reached home, he went straight to the kitchen, where Ma Miller was snapping green beans and tossing them into a large kettle.

Her eyes brightened when she saw him. "How did it go?"

"I'm hired."

"Thought so when you didn't come home all day. Congratulations, son."

Jack filched a piece of a green bean and popped it in his mouth.

"Thanks. I'm going in with Pa again tomorrow. He thinks I should be able to work on my own after that, but Mr. Bane will have to decide. Ma, I should be able to give you and Pa some toward my keep."

Her face melted, and he thought she might burst into tears. "Oh, Jack. There's no need for that. You're our son."

"I know. But I'm part of this family, and I eat my share. I want to help. With Elizabeth getting married ..."

"Oh, Jack." She waved a hand frantically for him to leave and lifted her apron to her face.

Jack tiptoed away. He was sorry he'd made her cry, but very pleased at the likelihood he would soon be able to contribute to the family's expenses.

He heard chatter and giggling from overhead, so he bounded up the stairs and paused in the open doorway to the girls' room. Caro and Ruthie were sitting on Caro's bed with another girl he didn't know. The other girl was wiggling her fingers at three-year-old Ruthie, in a threat of tickles to come. Ruthie shrieked with laughter.

Caro glanced his way. "Hey, Jack! You're home."

"Think so?" He enjoyed teasing Caroline mildly, and she was the only one of his sisters who took it well. "Who's this?" He nodded toward the visitor.

"Oh, that's Marilla. She's in Ned's class. Her mother said she could come help me watch Ruthie and keep her out of Ma's hair. I get to hem up my new skirt while they play."

"I see," Jack said.

"I'm teaching Marilla Morse Code."

Jack eyed the little girl, who must be about ten, with keener interest. "You like codes?"

She nodded with enthusiasm. "I want to be a telegraph operator when I grow up."

"Jack's going to be one," Caro said. "Aren't you, Jack?"

"Looks like it. Mr. Bane let me stay with Pa all day today, and I'm going in with him tomorrow. If Mr. Bane thinks I'm good enough, I've got a job."

Caro let out a whoop, and Ruthie mimicked it. Marilla just grinned at him.

"That's stupendous," Caro said.

"Yeah, all our practice paid off."

"You hear that, Marilla? You can do it too. All our games will help you gain an occupation."

"Do you want to be an operator too?" Marilla asked.

"Maybe." Caro considered that and shook her head. "I don't think so. I think I want to be an author. But I'll wait and see."

"Well, don't stop practicing, just in case," Jack said. He didn't want to lose his cryptography partner—although he might be too busy now to send pretend messages to his sister. He'd quit sending them to her doll a couple of years ago, when Caroline had placed Miss Juliet on a shelf, declaring she was too old to play with dolls anymore. But if Caro discovered selling poetry and novels was hard to do, she might fall back on her coding skills.

"Are you going to see the fireworks tomorrow night?" Caroline asked her guest.

Marilla's face fell. "Mama says we can't go into town."

"Well, you should be able to see them from your front porch."

"I hope so." Marilla sounded sad. She probably just wished she could go with her friends.

"She and her ma are staying with Mrs. Clayton," Caro explained to Jack. "Her ma and Mrs. Clayton are cousins."

Jack nodded, wondering where Marilla's pa was, but he didn't ask. The little girl looked sad enough when she wasn't laughing with Ruthie. He figured chances were good that her father was deceased, and he didn't want to make her sadder. She looked downright jolly when she laughed.

"I'll write you a message, Marilla, and you see if you can decode it."

"All right." She bounced a little on the bed, and Ruthie bounced twice as hard.

Jack determined to make his code message funny. He wanted to make Marilla laugh again.

4

1857, Philadelphia

"You watch that cat, now," Mama said. "I'll be filling the lamps, and I don't want him to come near."

"Yes, ma'am." Marilla picked up the wriggly ball of orange fur. She'd only been allowed to keep the stray a month ago.

She'd longed for a dog, since it was unlikely she'd ever get a little sister or brother, but Mama had always said no until now. They couldn't afford to feed a dog, she'd said.

Then Marilla had found Feathers. He'd hung around the narrow lane behind their house, mewing. When she went out to investigate, he'd allowed her to give him a bit of chicken skin and then to pet him.

"A cat will earn his way," Marilla had reasoned. "He'll catch mice and keep them from getting into things. That will save us money."

At last, Mama had given in. Mice had chewed her crochet cotton and invaded the pantry. So far, Feathers had caught at least two mice, and Marilla was terribly proud of him. But she had to keep him from getting into things too, and from bothering Mama when she was working.

She took him into the other room of their tiny house, where their beds stood. The front room served as kitchen and sitting room both. Mama hated it, but Marilla felt safe here.

It was small and cramped, but it was their own. Mama said living in their own little box was better than paying someone each month for the privilege of living in theirs.

Sitting down on her bed with Feathers in her arms, she stroked his glossy fur. "If we had a bigger house," she whispered to him. "We'd have a lot more room to play."

Most of her schoolmates lived in larger houses. Tears threatened, and she set the cat down on the coverlet. When Papa was alive, they'd lived in a big house with four bedrooms and a verandah. She didn't remember it exactly, but Mama had told her about it many times. But then Papa died.

The move was Mama's choice. Marilla wasn't really sure why she'd preferred living in the North in poverty to apparent ease in Georgia. Maybe Mama would have needed to get a job down there too, and it was easier to find work up here.

The first few years hadn't been so bad. Marilla had fond memories of the pleasant little cottage in Emmaus and Mama's cousin Anne. She'd gone to school and made friends. The Miller children were her favorites, and they'd treated her like part of their big, boisterous family.

But then Cousin Anne had died, and the last two years had been awful for Marilla and Mama. The cottage had gone to some relative of Anne Clayton's late husband. Mama and Marilla had been forced to move into this tiny place, in a Philadelphia neighborhood where they didn't know anyone. Mama found sporadic work, sewing or baking for other people.

Outside, a wagon loaded with lumber was passing, and the huge horses pulling it caught Marilla's fancy. She got up and went to the window. Those big steeds might be pulling a princess's coach. The owners would dress them in a fine harness though, not those plain, heavy straps. They'd have tassels on their browbands and shimmery bridles, without those square, black blinders on the sides.

She could just imagine the coachman jumping down in his bright silk uniform to open the door for the princess. In Marilla's imagination, that princess looked awfully like herself.

A crash and a scream from the kitchen jerked her from her fantasy, and she whirled around. The bedroom door stood open, and her mother's hoarse voice continued in broken cries.

Marilla ran to the doorway. Flames leaped all over her mother's body, speeding up her skirt to her basque, and even reached her hair.

With a yowl, Feathers tore past her to the front door. He meowed loudly and clawed at the crack between the door and the jamb.

"Mama!"

Her mother rolled on the floor, beating at the flames. Tongues of fire raced across the floor to a fallen lamp, and instantly the kitchen roared with searing flame.

Marilla darted to the door choking on smoke and ran out, the orange cat running before her and flitting off around the house.

She beat a path to the next house and found her voice as she ran.

"Mrs. Steele! Help!"

As she reached the neighbor's stoop, the door opened, and Mrs. Steele faced her, curious and then afraid.

"What's happened, child?"

"Mama," Marilla gasped. "Fire!"

"I'm so sorry about your mama," Mrs. Steele said. "You did fine at the funeral."

Marilla didn't think so. She'd sat mopping her tears and feeling miserable through the short sermon and then had to face the few neighbors and church people who came to the service. She'd had no idea what to say to them, but Mrs. Steele had stood beside her and made excuses and thanked everyone. Now they were back at the Steeles' house, where Marilla had stayed for the past three days.

She looked down at her stiff black dress. She hated the feel of the material. It was poorly made, compared to what Mama would have sewn, but Mrs. Steele and her daughter, Deborah, had stitched it up quickly. They'd insisted a black dress was imperative for the funeral.

Mr. Steele had gone into the Buckleys' old house with several men from the Fire Committee and brought out a few things—the miniature of her mother, a couple of books, Mama's small sewing box, and most of Marilla's clothes. Although the fire had been confined to the kitchen, Marilla wasn't allowed to go over there.

She hadn't seen the orange cat since. Nor did she want to see him, because then she'd have to think about how she hadn't latched the bedroom door tightly, and Feathers had escaped while she watched a team of horses pulling a wagon.

"May I change?" she whispered.

"No, dear. Mr. Doss is coming to talk to you. Have you met him before?"

Marilla shook her head. She turned the name over in her mind, but she didn't recognize it. "Who is he?"

"He's an attorney, dear."

That seemed odd, but Marilla said nothing.

She followed Mrs. Steele into the parlor. A tall man in a black suit stood looking out the window. He turned toward them and smiled when he saw her, but the smile didn't help Marilla feel better. All day people had smiled at her, and yet no one was happy. How did they expect to encourage her when all the people who'd truly loved her were dead?

"You must be Miss Buckley."

She wanted to hide her face, or better yet, run from the

room, but she pulled in a deep breath and stood tall. "I'm Marilla."

"Sit down, won't you? I'm Mr. Doss."

She perched on Mrs. Steele's uncomfortable horsehair sofa and eyed him uneasily as he claimed a chair opposite her.

"How old are you, my dear?" he asked, appraising her with sharp eyes.

"Twelve."

He nodded. "Your mother left instructions for your care in the event of ... in case she couldn't be here herself."

In case she died, Marilla thought. Why didn't people speak plainly? A tear escaped her right eye and dribbled down onto her dress.

"There, dear." Mrs. Steele settled on the sofa beside her and handed her a handkerchief.

"I have one." Marilla pulled the black-edged square of linen from her pocket and dabbed at her eyes. Would she ever stop crying, or would this go on forever?

"I sent a message to your great-uncle in Georgia," Mr. Doss said, "and he has responded by telegram."

Marilla caught her breath, and a sharp hitch pricked her in the chest. She knew her mother's uncle lived down South, but she'd never met him that she could remember. Perhaps when she was a baby.

He was Papa's uncle, at least she thought so. Grandfather Buckley's brother, that was it. When Papa died ten years ago, Marilla was just a tiny thing. After a short while living with the Georgia relatives, Mama had come back to her own people in Pennsylvania. But Cousin Anne was the only one to welcome them. Her mother's parents and sister and aunts had died, and now Mama was gone too. She had no kin left in Pennsylvania.

Mama hadn't wanted to stay in the South after Papa died. Marilla had a vague impression that Mama hadn't liked this uncle. She wasn't sure why she thought that, but she had the notion that the Buckleys hadn't offered a home to Mama and her baby after Papa's accident.

Pennsylvania was a good place to live, but she knew she couldn't stay at the little house alone, even if it hadn't been severely damaged by the fire. She didn't want to live with the Steeles either, but where else could she live? She was afraid to ask what would become of her now.

The lawyer consulted a paper. "Mr. Buckley is going to wire money for your train ticket, and you are to travel to Atlanta, Georgia, where you will be met and conveyed to his home. I don't have details, but I assume your aunt and uncle will welcome you into their household."

Mrs. Steele smiled. "There! Maybe you have some cousins living there too."

Cousins? Marilla couldn't remember anything about cousins. And it was Papa's uncle. Wouldn't his children be old?

"Now, I'll take care of your finances," Mr. Doss said. "The house won't bring much in its current condition, but I hope it will fetch enough to pay off the mortgage and leave a little something for you. If so, I'll send it on to Mr. Buckley, and it will be used for your upkeep."

She wanted to scream in protest, but she couldn't. A painful lump had formed in her throat. She didn't know what a mortgage was, but it sounded bad.

Mrs. Steele eyed her keenly. "Perhaps we should have postponed this conversation for a few more days."

"But her ticket is purchased," Mr. Doss said. "She'll have to leave first thing in the morning."

Mrs. Steele sighed and leaned toward Marilla. "Do you understand, my dear? Tomorrow you'll get on the train and travel to Georgia."

Marilla looked up at her. She was going all that way by herself? She wasn't overly fond of the Steele family, but they'd been kind to her this week, since Mama's death. She would rather stay here than go off on a train alone. Her stomach felt as though something was squeezing it.

"You'll be fine, I'm sure," Mr. Doss said. "You'll change in Washington, but it shouldn't be too difficult."

Change? How would she change? Marilla frowned. Would she be different at the end of the journey, then?

"If you need help, there will be all sorts of people in the station who can answer your questions and help you find the right platform," the lawyer went on. "Now, the money from your mother's house will be put in trust for you. That is, if any remains after the loan is paid off."

Oh, the loan. That must have been what he meant before. Mama fussed every month when she took the money for the loan payment to the bank.

"My office will send Mr. Buckley an amount each year for your upkeep. Anything that's left when you're of age will be yours, but I"—He coughed.—"I seriously doubt there will be any left by that point. Of course, should you marry ..."

Marilla's head spun. She stopped hearing what he was saying. "I—"

"Yes?" Mr. Doss eyed her expectantly.

"I don't understand, sir."

"There, now." Mrs. Steele patted her hand. "She's awfully young to go all that way alone, don't you think?"

He hesitated. "Well, my father came from Ireland alone when he was thirteen."

"But a girl—"

"I understand your concern, ma'am, but what would you have me do? Mr. Buckley is now her legal guardian."

"Yes, but ..."

"If you'd like to make the trip with her, that's your own affair, but I can't pay someone to accompany her."

Mrs. Steele shook her head. "I can't go. It would mean a week away from the shop. But it's not seemly, sending her off like that. Isn't there any money?"

"Not until the house is sold. Only a few dollars, which will not cover the cost of settling the estate."

Mrs. Steele didn't look happy, but she said no more.

That night Mr. Steele produced Mama's old valise, reeking of smoke. Mrs. Steele opened it and waved it about in the back yard. Even after she placed two sachets in the bottom, it smelled horrible.

They packed all of Marilla's clothing, along with the miniature of her mother. There wasn't room in the valise for both the tin that held Mama's sewing tools and the two rescued books. After an agonizing moment, Marilla held out the books.

"Would you like to keep these, Mrs. Steele? One's Hamlet, and the other's poetry. Mama loved them, but if take them I can't fit in her sewing box."

Mrs. Steele's smile wobbled a little. "Why don't you choose one, dear, and take your mother's needle case and scissors and her favorite thimble? You can replace the spools of thread once you get there."

That seemed a good compromise. Marilla opened each book and noticed the inscription in the front of the poetry book. *To my dearest Lila, from your husband, David.*

"I'll keep this one."

Mrs. Steele nodded, and Marilla placed it in the valise with the other small items, blinking at a fresh onslaught of tears.

Her hostess gave her a small, crocheted handbag to keep her money and tickets in.

"Now, dearie, here's two dollars Mr. Steele said to give you. Keep it in your purse, and don't lose it. That's for food, if you need to buy some along the way. Mr. Doss will meet us at the station and give you your tickets there."

"Thank you."

The woman nodded, her face pinched in a frown. "Here's our address. Write to me, dear, once you're settled. The firemen gave permission for my husband to salvage anything he can from your house. If we can sell any bits—dishes, maybe—I can send you the money."

"What about Mama's things?"

"Her clothes, you mean? They'll be all grimy from smoke, but I suppose I can wash them, same as we did yours." She made a distasteful face, and Marilla remembered the awful mess they'd made getting the soot out of her own meager wardrobe.

"You don't have to."

"What? Don't be silly. Of course I will."

"If there's anything you can use, just keep it."

Mrs. Steele's face softened, and she put an arm around Marilla. "That's kind of you, dearie, but if I find something I think would mean something to you, I'll send it on. Be sure to get me the address."

"Doesn't Mr. Doss have it?"

"I expect he does, but I don't like to ask him for anything."

Marilla met her gaze and felt, for the first time, a woman-to-woman understanding.

5

In the morning, Marilla and Mrs. Steele hurried through breakfast. They were about to leave for the train station when the postman came to the door. He gave Mrs. Steele an envelope and hesitated.

"There was a letter came for the woman next door, Mrs. David Buckley, but ... Well, there's no one left there."

"Her daughter is here with me." Mrs. Steele pulled Marilla forward. "This is Marilla Buckley, David and Lila's daughter."

"Oh. Well then, miss, I guess this should go to you." He held out a white envelope with her mother's name and address on the front in flamboyant script.

"Thank you," Marilla managed. She clutched the letter, wondering who had written to Mama. Never in her life had she received a letter, and her mother rarely got anything from the postman—an occasional bill, perhaps. She hoped it wasn't a bill she was expected to pay.

The postman tipped his hat and left.

"Well, dearie, you should open it," Mrs. Steele said cheerfully. "But do it in the cab, why don't you? Come, now. We mustn't dawdle."

Marilla followed her out to the closed carriage Mr. Steele had hired to take his wife and Marilla to the station while he went to work. The driver took her valise and placed it inside for her and then gave the two ladies a hand as they climbed in. He closed the door, and in a moment they were on their way.

Gingerly, Marilla picked at the glued flap of the envelope and drew out a single sheet of paper. She read the message silently and frowned, uncertain of what to do. When she held it out to her companion, Mrs. Steele took it.

"Do you want me to read it, dear?"

Marilla nodded.

"All right, let's see. 'My dear Lila, your mother-in-law, Alicia Buckley, has recently passed on to heaven. Since she was predeceased by both her husband (my brother) and their son, your late husband David, the bulk of her estate will pass to me as the eldest male of the Buckley family. However, she specified in her last will and testament that she wanted to leave her jewelry to your child. She always said little Marilla was a likely twig on the family tree.' Oh, my." Mrs. Steele looked askance at Marilla.

Marilla gulped and blinked at her.

"Seems this man—oh, my. Is he the one you're going to live with?" Mrs. Steele turned over the letter. "Hamilton Buckley. Yes, he's the one, isn't he?"

Marilla nodded.

"Well, it says here, 'I will await your response. When you inform me where to send a packet, I will ship one emerald necklace, matching eardrops, a sapphire ring, and a jet and diamond brooch to you, to hold in safekeeping for your daughter until she is old enough to wear them. Sincerely, Hamilton Buckley.' And that's it." Mrs. Steele folded the sheet and put it back in the envelope. "It seems your grandmother left you an inheritance, my dear."

Unable to think of a suitable reply, Marilla poked the letter into her handbag and tried to breathe slowly and evenly.

After a moment, Mrs. Steele said, "He must have written

that before Mr. Doss's telegram reached him, informing him of your mother's death."

Yes, he must have. Marilla nodded like some automaton doll. How pleased Mama would have been! The fact that she couldn't share this news with Mama smacked her like a slap across the face. Never again could she share anything with her mother— not good news like this, about jewels that might have allowed them to be free of that cursed loan, or bad news. But what could ever be worse news than her mother's dying?

"I expect he'll hang on to that jewelry for you until you get there," Mrs. Steele said. "Just think, when you're sixteen maybe he'll hold a big party for you. All your friends will come and dance, and you can wear that emerald necklace. Won't that be grand?"

Marilla struggled to imagine it. Other pictures in her mind were too vivid.

The mischievous orange cat, Feathers, leaping onto the table as Mama filled the lamps. A jar of lamp oil flying to the floor, shattering and spreading toward the fireplace. Flames leaping up Mama's skirt.

"Here we are," Mrs. Steele said. "I hope we've plenty of time before the train leaves."

WHEN THEY MET up with the lawyer on the platform, Marilla's terror threatened to overwhelm her. She tried to breathe slowly and evenly, but her heart pounded. People hurried past them on all sides. A man put her valise on a trolley and wheeled it away, and she wondered if she would ever see it again.

"This ticket will get you to Washington." Mr. Doss held out a piece of pasteboard. "This other one is for the last part of your trip, from Washington to Atlanta. You must be very careful of it."

She nodded, and he handed it over.

"Put it right in your handbag, dear," Mrs. Steele said. "And remember, the conductor on the train is there to help you. When you get off in Washington, if you need help, look for someone in a uniform. A policeman, a porter, anyone. They will see you safely on."

Marilla gulped. She thought she might be sick. As she put the second ticket away, it slid into the purse beside the letter. She glanced quickly at Mr. Doss, but he was looking toward the train.

No, she decided. She would not mention the letter to Mr. Doss. She hoped vehemently that Mrs. Steele didn't either.

"Train 507 boarding for Washington, D.C.," a uniformed man called from near the train cars. People moved toward the carriages that had rows of windows in the sides.

"Come quickly." Mrs. Steele grabbed her hand and pulled her toward the line that was forming outside the nearest car.

An elegantly dressed man and a woman stood just ahead of them.

"Excuse me." Mrs. Steele tapped the woman's arm.

"Yes?" The couple turned toward them.

"This girl has lost her mother, and she's got to travel all the way to Atlanta alone, to live with her uncle," Mrs. Steele said. "Is there any way you could—"

The woman flashed a glance at her companion.

"We're only going to Washington," he said.

"She needs to change trains there. Oh, please! I can't offer you anything, but I so hate to send her off unchaperoned."

"Darby?" The woman arched her eyebrows at her companion.

The man sighed, and the woman seemed to take that as a sign of resignation and acceptance.

"All right, we'll keep an eye on her as far as the capital. We're Mrs. and Mrs. Bell." She leaned toward Marilla with a smile. "What's your name, dear?"

"Marilla Buckley."

"And I assume you have your ticket?"

"Yes, ma'am."

"All right. Come along with Mr. Bell and me."

"Oh, thank you so much." Mrs. Steele squeezed Marilla's fingers. "You be a good girl, now." She dropped Marilla's hand and backed away.

Marilla sucked in a painful breath.

"Come, dear. Hold out your ticket." Mrs. Bell herded her toward the uniformed man at the bottom of the train steps. As the passengers reached him, he took each one's ticket and punched a hole in it. He gave Marilla's back to her.

"Now, keep that in your pocket or your bag," Mrs. Bell said.

Mr. Bell followed them into the car, and Mrs. Bell found an empty seat. She let Marilla enter first, so that she sat near the window. Mr. Bell found a place just across the aisle. He didn't look happy, but he stretched out his long legs and opened a newspaper he'd carried under one arm.

"Look, there's your friend." Mrs. Bell nudged Marilla and pointed out the window.

Mrs. Steele lingered on the platform. When she saw Marilla turn her way, she smiled and waved enthusiastically. Marilla gave a little wave back.

The train whistle blew, and the whole car jerked. Marilla caught her breath and grabbed the edge of the seat. As she watched out the window, Mrs. Steele got farther away, and Mr. Doss was nowhere to be seen. Marilla had the feeling he'd left the station as soon as he'd given her the tickets.

She waved once more, but Mrs. Steele was gone, and the train picked up speed with a lurch that put her stomach in turmoil.

IN ATLANTA, a porter found Marilla as she left the train carriage. He handed her a message telling her to take a local train to Covington.

Marilla gulped and looked up into the man's kindly, dark eyes. "But I—"

"Your ticket's done paid for, miss. Would you like me to show you to the platform?"

"I—yes, sir. Thank you." She'd spent most of the two dollars she left home with for sandwiches along the way.

Somehow she'd made it to Atlanta. Most of the time, after the Bells had seen her to the correct train in Washington, she'd cowered in the corner made by her seat and the wall, trying not to make eye contact with anyone.

As she hurried across the huge station with the porter, she was glad the Lord had sent her another guide. She could never had navigated this complicated maze alone.

The black man who picked her up at the Covington depot frightened her at first, but once they'd started out on the buggy trip to the plantation, he talked to her in an easy, friendly manner, and soon her heart slowed down and she began to listen to what he was telling her. Of course, he called her "Miss Marilla" all the time, but that was all right. His name was Thomas, he told her.

"River Lea is a big place," he said at one point.

"River Lea?" she asked.

"That's Mr. Buckley's plantation, where we're going. It be another hour before we get there."

"Oh." Marilla looked around at the wide-open fields they were passing. Right now they were cornfields, she could tell that much. Some of the crops they'd passed she didn't recognize. Another hour seemed like a very long time.

After a few minutes' silence, she dared to say, "I understand my grandmother died recently."

Thomas nodded. "That she did. It's been about two months now."

"Two months?" Marilla found this fact startling. She supposed it could have taken Uncle Hamilton's letter that long to reach Philadelphia. Or maybe he'd been too distraught to write for a few weeks. Papa's father was dead too. Mama had mentioned it once or twice that she recalled, as had the letter. She glanced over at Thomas. "My grandfather's been gone a long time, hasn't he?"

"Yes'm." Thomas adjusted the reins between his long fingers. "A good many years."

"Was he alive when my Papa died?"

"No, no. He passed on before Mr. David." Thomas shook his head dolefully. "We all miss Mr. David. He was a fine man."

Marilla thought about this for several minutes then asked, "Did my grandmother live at River Lea?"

"That she did."

"And my great-uncle does too, you said."

"Now he does, Miss Marilla. After your grandpa died, Mr. Hamilton Buckley moved to River Lea. He be your grandpa's brother, you know."

"Yes. But my father didn't live there."

"He grew up at River Lea. He and your mama had their own little house."

Marilla puzzled over that. Why hadn't her father continued to live at River Lea? She knew he didn't like having his farming done by slaves. Mama had been adamant about that. Maybe he'd disagreed with his parents on the subject.

Thomas turned a wide grin on her. "Your grandma, Miss Alicia, she thought you were somethin'! Yes, suh. She wanted to send for you and your mama to visit."

"Was she too poor to have us?"

"Well, depends on who you ask, missy. Mr. Hamilton, he say they can't afford it."

She raised her chin. "That means they were too poor."

"Maybe." Thomas shrugged.

"Do I have any cousins?" she asked.

"Well now, your papa didn't have any brothers or sisters, you know."

She nodded.

"Mr. Hamilton, he had three daughters. One died, but the other two married. They moved quite some distance away, though." Thomas shook his head. "You might see them and their families come Christmastime. And besides them, Mr. Hamilton has a son, William. He's off in New Orleans right now."

"Oh. How old is he?"

"Nigh on thirty."

"Does he have children?"

"Not yet. He gots his eye on a young lady, so maybe he'll get married soon and you'd have some more cousins. I expect he might come back to River Lea and settle down iffen he gets married."

Marilla sighed. Papa's cousin was too old to be a friend for her, and his children would be too young.

"What about Uncle Hamilton's wife?"

"Oh, she's here. Miz Olive. She be your great-aunt."

A huge weight lifted off Marilla's shoulders. At least there would be one woman in the house with her. She wanted to inquire about the jewelry her grandmother had left her, but she knew Thomas wasn't the right person to ask, so she kept quiet about that.

A big farm—no, plantation. That meant the neighbors would live a long way from them, if the size of the fields they were now passing was any indication. No cousins. In fact, it sounded like it would be just her and Uncle Hamilton, Aunt Olive, and their servants. She didn't want to think about them being slaves and belonging to Mr. Buckley. Maybe she would find a friend among them—if her great-uncle would allow it.

The sun beat down on them, and perspiration trickled down her back.

"What are those plants?" She waved a hand toward the field on Thomas's side of the road.

His eyes went wide. "Why, that's cotton, miss."

Of course. And it required a lot of slaves to cultivate and harvest cotton. She shivered in spite of the heat.

6

August 26, 1861
Emmaus, Pennsylvania

"Jack! Come quick!"

The look on Caro's face wasn't good, and he shouldered the hoe. Stepping high over the rows of lettuce and chard, he joined her at the edge of the large vegetable garden he was weeding.

"It's Ned. He's packing up his stuff. Says he's joining the army."

Jack pushed the hoe into her hands. "Take this." He ran for the house.

Ned stood beside their chest of drawers, pulling clothes out. He threw some aside and tossed others over to the bed.

"Ned, you idiot. You can't go," Jack said.

"Of course I can." Ned continued flinging his clothes onto the bed, where a rucksack rested. He turned and shoved a wad of them into the sack.

"But—Ma will be crushed." Jack pulled out the socks Ned had just packed and tossed them back into the drawer.

Ned scowled at him. "I want to join up. All the fellows are

going. The Union needs us." He took the socks out of the drawer again and stuffed them in the rucksack. "Half my friends are gone already. We're all joining the 47th Pennsylvania. I'm going, Jack."

"You're only seventeen, Ned."

"So? Lots of fellows my age are enlisting. We need to set the South straight."

Jack didn't waste time arguing with his logic—there was no persuading Ned on something about which he'd formed strong opinions. For the past couple of months, he'd talked about nothing but the war. "You'd have to lie about your age."

Hovering in the doorway now, Caro clapped a hand to her lips.

Ned's lips tightened. "Not if Pa will sign for me."

"You'll ask him?"

"Thinking about it."

Caro tiptoed away, and Jack wondered if she was heading for the kitchen to tell their mother.

He knew Ned would go, whether Pa endorsed his actions or not. If their parents refused to allow it, Ned would run away. Jack clenched his teeth. He could wrestle his brother to the floor, but what good would that do? Pa wouldn't keep him locked up until the regiment pulled out.

He stalked out of the room.

"Where are you going?" Ruthie called from the parlor as he passed the doorway. She was the youngest, at nine.

"To see Pa." Jack hurried out the front door before she or any of the other kids could join him and jogged all the way to the post office.

Pa was sitting behind his desk, working the telegraph key, but no customers were waiting in line in front of the metal grille that separated him from the lobby.

"Pa, I need to talk to you."

Charles held up his left hand. The telegraph was clicking away, and Jack forced himself to wait. He knew how important concentration was. Small errors in transposing a message could lead to all sorts of complications. He automatically translated what he heard in his mind: "... provision for troops to Camp Curtain quartermaster Wishard."

His father finished writing the message and sent a quick acknowledgment to the sender. He looked up at Jack with a weary smile.

"What is it, son?"

"It's Ned. He's going to join the army."

Charles sat very still for a moment. "Now? He's too young."

"He says he'll do it anyway, with your support or without it."

Charles sighed. "When does he plan to go?"

"Right away, I think. He was packing his things when I left the house. Says his friends are all going to Camp Curtain, where the 47th Pennsylvania is training."

"I have another hour here," Charles said. "Tell him I'll try to come home promptly and discuss this."

"Yes, sir."

Jack's father met his gaze. "Jack, we can't have him running off without saying goodbye."

"You'll try to stop him?"

"That may not be possible." Charles grimaced. "We'll do what we can, eh? Don't let him go just yet. If he insists ..."

Jack swallowed hard. "If he insists, I can go with him, Pa."

"No, Jack. We need you. The family, and the telegraph service."

"I know, but ... I can't think about Ned going off on his own and joining the army, Pa."

Charles nodded. "He's a difficult boy. I doubt we can stop him."

"He's the kind who gets into scrapes, Pa."

"Yes."

They looked into each other's eyes, and Jack thought what a deep, rich brown his eyes were. Jack was the only one of the eight children with blue eyes. Sometimes it made him feel like an outsider, but most of the time he knew he was as much one of the Miller boys as Ned, Peter, and Silas. This man loved him just as fiercely as he did the others.

"We'll figure it out," Charles said at last.

"I'll go and talk to him, try to make him stay until you get home."

August 31, 1861
Camp Curtain
Harrisburg, Pennsylvania

Dear Ma and Pa,

I hope this finds you all well. Ned and I are settled in at the camp, and for the past four days we have drilled and marched just about all day long. Let me tell you, it's been warm. These uniforms are not what I would pick to do heavy work in.

But I am not complaining, or if I am, I shouldn't be. We've had decent food, if very plain. Ned says to tell you, Ma, that we miss your cooking. We have met up with a few boys we knew—James Snow for one. He was with Ned at school, you know—from the farm out Allentown Road.

They say we'll be heading south before too much time has passed, but we are not ready yet. More training is needed all around. It's so different from home. No thinking for yourself in the army. You have to do as you're told, and that's it. Of course, Ned doesn't like that, but he's actually doing fairly well.

When we get to rest, we are generally too tired to do anything. Some of the boys play cards and chuck-a-luck in the evening. One fellow has a fiddle, and we'll hear him going at it after supper. I doubt he can take it with him when we join the Army of the Potomac. That's Major-General McClellan's domain, but I don't expect the likes of us will ever lay eyes on the general.

One thing that may interest you—yesterday our captain took me aside, much to my trepidation. He told me I am to be made a corporal. They will issue me a chevron for each sleeve, and I will have to sew them on, oh joy! Ma, I wish you or Caroline were here to do that. I'm sure I'll make a shambles of it.

Anyway, I will help the sergeant make sure our company follows orders. I feared Ned would be a little out of joint when he heard he'll have to answer to his brother, but he said, "It's no different from back home, is it?"

> *With love and kisses to all the family,*
> *Jack*

Oct. 1, 1861
River Lea Plantation

MARILLA STOOD on the verandah and gazed out over the fields. She hoped with autumn, cooler weather would come. No matter how long she'd lived here, she couldn't get used to the blistering heat.

Her great-uncle, Hamilton Buckley, paced slowly to the end of the porch and back, a glass of bourbon in his hand.

"They're bothering too much about Kentucky and western Virginia," he muttered. "Lee needs to consider where the valuable part of the confederacy is."

Buckley had expected to lead out the local troops, riding on his standing as a colonel in the Mexican War. But his age, cumbersome weight, and fractious temperament had gotten in the way—though Marilla would never cite any of those things in his hearing.

His cronies spent less and less time with him now, tending to their own business and preparing for invasion. Whenever they got together, Uncle Hamilton would fume and rage against Lincoln and the federal government in general. His acquaintances would try to calm him and assure him that when the Confederacy won, he would have a place in the new government.

But they kept away more and more. Buckley took to driving into town two or three times a week to gather news and make his opinions known. Marilla stayed home as often as she could, to avoid the embarrassment she inevitably felt when the colonel got loud and overbearing. He could start an argument over nothing—even things he and his friends supposedly agreed upon.

At the end of the verandah, he whipped around. "They'll attack here, and we'll have no army to defend us. No one to stand with us but the slaves."

Marilla cringed. Even though four years had passed since her arrival, she still hated the fact that her uncle kept dozens of people and forced them to provide a living for him. Even worse, she hated the way he treated them—and now he expected them to risk their lives to defend his precious plantation.

River Lea was a pretty place, she admitted that. The fields stretched right to the shimmering river, and the huge farm for the most part ran smoothly. She delighted in the mockingbirds, the magnificent trees, and the glorious flowering vines and shrubs. With a little effort, she could relax and ignore the objectionable parts.

And then Sadie or Reenie would bring her a glass of tea or tell her dinner was ready, and she would be jerked back into the real world of Hamilton Buckley.

If she tried to help the house servants, they protested. They knew that if Colonel Buckley found out, they would be punished, not Marilla. Even so, she tried to jump out of bed quickly each morning and smooth up the coverlet before Reenie could get to it. It was a small gesture of defiance, a proof that she didn't need to depend on slaves, that she was not incapable of performing such a small task.

How she longed to leave this place. She no longer wondered why Mama chose to go northward when Papa died. Their life in the little house in Pennsylvania had been hard, but they hadn't depended on other people's toil. Marilla wished she hadn't come here, wished she could go back.

But she had no funds. Uncle Hamilton provided her daily needs, but she had no way to put aside the price of a train ticket. As to the jewels her grandmother had bequeathed her, Marilla had never seen them.

She'd mentioned them once, about a week after she arrived at River Lea.

"All in good time," Uncle Hamilton had said with a frown.

When would that be?

If they lived closer to town, she might be able to find some sort of position that would earn her a bit of money. She wouldn't ask for much, as long as she could save for her escape. She'd heard of slaves escaping from some of the plantations. She wanted to escape herself, to draw a breath in a free land.

Her great-uncle stopped his pacing and gazed at her as if he expected her to speak.

"Maybe General Lee will drive them back," she ventured. "Maybe they won't ever come here."

"I want them to come here," he almost screamed. "I want those scoundrels to try to humiliate us. We'll crush them to powder!"

"Yes, sir." She stood on shaky legs. "If you'll excuse me—"

"Where are you going?"

"To my room. I've a ... bit of a headache." She turned and walked as swiftly as she dared into the house and up the curved stairway. If only other family members lived here to take some of his attention.

But, no. His daughters were married and living at least a day's drive away, and his son William had answered the first call to join Lee's army. Poor Aunt Olive had died the year after Marilla took up residence at River Lea.

While she was still alive, they'd entertained sporadically, and other plantation owners and businessmen from town had brought their wives. But now she was gone too, so Uncle Hamilton rarely had female guests nowadays. Invitations to other houses were even more scarce.

Sometimes Marilla hoped some nice young gentleman would offer for her hand, but with the death of his wife, Uncle Hamilton began acting strangely and few people came around. She didn't blame them. But still, she hoped she wouldn't have to stay here forever, an old maid, with just her great-uncle and the quiet slaves who watched her with wide eyes.

As she crossed the hall to her bedroom, Reenie appeared.

"You want help with your crinoline, Miss Marilla?"

"Thank you." She didn't like to accept help for such intimate tasks, but Uncle Hamilton insisted she dress fashionably, and that meant hoop skirts and corsets, which were difficult to get into and out of without assistance.

Under Aunt Olive's eagle eye, Marilla had learned not to try becoming too chummy with the slaves. Now she wondered if she'd made a mistake in distancing herself from the female servants. She loathed the whole idea of slavery, but maybe she was treating them cruelly as well—as though they didn't exist.

October 7, 1861
Near Fort Ethan Allen, Virginia

"Take me, Jack!"

Ned's eagerness pulled at Jack. His brother wanted to join him in scouting the road they were about to march, deeper into

Virginia, toward Lewinsville. Jack's sergeant had ordered him to pick three men to go with him, ahead of the column.

In the darkness, he peered at Ned. This could be a dangerous assignment. They'd heard there were Confederates camped somewhere in the area. On the other hand, they hadn't run into anything suspicious so far. They'd stayed at Fort Ethan Allen a week, and all was quiet. Now they were breaking camp at 3 a.m. and heading out.

He couldn't spend a lot of time choosing the men he took, but he hadn't planned on taking Ned. Logic told him his impetuous younger brother would be safer in the middle of the company.

Or would he? So far, keeping Ned where he could watch him had been Jack's strategy whenever possible. But they hadn't been in enemy territory long. When things got heated, he probably wouldn't be able to keep Ned close. The time would inevitably come.

But he'd promised Ma he'd stay as near his brother as he could. They all knew he couldn't protect him forever, but Jack would do his best. Memories of Baby Ned, an infant when the Millers took in Jack, always made him sentimental. Ned was only a couple of months older than Janie, and when Jack first saw him at the Millers' house, he'd been ambushed by sorrow and an almost crippling sense of loss and failure. He'd determined to keep his baby brother safe.

Of course, the Millers had three more babies after that, but the bond with them wasn't as fierce as that between Jack and Ned. He loved all his siblings, but Ned was special.

"I'll see what I can do," he mumbled and whirled to scan the rest of his outfit.

"Snow," he called, "you're with me."

Jim Snow shouldered his pack and ambled toward Jack.

"Potter," Jack called.

Willy Potter didn't look too happy, but he joined them. Ned stood by, practically panting like Pa's hound dog when he knew

Charles Miller was about to take him hunting. Jack could almost hear that hound whining.

"All right, Ned. Us four." He hated the decision as soon as he'd made it, but it was too late. Ned would never forgive him if he rescinded the order.

The three gathered around him.

"Remember," Jack said, "absolute silence. If you see or hear something, touch me and halt."

He spoke to his sergeant and then led the three men out of camp, past their sentries, and onto the wagon road. They had to make sure the way was clear without getting too far ahead of the column. If they found trouble, they needed to run back to the troops and warn them. In a dire situation, rifle fire would serve as the alert.

The air had cooled after sunset, and Jack was glad they were marching before dawn. They'd get the worst of it over with before it got hot. Beneath the trees all was dark. The sliver of waning moon wouldn't give them much light here, even if they could see it through the foliage. They walked along as fast as they dared, judging the middle of the road from the shadows of the trees around them.

Jack felt a bit of relief when they emerged and had open fields on either side, yet he felt exposed. Never in his life had he felt so vulnerable. When they'd crossed the invisible line into Virginia a couple of weeks ago, a wave of fear he hadn't known since the orphanage swept over him.

They weren't that far from the capital, actually, but everything felt different. They were in the South, the land of rebellion, the stronghold of slavery. He tried not to think about that most of the time, distracting himself with his duties and writing letters home.

But now he could think of nothing else. Thousands of men were out there wanting to kill him.

When the shot came, he stood stock-still. It couldn't be real, but it was.

Jim Snow let out a yelp, slapped Jack's arm, and ran back toward the column.

"Fall back," Jack yelled. They all ran amid the report of more muskets.

He caught up with Jim and Willy a few minutes later.

"Wait, boys!"

They stopped and looked back at him. Behind them, no more gunfire sounded. Were they out of range? Out of the enemy's sight?

Jack was shaking all over, and his rifle felt like it weighed a hundred pounds. "Where's Ned?"

Willy Potter stared back along the road. Dawn was near, and Jack could see a good hundred yards now.

"He was right with me." Willy sounded dazed.

Jack pulled in a deep breath. "Go to the captain. Tell him we ran into some rebel pickets."

Jim and Willy hesitated.

"Aren't you coming, Corporal?" Jim asked.

"I've got to find Ned."

"He didn't get past me," Willy said.

"Are you sure?"

The young man met Jack's gaze with wide, terrified eyes and nodded. "Could be he jumped in a thicket."

Could be not, Jack thought grimly.

"Go on."

"You can't go back there alone," Willy said.

"Then go get me some help." Jack was angry. Angry and scared. He was sweating, though the air was still cool, and the muscles in his neck and back felt tight. He swung around, fighting the feeling that someone stared at him from the shadows.

Willy took off toward the company. Jack could hear them marching now. His regiment was coming. But Ned was back the other way, somewhere.

Jack dropped his pack in the road and ran toward where

they'd been fired on. Jim Snow loped beside him, breathing in ragged gasps.

"Go back," Jack wheezed out.

"It's Ned," Jim said curtly, and they kept on.

Around a slight bend, Jack halted and peered into the gray light. Two men bent over a still form in the roadway. Their clothes didn't look like uniforms but blended in with the dirt and brown-leaved trees.

"We can take 'em," Jim whispered, raising his rifle to his shoulder.

"What if—"

Jim's rifle roared too close to his ears. Jack winced as one of the shadowy figures fell. The other straightened and stared at them, then turned and ran for the fencerow at the side of the road. Jack aimed his own rifle and fired. The man dove over the fence and rolled.

Jack didn't care if he got away. He ran to the two figures lying in the road.

"Ned!" He threw down his rifle and knelt by his brother.

Snow came panting up behind him. "Reload, Corporal."

Jack ignored him and lifted Ned's head and shoulders and held him. "Ned! Can you hear me?"

Ned's eyelids flickered, and he stared up at Jack.

"I'm hit, Jackie."

"I know."

"Tell Mama ... "

"No," Jack moaned. "You'll tell her. We'll get you back to Washington. The hospital—" He broke off as Ned slumped in his arms.

A horse galloped up from the marching column, and his captain reined in his mount.

"Miller!"

"Yes, sir." Jack laid Ned gently on the ground and stood on legs made of liquid. Jim Snow pushed his rifle into his hands, and

Jack was vaguely aware that Jim had reloaded for him while he spoke to Ned.

"Confederate pickets, Potter said?"

"Yes, sir. They've shot Private Miller."

The captain's lips twitched. "Your brother?"

"Yes, sir." Tear streamed down Jack's cheeks, but he didn't lift a hand to stop them.

The captain turned in the saddle and yelled, "Nelson, get the doctor up here." He turned back to Jack. "How many were there?"

"I don't know, sir."

"We heard at least half a dozen shots," Willy said.

Jack nodded. "There were two still here when Snow and I saw them. Snow shot that one." He waved a hand to the fallen man they'd ignored. "The other one ran and hopped over that fence. I might have grazed him. But there were more. I don't know where they've gone."

"We'll scour that farm and the woods over there." The captain wheeled his horse and rode back to give orders.

Jack went back to Ned's side as a wagon pulled by straining mules approached from the rear of the column. The doctor, no doubt. But gazing down at his brother's still face and vacant eyes, Jack knew it was too late.

7

October 12, 1861

D ear Pa,

I can't bear to write this to Ma. You probably received word already. Perhaps you took in the message yourself in a telegram. I hope not. I hope someone came in person to tell you, and that you didn't start decoding a message and see your own name at the top. It's been five days, but I still can't think about it or I'll go mad. I can't come home. I can only march on with the rest.

If only I was there with you now and could explain it. But there is no excuse. I shouldn't have chosen Ned as one of the scouts, but he was so keen to go. We'd done nothing so far but drill and train and lay about camp, then march and march and march. We knew it could end like this, but not so soon, Pa! We hadn't even got to a real battlefield. It's so wrong. I never should have let him go. I'm so sorry. Please forgive me.

Jack

October 28, 1861
Northern Virginia

"Miller!"

Jack looked up, startled. His name hadn't been yelled out at mail call since they'd crossed into Confederate territory. He wondered if his bleak letter had reached his father.

Numbly, he marched forward and accepted two slightly dirty, somewhat crumpled envelopes. Pa. A knot tightened in his chest. The second one was from Caroline.

When they were dismissed, he carried them back to the tent he shared with six others. Most of the men were lining up for chow, but Jack wasn't hungry. He ought to eat to keep up his strength, but he thought he'd be sick if he put anything in his stomach before he opened his father's letter.

He sat down on his bedroll and stared at the envelopes. Finally he laid Pa's letter aside and carefully tore open the one from his sister.

Dear Jack,

We heard about Ned yesterday, and we are all ill. But we have each other here, and I keep thinking about you, all alone out there, with nobody to share this with.

Dear brother, I know you are mourning. Don't let this drive you to despair. We need you to go on, Jack. We need to keep hearing from you and holding on to the hope that you will come home to us. We love you so! Don't let us down. Take care of yourself. And don't blame yourself for Ned. You know he wanted to go. It was his decision.

I've been helping Ma and fixing food for the troops that go through on the trains. But this week, I've actually been working at the post office too. Mr. Bane has been driving Pa crazy since you left. He can't get anyone to take your place on the telegraph key. He's made Pa and Mr. Lowe work such long hours that I finally asked Pa why I couldn't help.

I know I'm not as good at it as you and Pa, but I still remember Morse. You and I spent so many hours tapping out messages to each other when we were kids, and now it's paying off. I'm earning a few coins and giving Pa and Mr. Lowe a few hours off work.

Of course, Ma didn't want me to start working, but Pa talked to her. I don't know what he said, but they've let me do it. Sometimes I make mistakes, which is not good, but I'm getting better every day. So when you need something to think about on your long marches, think of me, sitting at the telegraph desk like I was important!

Your loving Sister,
Caro

Jack couldn't help smiling, for the first time since Ned's death. His face felt stretched and brittle, as though it might break. He read Caroline's letter again and drew from it a bit of her spirit. Good old Caro.

He remembered when Pa Miller took him home from the orphanage. Caroline had padded downstairs, that first night, saying, "I want to see Jack." He loved all his siblings, but Caro was the one he'd felt closest to, in a different way than he had Ned.

Funny, he'd never felt she needed protecting the way Ned did. He supposed it was because Ned was so tiny when he first laid eyes on him, helpless and scrawny, like Janie had been. Ned was a responsibility. Caro was a friend.

He wasn't sure he was ready to open Pa's letter. He cradled it in his hands, looking down at the firm, strong lettering that spelled out his name and his company. Surprisingly, both letters had tracked him down in three weeks or so.

Unless this one was written before they knew about Ned. Caroline's was written after, but the way the mails were these days, Pa's could be one written weeks earlier.

When he opened it, he found a very short message, like the telegrams Pa sent out every day.

Son, our prayers are with you. Know that we love you. More later. Pa

Jack exhaled heavily and slipped the note into the pocket over his heart.

October 29, 1861
River Lea Plantation

LAZARUS, the huge house slave, came into the dining room while Marilla and Uncle Hamilton were still at luncheon. Marilla often wondered why the giant of a man wasn't made to work in the fields, but for some reason, Uncle Hamilton kept him on duty around the house since the war started. Maybe he felt more secure with the big man nearby. They'd heard rumors of skirmishing along the railroad lines.

"Suh, they's two soldiers on the verandah askin' for you."

Buckley jerked his head up. "Soldiers?" He sat still for a moment then tossed his napkin on the table. He rose, cleared his throat, and tugged at the tails of his jacket. "It's about time."

He left the room, heading toward the front door. Lazarus lingered, as though reluctant to hear the impending conversation.

Even though he sometimes looked fierce and was always imposing because of his bulk, Marilla found Lazarus surprisingly kind. They weren't friends by any means, but she could ask Lazarus questions and he would answer in a reasonable manner. Through him, she'd begun to make progress in befriending the housemaids.

"Do you know what's going on?" she asked, remaining in her chair.

"I expect Colonel Buckley thinks they've come for him to lead a regiment," Lazarus said.

Something about the way he said it made Marilla look at him more keenly.

"You don't think that's it?" In some ways, it would be a relief if Uncle Hamilton went off to help the army, but Marilla couldn't imagine being left alone here. The very idea of trying to run the plantation, and especially having to deal with the ruthless overseer, Zeke Vernon, terrified her.

"I see they wearin' black armbands, missy."

"Oh. So it's bad news?" A sudden, dreadful thought hit her. "Oh, surely not William!"

Buckley had left the front door open, and his tortured wail carried all the way into the dining room.

Marilla shoved her chair back and sprang to her feet. She dashed past Lazarus and through the hall to the open door. The two men in gray uniforms, their black armbands stark against their pale woolen sleeves, stood looking helpless as Uncle Hamilton leaned over the verandah railing moaning, his blanched face distorted in agony.

"Uncle!" She ran to his side and touched his arm.

He stared blankly at her for a moment, then he lurched forward and retched into the rosebushes.

8

June 5, 1862
Key West, Florida

O n his last evening at Key West, Jack sat leaning against a palm tree, looking out at the boats in the harbor. They were finally leaving Florida. He could hardly believe it. The regiment had been in this oven much longer than he liked.

All last fall they'd been shuffled about from place to place, on trains, steamships, and their own sore feet, doing manual labor at various locations. They'd even traveled to the Washington Arsenal in January, where they'd all been issued new Springfield rifles and had a nice dinner at the Soldiers' Retreat.

Next was a train trip to the U.S. Naval Academy in Annapolis, Maryland. There they'd carted weapons and all the other equipment and supplies they'd need onto the steamship *Oriental*. The loading process had taken three days, but eventually they were ready, and the steamer set off southward.

The voyage might have been pleasant if they hadn't constantly been on watch for enemy vessels and blockade runners. In some shadowy corner of his mind, Jack remembered his older brother Zeph saying he planned to be a cabin boy on their grandfather's ship one day. Jack put a hand to his chest as he gazed out over the vast ocean, feeling the Chinese coin he and his brother wore. Did Zeph still have his? Had he gone to sea, as he'd once longed to do? And would they ever see each other again?

The journey had taken several days, and the ship had landed the entire regiment on an island called Key West early in February. On Valentine's Day they paraded through the small city, to the cheering of the residents.

"So, we're leaving at last." Jim Snow plopped down beside him on the ground.

Jack gave him a lazy smile. "Oh, Florida's not such a bad place. In January."

Jim guffawed. "Well, it's June now, and I'm tired of baking in my skin."

During their first month on Key West, when Jack wasn't on duty, he wandered around the island, gawking at the strange trees and birds. It was like another world.

Apparently a lot of New Englanders and other Union sympathizers had migrated here, outnumbering the southerners. The regiment's job was to improve Fort Zachary Taylor, the harbor, and the roads on the island. It was hard work, but they didn't have to fear enemy gunfire while they were at it. The officers thought the Confederates would eventually attack the island, but it didn't happen while Jack was there. He was even able to get in a little fishing.

He and Jim were also part of a detail that went to a tiny island seventy miles west called Dry Tortuga, which he learned meant turtles, to work on a fortress there—Fort Jefferson. Ships stationed at the two outposts were expected to keep a lid on the blockade running.

"I heard they might use that fort on Dry Tortuga as a prison," Jim said.

Jack nodded. "Might be a good place to keep captured Rebs. It would be hard to escape."

Jim sighed and looked out over the beach. "There's been a lot of skirmishes in Virginia."

"Bigger battles too," Jack said. "All across the South. Be glad we weren't in 'em." At once he felt a flash of guilt. He wouldn't shirk his duty. But sometimes he got to feeling he wasn't really doing anything to help the Union. Fixing up the forts and building roads was important, he supposed, but would these isolated islands really see action?

He wasn't sorry they were leaving the islands, though. The sun was ruthless here now, and the skin on his face and arms was dark brown. They had to keep drinking water all the time to keep from shriveling up—which was a real problem on Dry Tortuga, where there was no freshwater source. All their drinking water had to be brought in on ships. Jack wondered how that would work out if a prison was indeed established there.

The turtles were something. He walked along the beach mornings, seeing hundreds of them, of different kinds. They were more plentiful than the squirrels back in Pennsylvania. He could tell the Miller youngsters about them when he went home —which would be better than gory tales of battle.

"So, we ship out on the early tide." Jim leaned forward and wrote his initials in the sand with one finger.

"Yeah. Can't believe it. I kind of like this place, but I'm glad we're going."

"They say it will only get hotter for the next two or three months." Jim stretched out his long legs. "Wish I could take some of this sand home to show the folks."

Jack laughed. "I was just thinking how my sister Ruthie would love it if I could take her a turtle."

"How long we got left?"

Jack knew he meant how long on their enlistments, not in Key West. He looked up at the darkening sky through the palm fronds. The moon was hiding tonight, but stars began glittering like diamonds. "Two years. A little more."

Jim sighed. "Didn't expect it to last this long."

"Nobody did.

"Think they'll send us to the front now?"

"I dunno," Jack said. "We've had it pretty easy the last four months."

"Yeah, if you call building roads easy. Beats cannon fire, I guess."

August, 1862
Emmaus, Pennsylvania

CHARLES MILLER WAS CLICKING AWAY RAPIDLY on the telegraph key when a uniformed man walked in. He carried himself with authority and was no doubt here on military business. Charles kept his head down, focusing on the code he was sending, and didn't look up again until he'd finished his message.

"Yes, sir, may I help you?" He swung his gaze upward and was met by the steely eyes of a Union officer.

"I'm Colonel James Leonard, from the office of the Secretary of War."

"Do you want to send a message?" Charles asked.

"No. I'm here to recruit you."

Charles almost laughed but quickly sobered. "I beg your pardon."

"We need people like you, Mr. Miller. I understand you're the best telegrapher in these parts."

"He is," postmaster Edward Heinz said from behind his high counter. "Miller took it up the minute we got telegraph lines through town, and he's faster and more accurate than any of our other operators. But we'd hate to see you take him away from us, that's for sure."

Charles looked from the postmaster back to Leonard. "Are

you saying you want me to go and run telegrams for the army?"

"That and more," Leonard said.

Charles arched his eyebrows and thought about that.

Leonard leaned close over the desk. "We find that people who are good at Morse Code are good at ciphers as well."

"Ciphers?" Charles frowned. "Codes, you mean?"

"Both." Leonard nodded curtly. "The country needs your talents."

Charles's stomach knotted. "Well, I don't know, sir. I like my job here, and I have a large family to provide for. Not just my own—I've got a son-in-law and two nephews off to war, and I'm helping look out for those families too." Not to mention, he was forty-seven years old, but he didn't suppose the recruiter would blink at that for a telegrapher.

"Please consider it, sir." Leonard straightened his back. "It wouldn't pay what you're no doubt making here, but the service to the United States would be invaluable."

"What about my wife and children?"

"We all make sacrifices, Mr. Miller."

Charles sighed.

"There's his boy, Jack," Heinz said. "He's a good telegrapher —almost as good as his papa."

Leonard's eyes brightened.

"How old is he?"

"Twenty-three, just. I taught him the code, and he excels at it." Charles grimaced. "But he enlisted last year."

"More's the pity." The postmaster spat into the cuspidor he kept behind his counter.

"He enlisted?" Leonard frowned. "In the regular army?"

Charles nodded. "Forty-seventh Pennsylvania Infantry. He and his brother both." A bleakness settled on him, but he didn't mention that Ned had been taken from them.

"Jack worked here before he joined up," Heinz offered.

Charles scowled at him, but the postmaster ignored him. He and Mr. Bane had both resented losing Jack, who by then was one of their best operators. Charles and Frances had actually been relieved when Jack said he'd go with Ned to the enlistment officer. A lot of good it did. Ned would never return. How he wished he'd forbidden Jack to go. He might be older, but Jack at least would have listened if he'd told him to stay.

Charles's throat ached. Jack had only gone to keep an eye on Ned. At seventeen, the younger boy was grown, but he didn't have the good sense Jack had.

His wife mourned continuously, having both the boys off to war. When they got word of Ned's death, she'd fallen into a dark slump. Ironically, she seemed to be coming out of it now.

She didn't worry as much about Jack as she had Ned, and Charles understood that. Jack was able to take care of himself. He had some innate sense, and Charles suspected it came from his mother's side. Apparently Jack's real father had been a wastrel, but his mother came from old New England stock. Smart, hardworking people. Ned had never been the steady, level-headed boy Jack was. Funny, his adopted son seemed to take after Charles more than his own progeny.

"I tried to talk him into staying," Charles said softly, though he hadn't tried all that hard. "He's needed here too, but—well, he and his brother went in together. We thought that was best at the time."

"The younger boy was kilt," Heinz said with a fierce nod.

The look on Leonard's face was so plain, Charles could almost read his thoughts. Two sons off to fight the rebels. Now one was gone, and the Millers could lose the other.

"I'm very sorry. Do you have other boys, Mr. Miller?"

Charles nodded. "Silas is fourteen, and Peter is twelve." He knew Silas would have gone with his brothers, if they'd let him. He was keeping a close eye on the lad and had tried to impress on him the importance of his presence at home. He'd even tried to interest him in telegraphy, but Silas didn't take to Morse Code the way Jack had.

Caroline was the only other of his children who hadn't

become bored with it. She now worked a couple of shifts a week here at the post office. But Charles wasn't going to tell the recruiter that—he'd probably start hauling off girls who were proficient at the telegraph key.

"You shoulda come sooner." The postmaster shook his head. "Jack worked here for nigh on seven years, and he was second best at the job. I haven't been able to find anyone as good to replace him." He turned away to wait on a woman who had come in with several letters in her hand.

"Ned was keen to enlist," Charles said. "Jack would have waited, but his brother was determined and ... well, his mother and I saw the sense of Jack going at the same time. They got into the same outfit, and Jack took a corporal's stripe."

"Most of our employees are civilians, not military men," Leonard said. "Still, a young man as skilled as you say ... Where is his regiment now?"

That brought a smile to Charles's face. "He's been down in Florida since last winter."

"Florida?"

"He said he couldn't tell me exactly where, but they were working on some fort or other."

Leonard nodded sagely. "I see. Perhaps he'll be transferred somewhere else soon."

"Do you think so?" Charles eyed him sharply. Would his man be privy to troop movements?

"I may look into his current assignment."

Charles caught his breath. "You wouldn't—I mean, he signed up for three years, and it's only been one."

"Sometimes special arrangements can be made," Leonard said. "I can't force him, you understand, but if I can locate him, I'll make him an offer. The army might agree to muster him out so he can come work for us. This is critical work, Mr. Miller."

A glint of hope kindled in Charles's heart. Would Jack be working in an office, somewhere away from the fighting?

Leonard frowned and whipped a small leatherbound notebook from his pocket. "Jack Miller?"

"Yes."

"Is that a nickname for John?"

"No, it's ..." Charles shook his head. He didn't want to have to explain Jack's background and how he'd become part of the Miller family.

"Who's his commanding officer?"

Still Charles hesitated. "Would he be safer with you than he would be with the infantry?"

"I can't guarantee that. He'd be in the capital area for a while, for training. Most of our operators go out into the field with the construction units."

"The field?"

Leonard said slowly, "They build temporary telegraph lines so we can get messages back quickly from the battlefield. It's their job to maintain communications between Washington and the field commanders. Some of our operators are out there collecting the messages. Of course, some stay in Washington, but I can't guarantee it. We need more good operators, Mr. Miller, and you say he's good."

Charles sighed. "Well, you'd have to ask Jack if he wanted to do it."

"Of course. As I said, I can't force him to leave his regiment. But your son has a rare talent that we need right now."

Charles couldn't guess what Frances would say when he told her. But he thought he knew what Jack would say.

September 15, 1862
Beaufort District, South Carolina

"Miller, take eight men and establish the western perimeter of the work area, along the tree line over there." The sergeant pointed toward a patch of woods, where enemies could slink about and spy on them. The other sides of the camp were open, and anyone approaching would be seen before they got close.

"Yes, sir." Jack quickly alerted Jim Snow and the other men. "Form a picket line on the west side, on the edge of the woods. Not too far apart. We need to protect the telegraphers while they work, and this seems like the only place a surprise attack could come from."

Four wagonloads of equipment lumbered into the field. Their supplies included everything from poles, wire, spikes, and insulators, to the precious telegraph key that would eventually transmit and receive messages. If these men couldn't set it up right, the officers wouldn't be able to communicate with headquarters when it came time for battle.

"How do they know where to set up?" Willy Potter asked, shouldering his Springfield.

Jack shrugged. "I expect they've had scouts out for weeks, monitoring the Rebs and intercepting their communications."

"So, they're going to fight us right here?"

"No, they wouldn't plant the telegraph station smack on the battlefield," Jack said. "But it has to be nearby. Close enough so they can run back and forth when they hear something."

Willy shook his head. "If you say so."

Jack smiled and turned away. Willy wasn't his brightest comrade, but he was loyal and hardworking. When they'd labored away for weeks in Beaufort, converting several buildings into a military hospital, Willy worked like a plow horse. The small South Carolina city, in the Beaufort District on the coast, was the first Southern city occupied by Union forces, and was now headquarters for the U.S. Army's Department of the South.

Since leaving Florida, the men of Jack's unit continued what they'd become good at—construction of one sort or another. In their travels, they'd become embroiled in a few skirmishes, but so far they hadn't gone into the thick of a major battle.

No room for guilt about that, Jack reminded himself. Their work was important, and he needn't be ashamed that he wasn't being shot at day after day.

His men did well all morning, keeping guard while the telegraph crew dug holes and raised the poles, then strung the wires. They ate dinner in shifts, and when Sergeant Taft came to relieve Jack so he could eat, the sun told him it was at least two hours past noon. His stomach had been rumbling for some time.

"All quiet?"

"Yes, sir." Jack pointed into the trees. "Haven't seen any activity. I've got two men out nearer the road, one on that knoll, and I think you can see the rest if you look hard. They've all been fed."

Taft nodded. "All but you, eh? Get some chow, Miller."

"Yes, sir." Jack went to collect his plate from the wagon

where the camp cook had set up shop. No fire today, so the meal was cold—if anyone could call it cold in this torrid climate. He doubted Florida was worse than this right now. Wistfully he imagined sitting on a rock on the edge of Dry Tortuga with a fishing pole in his hands and a warm breeze ruffling his hair.

One of the telegraph chaps was fussing at something in the bed of a canvas-topped wagon, and Jack wandered over, shoveling in mouthfuls of beans as he walked. He perked up when he saw the brass telegraph key, mounted on a makeshift desk of rough boards.

"You an operator?" he asked.

The man nodded. "Nash. Out of New Jersey."

"Corporal Jack Miller. I was an operator before the war."

"Really? Whereabouts?"

"Emmaus, Pennsylvania. My father's their head telegrapher."

Nash grinned and stuck out a hand. "Pleased to meet you, Miller."

A man perched twenty feet in the air on one of the poles yelled down, "Give it a try, Nash. Should be in business."

"All right," Nash roared. He leaned over the apparatus and tapped out a quick message—TEST, and the signal to acknowledge, to headquarters in Beaufort. Nothing happened.

Nash swore under his breath and reached for a set of headphones. "Looks like I'm climbing again."

Jack finished his beans and cornbread, keeping an eye on Nash, who fiddled with the wires at the top of the pole.

"Hey, Miller, go over to the wagon and see if you get this," Nash called.

Jack went to stand at the rear of the wagon and set down his plate. After a short pause, the telegraph key inside began to let out a series of clicks. He turned and held up a thumb. "Test to Miller."

Nash laughed. "That's it all right."

Jack grinned at him. "Sounds like a good line to me."

A man rode in from the road on a sweating bay horse. He

leaped down and ran toward the wagons. The lieutenant in charge of the detail intercepted him. "What's going on?"

"We spotted Confederate pickets two miles west. Can you transmit yet?"

"We sure can," Nash yelled down.

Jack's skin crawled and sweat ran down his back. He shouldered his rifle and ran back to his sentry station.

"Sarge, did you hear that? Enemy two miles away."

Taft's mouth was set in a grim line. "I heard." He swore. "We're too far from the main force."

"Nash will send out a message for reinforcements."

"They've got a connection?"

"Yes, sir." Jack turned around and looked toward the towering telegraph pole. Nash had started to climb down.

"Thank God. Pray they get in position before the Rebs find us." Taft clapped Jack on the shoulder and strode off to make the rounds of his meager troops.

Gunfire erupted so suddenly Jack thought his heart would leap out of his chest. He whirled back toward the camp and saw Nash, his arms flailing, fall the last ten feet to the ground.

Jack ran across the clearing. A few shots rang out sporadically, mostly in the direction of the woods. One of the construction crew, Twining, had reached Nash and crouched next to him. Most of the others were huddled behind wagons and piles of equipment.

"Is he alive?" Jack skidded to a stop on Nash's other side.

"Yeah." Twining was pressing a blood-soaked neckerchief to Nash's side.

Jack swallowed hard. Nash's right leg was twisted beneath him, and his bluish lips quivered as he sucked in short, choppy breaths.

"Can we get him in the wagon?" Jack asked.

"Better not move him."

"We're right in the open. They could pick us all off."

Twining gritted his teeth and nodded, looking around the encampment. "All right, on three. One, two—"

Jack got one arm under Nash's back and supported the dangling leg as he lifted, and Twining raised the telegrapher's head and shoulders. Nash let out a yell and passed out. Probably best.

"Hurry," Jack said.

They lugged Nash awkwardly the ten yards to the wagon. Twining muscled the man's head and shoulders in at the back and then scrambled up to pull him the rest of the way inside.

Jack climbed in and pulled Nash's shirt back. The side wound was bleeding copiously.

"Get me something, some cloth," Twining said.

Jack rooted around and found a towel and someone's clean shirt. He took them to Twining, who balled up the towel and pressed it to the wound.

Nash's eyes flickered open. "Have to get a message to HQ," he gasped.

"What is it?" Jack asked. "Tell me and I'll send it. I know how."

"The key word is guard."

"What?" Jack leaned closer.

"Key word. Put that first. Guard. Then ... code name ..."

Nash's eyes were glazing over.

"What does it matter?" Jack demanded. "I'll just tap out a message to Beaufort."

Twining shook his head as he pressed on Nash's wound. "They have code words, and you have to write the message in a certain order."

Jack scowled at him. "We don't have time for that. The Rebs already know where we are. What can it hurt if it's not encrypted?" He gazed down at Nash.

"Do it." Nash closed his eyes.

More gunfire sounded—too close. Jack threw himself prone next to Nash as the sideboard of the wagon splintered.

Twining grunted and sprawled forward, onto Nash's torso.

"You hit?" Jack asked.

Twining stirred. "My arm."

Heart racing, Jack listened. The rifle fire seemed to be moving away, but maybe it was just that his hearing was impaired by the noise. He didn't dare wait.

He rose to his knees and crawled around Twining and Nash to the telegraph key. He hesitated only a second before touching the brass lever. He wasn't sure what to say, but telegrams always started with the name and location of the receiver. He entered his commanding officer's name and Beaufort District, SC.

The Morse symbols came back to him like old friends in his time of need. The words flowed through his fingers, through the key, into the wire.

UNDER ATTACK SEND RELIEF JNASH WOUNDED CPL JMILLER.

Was there a closer station he could notify? He didn't know of one. He waited a couple of minutes.

"You're going to be all right," Twining assured Nash. "Hold on." Though his left sleeve was soaked with blood, Twining's voice sounded calm, and he was using his right hand to once more press the cloth to Nash's wound.

Jack pulled in a shaky breath and resent the same message. A couple of shots sounded to the north of the camp, but then quiet. He stared at the silent telegraph apparatus, wondering if their lines had been cut.

Sergeant Taft peered in at him from the back of the wagon. "Can we get a message out?"

"Nash is hurt," Twining said. "Miller's trying."

"Miller?" The sergeant eyed him sharply.

"I was a telegraph operator before I joined up," Jack said. "Twining's hurt too. Do you have medical supplies?"

"Bandages in the cook wagon. I'll get some."

The receiver began to click, and Taft stopped, staring at it.

Jack had no paper or pencil for the message, so he concentrated on it and spoke the words aloud as they came through.

"Raines five miles out. Hold fast." Then the signal for end of message.

Hastily, Jack sent an acknowledgement of receipt and looked at Taft.

"Raines will be here in an hour."

"If they can get the message to him."

"What can we do?" Jack asked. "Should I come out there?"

"No, the Rebs have pulled back, but they could launch another attack. Our men are in position now, and most of them have good cover. Two of the construction men are wounded. There aren't many enemy out there—I think a scouting party must have stumbled on us and heard the crew working. We can hold out. Just don't go making yourself an easy target." He glanced at the other men. "Any of you, but especially you, Miller. We may need you."

"Yes, sir."

September 25, 1862

JACK WAS ENJOYING this first letter from home in more than a month, letting the nostalgia and comfort warm him, when running footsteps pounded outside and a private stuck his head in at the tent flap.

"Miller, quick! Captain Raines wants you at his tent."

Jack tucked his father's letter inside his bedroll and strode across the camp. What could the captain want with him? Dread and uncertainty swept through him, making him shudder. Would they strip him of his stripes, so that he was no longer corporal of his company? In a way, that might be a relief. It wouldn't be up to him who went into danger.

He paused outside the commanding officer's tent and told the sentry, "Corporal Miller to see the captain."

The private nodded for him to go in.

Captain Raines's tent was the same size as the ones eight soldiers occupied, but his had a cot, a chest, a folding table, and two folding wooden chairs. The captain was seated behind the table, with letters and other papers spread before him. A second officer occupied the other chair.

Jack halted two steps inside and came to attention.

"At ease, Miller," Raines said. "This is Colonel Leonard. He's come a long way looking for you."

Jack's throat went dry. Had he done something wrong? Other than getting his brother killed? Maybe it had to do with Nash, the telegrapher, and Jack using the key to send a message to headquarters without authorization. Or was there trouble at home and they'd sent someone to break it to him gently? He should have finished reading Pa's letter first.

Leonard stood and extended his hand to Jack.

After a quick glance at the captain, who nodded almost imperceptibly, Jack shook the man's hand. Leonard's uniform looked almost new and well cared for. Jack wondered if he'd recently been promoted.

"I'm pleased to meet you, Corporal Miller." Leonard looked him up and down.

Jack waited, wanting to pepper him with questions.

Raines cleared his throat. "Colonel Leonard is with the Military Telegraph Corps."

"Wh—" Jack clamped his lips tightly together, but his heart pounded. What was going on? This must have to do with Nash. He hoped the man hadn't died of his wounds. They'd heard only that he was transported to the nearest hospital.

"I understand you're a proficient telegrapher." Leonard smiled as though this were idle chitchat at a tea party.

"I ... I did work at the telegraph desk in the post office back home, sir."

"I heard about how you helped out a Military Telegraph Corps unit when they were attacked."

"My company was there to guard them, sir."

"Yes, but you were able to send a telegraph message when it was needed."

Jack swallowed hard. "Mr. Nash was wounded, sir. I wouldn't have touched the equipment if I hadn't thought it was urgent." He pressed his shaking hands against his thighs.

After a pause, Leonard gave him a nod. "You did the right thing, son."

Jack exhaled. "Thank you, sir."

Captain Raines stood. "Before Colonel Leonard explains why he's here, I have something to tell you, Miller."

Jack looked from Leonard to the captain and back. So, there was more? He doubted Leonard had requested to see him just because of the incident where Nash was wounded. He rethought the captain's earlier words. The telegraph officer had come a long way to find him. Why?

Raines came to stand directly in front of him. "Miller, because of your ingenuity and quick thinking in the field, I'm recommending you be promoted to sergeant."

Jack's pulse raced. "Thank you, sir." Relief and gratitude washed over him, but also a bit of apprehension. What would the promotion mean? Would he stay with his company of Pennsylvania boys? Would he be transferred? Sent into battle? He could feel sweat soaking his hair and his uniform shirt.

"Yes, well, I had already decided on that, but Colonel Leonard has a different proposition to offer you." The captain turned and walked back to his table. He sat down and leaned back in his chair, watching Jack for a moment. Then he nodded to Leonard.

Colonel Leonard walked between him and the captain. "Son, I'd like to offer you a position in our department. It would mean going back to Washington for special training, and then you'd likely do field work."

"Sir?" Jack's pulse still raced as he tried to make sense of what he was hearing. "I'm in the army, sir."

"Yes, well ..." Leonard looked over at the captain for a moment. "The Secretary of War deems this an essential mission. Our telegraphers are responsible for maintaining communications with our officers in the field, and as you know, they can help prevent many casualties and strategic losses. We're short on men who are already proficient in using the telegraph."

Captain Raines stood with a sheet of paper in his hand. "It's my understanding that you'd be officially discharged—honorably, of course—and taken into the Military Telegraph Corps as a civilian."

"I see," Jack said, but he didn't. "I've served less than half my hitch, sir."

"You've had a rough go of it so far, Miller," Captain Raines said almost gently. "This might be a good change for you."

Jack stared at him, stricken. Raines knew about Ned's death. Did he think that made him weak? Had he been watching Jack all this last year to see if he could hold up under pressure? Did Raines want the bumbling corporal out of his regiment with no fuss? Or was he genuinely concerned about Jack's grief?

Everyone in Jack's company had been shocked by Ned's death, but as the war progressed, they all knew more casualties were coming. Was Raines afraid he couldn't stand up at the next clash? Or would he look at him as a deserter who wanted out as soon as things got tough?

No, he told himself firmly. The offered promotion wasn't a bluff to make him feel better. Raines really planned to recommend him for a sergeant's stripes—if he turned down this stranger's proposition.

"I ... don't know what to say, sir."

"There's no dishonor in this, Corporal," Raines said. "You are a staunch man with a quick mind and unquestioned loyalty. It's an honor to be considered for this position. You should look at it as such."

"Yes, sir." Jack managed to hold the captain's gaze while the alternatives tumbled about in his mind. Was it truly his choice whether to become a sergeant or a telegrapher?

"Then you'll come with me?" Leonard asked. "We'd have to leave immediately. I've got a horse for you, and we've been promised seats on the last train out tonight, but we've no guarantee there will be one tomorrow."

Jack blinked, wondering if the rebels had attacked the railroad lines close by. He could see the need for good communications. Already his mind tore over the possibilities and the ways the Telegraph Corps would deal with sabotaged lines. They'd be out there stringing new ones. Lines to battlefields where no wires had been before, and new ones to replace the main lines now in existence when traitors and spies managed to put them out of commission.

"You know, Miller, the decision is up to you," Raines said. "I'd be happy to have you stay on under my command. But the truth is, a lot of men can serve as sergeants. Only a few have your training and talent."

Jack met the captain's eyes once more and drew courage to replace his doubts. He could help win the war in a bigger way than he'd imagined. He'd be away from his friends, but maybe it was best to separate from those who were beside him when Ned was killed. The memories might fade sooner if he didn't see Jim Snow and Willy Potter every day.

He knew what Ma Miller would tell him—God had opened a door for him, and he ought not to dawdle going through it.

10

Marilla stood at the stove, stirring the gravy while Sadie fixed the sweet potatoes and Reenie, under protest, whipped the cream to top the pies for the dessert course. It was a job Reenie hated.

Another of the field hands had run away. Uncle Hamilton was out on the porch ranting about it to the three men who'd come out from town to join him for dinner tonight.

"How are we supposed to plant come spring, if the hands all think they can up and leave? And there aren't enough officers to chase after them."

"There's a war on, Buckley," said Dr. Riley.

Uncle Hamilton had invited his overseer, Zeke Vernon, to eat with them, mainly to fill out the table, Marilla figured. Vernon was the leader of the small squad of white men her uncle had gathered around him to keep him and River Lea safe. And Marilla, of course. But she didn't feel safe around those men. They were Hamilton Buckley's private little army.

"This is ready," she said to Sadie, who was the sweetheart of the man who'd run away.

Over the year since her cousin William died in battle, she and Sadie had developed a truce. It wasn't a slave and mistress relationship, and it certainly wasn't a friendship. Marilla wasn't sure what to call it, even in her mind. She abhorred the thought of owning Sadie, yet she could tell the cook still didn't trust her completely.

The situation at River Lea had deteriorated. Uncle Hamilton's rants and rages had become more frequent since he got the news of the Battle of Ball's Bluff on the Potomac last fall. His temper flared seemingly at random, and he rode off on sporadic jaunts without telling anyone where he was going, only to return later exhausted and incommunicative.

Since the number of their staff, as Marilla preferred to think of them, had dwindled, she started going into the kitchen regularly. For the last six months she'd done her best to help Sadie with the burden of providing meals.

The cook had opposed her presence from the beginning. But over time Marilla proved her proficiency at food preparation, and with more slaves sneaking off in a bid for freedom, Sadie tolerated her.

Four times Uncle Hamilton had sent Zeke Vernon and his men to track down runaways. They'd only succeeded once, and Marilla felt ill every time she thought of what they'd done to the man—so she refused to think about it. She had to go on living here, and that would be impossible if she thought too much about what went on around her.

Sometimes she imagined herself as one of the runaways. She'd heard whispers of the Underground Railroad. Slaves ran away into the night, guided from one hiding place to another. The guides, or conductors, risked their own lives by helping the escaped slaves. Marilla admired them for their courage and their passion.

Reenie had been whipping the cream for at least ten

minutes. Her arm must ache as though it would fall off. The task was a thankless one, though not as hard as working in the fields.

Marilla stepped over to her side and put her hand over Reenie's, stilling her circular motion with the wire whisk.

"I'll do that."

Reenie stared at her for a moment, her face a blank, then let go of the handle.

A bell on the wall jingled, signaling that the master wanted his dinner.

Marilla smiled at Reenie as she took up the beating rhythm. "Help Sadie serve. This will be ready when you come back—you did most of it."

The two black women carried trays up the stairs to the dining room. A minute later, Sadie was back.

"Mr. Buckley wants you to go in and eat with them."

Marilla had half expected the summons. She'd excused herself earlier, while the gentlemen enjoyed a preprandial glass of Bourbon. She'd told her great-uncle she didn't enjoy dining with a room full of men, hoping he would invite the wives and daughters, but he hadn't taken the hint. He wanted to talk to his cronies without feminine influence. But he still liked to show off Marilla as his hostess, and she loathed that role.

Hosting dinners and parties had seemed glamorous while Aunt Olive was alive. In the North as a girl, Marilla had only attended informal gatherings, so the social events of the plantation community dazzled her at first.

She'd been here five years now, spending four of them as the only white woman residing at River Lea. When she'd turned sixteen last year, Uncle Hamilton had insisted she take over the role of hostess whenever company came.

Working in the kitchen alongside Sadie and Reenie was a job she found preferable. At least in the kitchen, men weren't ogling her and making excuses to touch her hand or brush up against her.

She reached behind her to pull the ties of her oversized apron. "Set the cream in the ice box until it's time."

Pulling in a deep breath, she went to the dining room.

"Ah, there she is," Uncle Hamilton said jovially.

The other men shot to their feet. Her great-uncle came to hold her chair for her, and Marilla gave the guests a stiff smile. She couldn't wait for the moment the meal was finished, when she could slip away without censure while the men enjoyed their cigars and bourbon.

December 21, 1862
Washington, D.C.

"HERE IS YOUR CIPHER BOOK," the supervisor said as his aide circled the room, handing out booklets. "As you've learned, these are much smaller than those our colleagues use in the navy. Since we use fewer code words than they, and we change our key words more frequently, this is all you need."

Jack was well acquainted with the thick leather binders with lead-lined covers the navy's Signal Corps used. The army used a different system altogether, allowing for smaller and lighter references. Whereas the navy men would throw their weighted codebooks overboard if capture was imminent, army men would have much less on them to lose. Even so, extreme caution must be exercised with their cipher books.

"This has all the key words for our current ciphers. These will tell you the routing instruction. Also included are the arbitraries you will use for encrypting names and places. If these change, you will be informed. Do not let this book out of your sight. Do not give it to anyone else, not even a high-ranking officer. Guard it with your life."

Jack ran his fingertips over the smooth leather cover. It bore no title, as was fitting for a secret book.

"Open to the front."

Along with the twenty other new operators, Jack turned to the first page. Inside, the leather was incised with the words United States Military Telegraph Corps and #107. He noted the blank lines on the following pages, where he could pencil in new code names for various commanders, places, and military units as needed.

He drew in a deep breath. This was real.

It seemed more real than Ned's death or anything since. The palm trees in Florida and the steamship voyage around the peninsula were foggy memories now.

His heart still pounded when he recalled the train ride from South Carolina to Washington with Colonel Leonard. As the wheels clacked over the tracks, he'd wondered whether they would be hit by a hostile force. Throughout Maryland and southern Virginia, disruption of the rail lines was commonplace now, and the threat was almost universal.

They'd made it through, and with a handful of other recruits, Jack had been introduced to Anson Stager, who had been pulled in from Ohio, where he'd managed secret telegraph communication for the governor, and was now head of the United States Military Telegraph Department.

With the other latecomers to the special unit, Jack was shuttled to a boardinghouse, where he was assigned to a room with a man five years his senior, Wilfred Carson. It wasn't bad, since Jack was used to sharing a room with several brothers and then a tent with half a dozen or more soldiers. Though Carson complained of the morning chill in the third-floor room, Jack found it quite cozy and enjoyed the relative privacy they had in their free time.

For eight weeks, each day was filled with training, but not the kind he'd experienced when he enlisted. First, they spent two weeks preparing to work with construction crews, learning to handle the tools and equipment and string new lines. Repairs and emergency measures were included. During that phase, Jack went back to the boardinghouse each night more tired than when he'd marched all day.

The next six weeks entailed sitting at a desk ten hours a day, working out substitutions and mathematical puzzles and memorizing routing sequences. The mental fatigue was more welcome than the physical grind. Each afternoon, one of the instructors updated them on anything new their field telegraphers and spies had learned about Confederate communications.

The men in Jack's unit were coached on unraveling dummy messages to prepare them for real ones that would—they hoped —be intercepted. They focused mainly on two cryptography systems—the one known to be used by the Confederates, and that developed by the Union codemakers.

Jack found he was quite good at solving, and he actually enjoyed decrypting more than he liked encoding sample messages from American headquarters in the cipher for which they had a key. The challenge of breaking a message from the enemy excited him.

"You won't be able to leave over Christmas," the supervisor said.

Carson groaned, along with a few others, but Jack wasn't upset. He didn't expect time off. If they slacked off, the Confederates might take advantage. He would work even harder. With his training complete, he was ready to work on real dispatches.

The supervisor paused in his pacing. "You will, however, be allowed to send one private message each by telegram to your families, at no cost to you. This should be a message no longer than ten words."

Jack grinned at Carson. This was reward enough for him. Carson just shrugged, but Jack was already planning his holiday greeting in his mind.

MERRY CHRISTMAS TO ALL. NEW JOB FINE.

LOVE JACK

Only nine words. It would be a shame to waste one. He'd have to refine it tonight.

The following afternoon, after he'd sent his telegram, Jack would sit down and write a longer letter, detailing his circumstances, though he knew it would be heavily censored.

On the train two months ago, Leonard had told him about meeting his father in Emmaus, and Jack had sent a brief letter as soon as he could, telling of his changed situation. He imagined both his parents were relieved to know he wasn't on the battleline. But since coming to Washington, he'd only had time to dash off quick notes, and he knew the family would want more details.

Of course, he'd be going out into the field again, perhaps soon, in advance of the troops, to build new lines. He'd be in at least as much danger as he had been with the 47th Pennsylvania.

Wilfred Carson sat next to him in the classroom where they'd trained. He wiggled his bushy eyebrows, and Jack smiled. They were ready to work in earnest.

"Mr. Simpson will now hand out the assignments," the supervisor said, and his assistant took a stack of envelopes off the front desk.

"Those of you who drew field duty, your deployment orders will come within the week." Simpson spoke as he walked among them, handing each man an envelope.

"You'll travel with one of the armies. When the commanding officer gives you messages, you'll relay them back to headquarters. If they intercept Confederate messages, they'll bring them to you to try to decipher. As you've learned, you will also send a copy here. And when the construction crew goes out to build a new telegraph line, you'll go with them."

Jack swallowed hard, remembering Nash's fate and wondering if he would be assigned field duty.

When he received his envelope, Wilfred was watching him, holding his own in his hands.

"Together?" Wilfred whispered.

Jack nodded, and they lifted the flaps. Jack took out the paper inside and scanned it quickly, then drew in a deep breath. He hadn't been assigned to field duty yet. A stark office in Washington was his lot for now, where he'd work with a dozen other fellows. He didn't mind a bit. But his turn would come if the war went on for more than a few months. All of the telegraphers were told to expect marching orders sooner or later, probably sooner.

He looked over at Wilfred. His friend's face twitched. "I'm for field work. You?"

Jack shook his head, feeling suddenly selfish. "War Department."

"Congratulations," Wilfred said softly.

"Now remember, all of you, this is our current code." The supervisor tapped his own copy of the precious cipher book. "Take it with you, and have it on your person when you report to your new post. I don't need to tell you how imperative it is that you don't speak of it to anyone outside your department, and that you don't carelessly leave this book lying about."

Jack gritted his teeth. He'd failed to protect Ned. He would not fail at this.

"New items will be added to the arbitraries as the theater of war changes. You will be updated, wherever you are working. And if there is any danger the code has been intercepted or cracked by the enemy, you'll receive an entirely new codebook."

They'd learned this during training, but Jack had been stymied. How would they know if the cipher was compromised? And how often could that possibly happen? How would they get the new codebooks to the men in the field, or pass on the new arbitraries—the words they would substitute for names? It was all beyond him, but he was sure clever men would figure it out.

They were soon dismissed. Jack could tell Wilfred was

unsettled as they walked home, but he wasn't sure he could help his friend so he kept quiet.

When they reached the boardinghouse, Mrs. Grayson, the landlady, met them in the hallway.

"Mail for both of you today, lucky boys." She handed them each one item.

"Thank you, ma'am," Jack said, hurrying to their room, while Wilfred trudged behind him up the stairs.

Jack tore open the bulging envelope. It was full of notes from his siblings and his mother. Caroline described their outing to cut down a Christmas tree on a neighbor's farm, complete with a sketch of Pa pulling their older sister Elizabeth's two toddlers on a sled. At the bottom she spelled out "I miss you" in Morse Code.

His mother's letter was two pages of cramped script, telling of their plans for Christmas and how much they wished he could get leave and come home. Of course she mentioned how much they would miss Ned as well, and Jack's eyes filled with tears. He pulled out a handkerchief to blow his nose.

Pa had simply scrawled at the bottom of Ma's letter, "Proud of you, son!"

Wilfred had finished his letter and was sorting through his clothing.

"I'll need to do some laundry, I suppose." He gazed bleakly at a frayed shirt and gave it a cautious sniff.

"Anything I can do to help you?" Jack asked.

"Don't think so. Here." Wilfred tossed him a worn leather belt.

"What's this?"

"It's an extra. We can only take one small bag. I expect they'll put our stuff in a wagon, but we might have to carry it sometimes. I doubt I'll need my heavy coat."

"Take it," Jack said. "They might send you into the mountains. You just never know."

Wilfred frowned and nodded. "Well, here. My ma knit me

some new gloves. If you think these will do you any good ... " He passed Jack a pair with a small hole worn in each index finger.

"Thanks. If you're sure." He didn't have any since his trip to Florida. Colonel Leonard had found him a secondhand shirt and a pair of trousers along the way, and he'd bought another shirt since arriving in Washington, but Jack's civilian wardrobe was pitifully meager. He had no doubt his mother or sisters would knit him some socks, but he hadn't yet received any parcels from home.

"When do you go?"

"Tomorrow," Wilfred said. "You?"

"I report to the War Department the day after Christmas."

"It's farther from here than where we've been working. Will you move?"

"I don't think so, but I thought I'd practice the walk this evening. If it's not too far, I'd like to stay here."

Seeking new lodgings would be a bother. And while the food at the boardinghouse wasn't as good as what Ma Miller cooked, Jack knew it was much better than what the infantrymen were getting. He'd as soon stick with Mrs. Grayson as take a chance on a new landlady's cooking.

"Lucky you. Guess I'd better write to my folks." Wilfred swallowed hard and sat down in their only chair, at the tiny table they used as a desk.

"You'll be all right," Jack said, feeling guilty.

"Well, I knew it was coming. It's what we signed up for."

Jack didn't know what to say. His turn would come, but saying it wouldn't make Wilfred feel better.

"They didn't tell us where we're headed," Wilfred said, not looking up from the letter he'd started, "but I'll warrant it's south. I'm to be at the railroad station at six."

Jack's throat went dry. "At least you won't start out with a long march. Good luck. I'll miss you."

"Same here."

Wilfred gazed at him with troubled eyes. "Look, Jack, not to be morbid or anything, but I'm writing out a message, and if I don't make it, I'd appreciate it if you'd send it to my family."

"You'll be back, Wil. You can send your own message."

"A construction crew was attacked in western Virginia last week. Three of our men were killed."

Jack's heart plummeted. "Telegraphers?"

"Construction men, but still ... Please take the message. I'll feel easier."

"All right, give it to me when you're finished." Jack walked over to the washstand and poured water into the basin. As he scrubbed the long workday's grime off his hands, Jack wondered if he'd ever see Wilfred after tomorrow.

His two families sprang to his mind—the active, boisterous Millers, ten people crammed into a little frame house. They were fewer now, without him and Ned or the two older girls who'd married and gone to their own homes, but four children still made a full home.

Caroline was twenty, and many people were surprised she hadn't married yet. But Jack recalled her heartbreak three years ago, when the young man she'd set her heart on died of diphtheria. She stayed home with her parents and the three younger children, Silas, Peter, and Ruthie. She never spoke of Andrew Collins, but Jack knew she still mourned him.

His other family were shadows of memories now. Jack dried his hands and touched his chest. Through his shirt front, he could feel the small disk on its cord—the Chinese coin his grandfather had brought to all his grandchildren years ago. Not Grandfather Miller, who had passed on when Jack was ten, but Grandfather Rose, the sea captain he couldn't remember.

Zeph, his older brother Zephaniah Joseph, had clearly remembered the old man he was named after, and their Grandmother Rose too. They had a cousin, Abby, somewhere in Maine, but Jack didn't recall her at all. Just Zeph, or Joey as he'd sometimes called him due to his middle name, and their mite of a baby sister, Janie.

Jack had been sick with terror when first Janie, then Zeph had disappeared from the orphanage and he was left alone. At least someone had wanted them and taken them. He'd feared he would stay in the orphanage until he was old enough to go to work. His own dear mother was a ghost of a beautiful face now, and his birth father was gone, both from his recollection and from his life.

He sighed and sent up a prayer for his first family, wherever they were now. The ones in Maine were probably well out of the war. He hoped his grandparents and Abby were safe. Of the others, he had no idea. Zeph could be in the army now. He might even be fighting for the other side. Or worse—he could be lying dead on some battlefield. Jack shuddered, thinking of Ned.

God, keep my big brother safe. Please keep Zeph safe!

Mrs. Grayson's dinner bell clanged ten minutes later, and Wilfred rose with a sigh. Jack accepted the folded paper handed to him and put it in his Bible on the shelf by his cot.

"You'll be all right," he said without believing it.

"Sure." Wilfred gave him a tight smile. "Well, I reckon it's time to eat. You coming?"

"Yeah." They walked down to the dining room for their final supper together.

11

Because Wilfred was leaving so early, Jack had time to walk with him to the railroad station in the morning. The gray promise of dawn surrounded them as they approached the platform. A large group of men in civilian dress and a company of infantrymen milled about, talking quietly in the chilly air.

"Do you suppose they're actually fighting, so close to Christmas?" Wilfred asked.

"I hope not. Maybe you'll be repairing lines the Confederates have interfered with."

"Why not just send out laborers for that?"

Jack sighed. It probably seemed a waste to Wilfred, after all his training. "They need someone with them who can test the lines and send messages back to headquarters. And you'll be the one to make sure the apparatus is kept in top condition and the batteries are fresh."

Wilfred pressed his lips together and nodded. He shifted the straps of his rucksack then held out his hand, a somber expression on his face. "So long."

Jack shook his hand. "Stay well, friend. I hope we meet again."

"Same here. And don't you feel guilty because you're staying."

Jack gave him a weak smile. "But I do."

"Hey, you've been out on the lines before. I haven't. It's my turn."

"Right. I hope the worst thing you encounter is helping lug those heavy poles."

Wilfred laughed. A train pulled into the platform with a shriek of brakes. Wilfred gave Jack a casual salute and went to join the other men of the telegraph unit.

Jack stayed until the train pulled out. He hurried back to Mrs. Grayson's wishing he could begin at the War Department today, but he had a few more shifts in store at his old office. When he made the change, he would work under David Strouse, who had formerly served as a telegrapher with the Pennsylvania Railroad. Jack wondered if he'd ever taken a message from Mr. Strouse in the days when he worked at the post office.

At the boardinghouse, he went upstairs to the room that seemed hollow without Wilfred in it. He gathered a couple of pencils and slipped a few coins in his pocket. He was fortunate that Mrs. Grayson packed lunches for her boarders for a small fee. He went downstairs to collect it and eat a quick breakfast of one egg, toast, and tea.

"Sorry, it's not more," the landlady said.

Jack smiled at her. "At least you got a few eggs. This is great."

Though it was a meager spread, Jack sent up a prayer of thanks and filled the empty corners of his stomach with toast. He hoped his family back in Emmaus wasn't hungry this morning.

"Here you go, Corporal Miller." Mrs. Grayson handed him a covered lard bucket with tears in her eyes. "We'll surely miss Mr. Carson. He's a good lad." Her voice choked and she put a hand to her mouth.

"There, now," Jack said awkwardly. "He's got a good head on his shoulders. I'm sure he'll be fine."

"Oh, I do hope so. Now, you have a good day, you hear me?"

Jack smiled. She did remind him of Ma Miller sometimes.

"I'll do my best." He wondered if she would put another man in the room with him right away. Of course, the widow had to take all the boarders she could get to eke out a living. Jack just hoped the newcomer was as easy to get along with as Wilfred, whose most annoying habit had been leaving his dirty clothes on the floor overnight.

His last few days at the training office passed without incident, and on Christmas Day he worked the evening shift. It seemed like any other workday, except for the small parcel of ginger cookies Mrs. Grayson handed each boarder in the morning. Jack gave her a packet of needles he'd bought at a haberdashery, and she fussed over the little gift as if it were a golden brooch.

The next day, his walk to the War Department took him past some of the entrenchments and a battery of field artillery that General McLellan had ordered built to defend the capital. With the four new forts that had been constructed nearby, Washington was said to be the best defended city in the world.

Once past the sentry at the door to the imposing building, Jack was shown to a room where he sat at a table with three other men. In all about twenty occupied the chamber, all in civilian clothes except the officer who occasionally entered and paced between the tables for a few minutes.

Messages were delivered frequently—from where, Jack didn't know. He supposed telegraphers in another part of the building received coded ones from field officers over the wire. The ones they were to encrypt reached them via couriers, from government officials and military officers within the city.

He'd hardly sat down when he was handed several messages to encrypt for sending to army officers in various places. Details about troop movements, supply wagons, and strategy sessions flew through Jack's fingers. He enjoyed using his telegraphy skills, but the encryption and decryption parts of the job became a passion.

Each message had a key word—the mystery Nash had tried

to impart months ago. Now Jack understood it. The key word told him how to route the message. He was to copy it out in grid form—so many columns, and so many words to each row. He did that on a slate, as paper was scarce. In columns that didn't come out even, he filled in blanks with random words. The routing element told him in what order to send the columns, and whether to read each one up or down.

Two months ago, he'd found it baffling. Now it was his everyday way to communicate. When he sat down to write a plaintext letter to his family, it seemed odd. He wondered if Caroline would like to learn this type of code. She'd be good at it, but it didn't seem they recruited women for this job.

At the end of his first week in the new unit, his supervisor spoke to him as he left the room. "Good work, Miller. I'm getting reports of accuracy on the messages you handled."

"Thank you, sir." Jack still felt a warm pride as he walked to his boardinghouse. He'd done well. He wouldn't brag about it, but he knew his parents would be pleased.

On his way home, he met a troop of soldiers marching down the street. Jack stood aside and watched them pass. They looked smart in their dark blue jackets and trousers. He looked down ruefully at his plain work clothes and realized he didn't really miss the uniform and taking care to make it always presentable for inspection.

He and Ned had taken pride in keeping up their gear, but now Jack had no regrets. If he were still wearing a uniform, he wouldn't be doing code work. He raised his chin a fraction of an inch. Knowing he was doing crucial work for his country—work that might save the lives of many soldiers—was worth the trade-off. If anyone asked him why he wasn't wearing blue, he could tell them rightfully that he did important work for the government.

"Well, sir, you got a parcel today," Mrs. Grayson said when he walked in the door.

"Really? Me?" Jack took the box she brought him and smiled

as he scanned the address. "My father's hand. I expect it's my Christmas gift."

"Better late than never."

"Right." Jack sniffed. "What's for supper?"

"Got a bit of chicken, I did, so I made a stew."

"It smells delicious."

The lines at the corners of Mrs. Grayson's eyes deepened as she smiled. "Well, it's the only way to make a half chicken go 'round with so many at the table." She straightened her shoulders. "But I'm not complaining, no sir."

"Of course not." Jack hid his grin. "I'll just take this upstairs."

"Ten minutes, that's when I serve supper."

"I'll be there."

He cut the string from his box and lifted the lid. Bless Ma Miller. She'd made him a new shirt and bought a new set of drawers. He was truly grateful. Wouldn't Ma be shocked to know how many soldiers were marching around without underclothes?

Caroline had somehow got hold of a small pocket ledger and wrapped it separately for him, and Ruthie contributed the first pair of socks she'd ever knitted. Jack laughed as he examined them. They had quite a few lumps, and several gaps between stitches, but those wouldn't show beneath his trouser cuffs. At least they were roughly the same size. For an eleven-year-old, she'd done a creditable job.

The dinner bell rang, and he quickly washed his hands and scuttled down the stairs. He didn't want to miss Mrs. Grayson's cooking, and she took umbrage with those who entered her dining room late.

At the supper table, he sat between Caleb Ritter, who was also part of the Telegraph Department, and Robert Jasper, a man who worked for the *Washington Star*, one of more than two dozen newspapers in the city. Jasper always had stories to tell while they drank their coffee after a meal.

Mrs. Grayson offered cake that night, drizzled with a sparse glaze.

"Couldn't get any sugar today," she said regretfully as she distributed the plates. "This is the last of it until I can get more."

"I've heard a lot of foodstuffs are in short supply," Jasper said. "Especially when it's got to be brought in."

"Yes, coffee's very dear now." The landlady gave them a meaningful look.

When she'd left the room, Caleb whispered, "I think she's going to ration our coffee even tighter than she has been, boys."

"I wouldn't blame her," Jack said. "If it's hard to get, or if she has to pay more, she ought to charge us more."

"Oh, please." Jasper held up a hand in protest. "Don't even think it."

After they finished eating, Jack and Caleb sat on the back porch. Jack sat upwind of Caleb, who enjoyed smoking. Mrs. Grayson wouldn't allow it inside, so they often wandered to this haven in the evening.

"Heard from my pa today," Caleb said.

"What's he say?" Not that Jack really cared, but any news outside their world of military jargon and clandestine messages was mildly interesting.

"He's still under the illusion that I'll be safe in this job."

"And so we are, for now," Jack said.

Caleb grunted.

A chilly breeze struck them, and Jack shivered. "We'll have to give this up soon. It's too cold to sit out here."

"All right. Let me finish my cigar."

Jack wished he was up in his room. It would be cool up there tonight, but not a bad as out here in the wind.

"How'd they get you?" Caleb asked. "Did you volunteer?"

Startled, Jack asked, "You mean for the Telegraph Department?"

"No, for the war in general. You started out an infantryman, right?"

"I enlisted."

Caleb tapped his cigar on the porch railing, letting the ashes fall into Mrs. Grayson's dormant flower bed. "I heard you was a corporal."

"Yeah." Jack stared out at the street, where pedestrians and occasional wagons passed.

"So how'd you get here?"

"The story is, they tried to recruit my pa. He's a telegraph operator up in Pennsylvania. He taught me when I was small. By the time I was sixteen, I started working a key for pay. Not much at first—not nearly as much as my Pa earned, but after a couple years, I was considered a regular telegrapher."

"So, did your pa sign on too?"

"Nope. He was needed where he was."

Jack supposed some people might look down on Charles Miller for not going to Washington to serve, but he truly was needed back home. Jack would never think less of him for staying in Emmaus.

Still, the work he was doing here impressed him more each day, as he was handed messages addressed to the likes of McLellan, Scott, and Halleck. And this morning he'd been handed a Rebel message to try his hand at. It was a tricky cipher, and Jack surprised himself by cracking it in under two hours. It wasn't of vital importance, just word of supply shortages in the Carolinas, which they already knew, but Mr. Strouse had been impressed with Jack's prowess.

No doubt he would be given more important assignments in the future. Or sent out into the field like Wilfred. That thought was daunting, but field work was critical as well. He prayed daily for the strength to accept whatever duty was handed him and do it well.

He huddled on the cold porch, waiting for Caleb to finish his smoke. Jack missed the big, noisy Miller family terribly, but surely now he was where God had placed him.

January 3, 1863
River Lea Plantation

MARILLA and her uncle were finishing their luncheon when a loud knocking on the front door reverberated through the house. Startled, they stared at each other.

"Mr. Buckley! Mr. Buckley, open up, sir!"

"It's Vernon," Marilla said. The overseer frightened her a little, and she avoided him whenever possible.

Uncle Hamilton shoved back his chair and strode into the front hall. Marilla rose and followed him, hanging back when she reached the dining room doorway.

Reenie had already reached the front door. She opened it, and Vernon pushed past her.

"He's done it, Mr. Buckley. That Lincoln's saying his proclamation takes effect now. All the slaves in the Confederate states can—" The overseer paused and shot a sidelong glance at Reenie. "You know what they been talkin' about, sir."

Reenie closed the door and stood with her head bowed, as though she didn't hear their conversation, let alone understand it, but Marilla knew better.

Buckley tipped his head back and gave out a roar.

Vernon jumped and eyed him cautiously. "What you want us to do, sir?"

Buckley turned on Reenie. "Get my coat, you worthless clod!"

When Reenie had scrambled out of the room, Buckley moaned. "It's all Davis's fault. Nobody else would have made such a mess of things. Why, oh why wouldn't the council listen to me?"

Marilla stepped forward, not wanting to incite more anger from her uncle, but unable to help herself.

"Mr. Vernon, what is it?"

He swore. "That ape Lincoln says all the slaves in our nation are free now. Did he include the slaves up North? No, ma'am, he did not. Just those in Confederate states. It's below criminal."

Marilla caught her breath. She'd heard months ago that President Lincoln would issue such a proclamation, but the plantation owners hadn't believed it. They'd all thought the South would have won its independence before that could happen. And even if they didn't, how could Lincoln enforce it?

She inhaled slowly. What would it mean at River Lea? Would Reenie and Sadie and the rest leave them now? And if they did, what would become of her?

She had a sudden vision of her uncle wearing filthy clothes, because he had no idea how to do laundry, and eating raw vegetables because he'd never cooked a meal in his life. A second picture followed—of Marilla herself doing all the chores the house slaves now performed. Would she become a slave herself, forced to take care of the big house and do all the cooking, cleaning, and laundry alone? Forget about the crops. They would starve to death.

Reenie came on tiptoe with her master's coat and gloves. She stopped two yards from Buckley and held them out at arm's length. He stepped toward her and grabbed them.

"Come on, Vernon, we've got to make sure the guards are alert. Once this gets out, they'll try to run for it. We need to keep them in the quarters—"

The door slammed behind them.

Reenie stared at Marilla. "What does it mean, Miz Marilla?"

Marilla drew in a careful breath. "God only knows, Reenie."

12

February 4, 1863
Emmaus, Pennsylvania

"I don't think we're safe here, Frances." Charles Miller was not accustomed to pleading with his wife. She usually went along with whatever he proposed—at least when she had time to think it over. Look at Jack. She'd opposed the adoption at first, but inside a week she'd admitted he'd done a good thing when he brought the boy home.

"But, Charles, what about Elizabeth and Jenny? We won't see our grandchildren again if we leave here. And Jack! Poor Jack. If he gets leave, he'll come home, and there'll be no one here for him."

"We'll let Jack know. He'll understand. I'm sure he knows how those Rebels keep raiding and pushing farther north. Think of the little ones, Frances. We need to keep them safe, but Jack can take care of himself."

Her eyes teared up, and Charles knew what she was thinking. *That's what we thought about Ned.*

"But why Connecticut?" she wailed.

"We can go farther north if you want, but there's a job in Bridgeport if I tell them today that I want it."

"Bridgeport." Her brow wrinkled. "Where is that?"

"It's on the coast. Not too far above New York."

"But won't enemy ships be in and out of there?"

"I don't know, maybe. I doubt it."

The truth was, nobody knew what Jefferson Davis and the Confederate Army would do next.

"Pa, can I get a job there too?" Caroline asked plaintively.

She'd helped out enormously since Jack left, working hard at home to help her mother and then hiring on at the telegraph office, contributing nearly all her wages to the family's coffers.

"I'm sure you can." But that wasn't true, so he amended, "Well, I'm not really sure, but I think it's as likely as here."

Caroline walked over to her mother and put an arm around her. "We can do this, Ma."

"The boys—"

"The schools are supposed to be good in New England."

Frances eyed her daughter tearfully. "What about Jenny? With Luke gone to war, we can't leave her alone. She's expecting."

"She can go with us," Charles said quickly. "We'll write to Jack and Luke tonight and tell them."

Caroline turned to look at him. "Shouldn't we ask Jenny first?"

"Well, yes, of course." Charles stood. His lunch hour was more than over. "I've got to get back to the post office. Caro, you talk to Jenny. If she agrees, come and tell me. But I have to let them know in Bridgeport by five o'clock, or the job goes to someone else."

"Put in a good word for me." Caroline grabbed her woolen cape and dashed out the door.

"Oh, Charles," Frances said, lifting her apron to wipe her tears. "This has been our home for over twenty years."

"And too small for at least ten." He walked over and drew her into his arms. "We'll get a bigger place, Frances. Something with more than three bedrooms, and a bigger kitchen. You'll like that."

"How do you know?"

"The Lord will find us a place."

Dear Jack,

I have decided to move the family. I know you hoped to come home to us in Emmaus, but I've an offer of a position farther north, and I think the family will be safer there. We hate to leave Elizabeth and her family behind, but she has her in-laws. I have to think of your mother and the little ones.

Luke has gone to war now. He kept out of it for a good bit, but he had to go. Jenny is coming with us. We expect a new grandchild next summer.

We're going to Bridgeport, Connecticut. You can reach us through the post office there. I will actually be doing my work at the train station in that city. Ma will send you the address of our new home when we find a place and settle in. My new supervisor with the railroad has promised to help us find something.

It's still cold, and even colder up there. I am going up next week, but I'll come back on the train if I can in a month or two, to get Ma and the kids. Caroline hopes to get work as a telegrapher as well, and we are told they're much needed, as so many have gone to work for the government. She could stay here and work, but your mother forbade it. I was glad—we'd all be heartbroken if our Caro didn't go with us, and I don't think it's safe for a young woman to be alone.

That's all for now, Son. We're glad you are attending church. We pray for you every day.

Pa

JACK READ the letter over twice. He wondered if Pa hoped to keep the younger boys, Silas and Peter, from running off and trying to enlist. Silas was only fourteen, and Peter twelve, but boys their age and younger had left home to join the army, whether officially or not.

Connecticut. He didn't think he'd ever been there, but still, it wasn't too far from the area where he was born, was it? He'd have to look at a map and find out exactly where Bridgeport was.

13

August 11, 1863
Boston, Massachusetts

Ryland Atkins held out his train ticket. "But I was told I could get through now."

"No, no. Haven't you heard? Pennsylvania is still in chaos—ever since that huge battle last month. And Meade's army is being harassed right and left. You can't go down there."

"Please, I—"

"Are you deaf, man?" the stationmaster all but screamed. "I have orders. Even if I thought it was safe, these trains are only for military detachments and diplomats right now, and until I hear otherwise, nobody's going that far south. Now, you can get a train to Worcester or Hartford, but nothing outside New England right now."

Ryland turned away. He couldn't go back to Maine without some news for his client. Mrs. Rose was paying dearly for him to continue his search for her grandchildren.

A porter directed him to a telegraph station, and he stood in line.

"I'd like to send a telegram to Emmaus, Pennsylvania," he began when he reached the window.

"Not today, you won't," the woman behind the grille said.

"I beg your pardon?"

"Lines are a mess down there. Is it military business?"

"No."

"Is it urgent?"

"Well ..." Ryland supposed it wasn't, not in the sense that war communications were urgent.

"Best wait a while," the operator said.

"How long a while?"

"A few weeks, maybe?"

He sighed. "Can I send a message to Portland, Maine?"

"If it's short."

Ryland crumpled the form he'd made out for the postmaster of Emmaus and took the new form she slid under the grille. Quickly he spelled out Mr. Turner's name and address.

TURNED BACK AT BOSTON.

Ryland named a hotel where he hoped he could get a room for the night. He also hoped they had a telegraph station of their own—many large hotels did nowadays.

He finally left the train station carrying his bag and sought out a café. The soup he ordered had barely a hint of meat in it, and what passed for coffee wasn't worth drinking. The biscuits were good, but that was the best he could say about his meal. Butter was nonexistent, but the waitress brought him a small pot of apple jelly that looked as though every customer all day had stuck his knife in it.

This was insane. How was he ever to find the two lost Cooper children, who disappeared in New York twenty years ago, if he couldn't get past Massachusetts?

He was reasonably sure the middle child, Elijah, had landed in Pennsylvania, at least for a while. The client was praying the family that adopted Elijah hadn't moved. Then there was Jane, the baby. Ryland had no clue yet where the Weaver family had taken her when they'd left Brooklyn. He'd hoped to bring Elijah and little Janie back to their grandmother before this, but the war had shackled him.

With a sigh, he picked up his luggage and headed for the hotel. At least he'd found the eldest, Zephaniah Cooper, now known as Matthew Anderson, and a wild adventure that had been! But the trains had been running then, and he'd managed to get messages through, even from the wilderness of Colorado Territory.

Now he wondered if the Andersons had been able to get back to their ranch after their visit to Mrs. Rose in Maine. What if they'd been sidelined along the way?

No sense worrying about them right now.

He entered the huge hotel and stepped up to the desk, where the clerk greeted him with a smile. "May I help you, sir?"

"I'd like a room for the night."

"I'm so sorry. We're full tonight."

Ryland huffed out a breath. "Of course you are."

"So many train cancellations and whatnot," the clerk said.

"Trust me, I understand. Can you recommend a likely place where I can lay my head tonight?"

"Well ..." The clerk seemed doubtful at best, but he named a few establishments within walking distance.

Ryland hefted his bag and set off again. He'd slept in all sorts of odd places on his trip west last spring. Haylofts weren't easy to come by in Boston, however.

He stopped by the telegraph station and gave his name. Nothing yet.

Two hours later, discouraged and exhausted, he went back to the first hotel. He'd not only found no lodgings, but there were no trains heading northward until the next day. Darkness was falling, and he didn't want to be left on the streets all night. If

Mr. Turner was going to answer his message, it would come here, to the hotel Ryland had named.

The telegraphers had swapped out, and a man sat behind the grille now.

"Oh, yes, sir. You just caught me. We're ready to close for the night. I asked at the front desk, but they couldn't find that you'd registered." He handed Ryland an envelope, and Ryland ripped it open.

With relief he saw that Mr. Turner was including the name and address of a colleague—Robert Donleigh, Esq. Ryland didn't hope for much, but he turned to the telegrapher.

"Did you by any chance take a message for a Mr. Robert Donleigh, Esquire?"

"Well, we're not supposed to say as much, sir, but seeing as how he's named in your message ..."

Ryland smiled. The man had taken both messages and knew the connection.

"He's a friend of my employer, and he suggests I go to him for assistance."

"Very good, sir. I recommend a hackney. You should be able to catch one outside, although it's growing late."

"Thank you." Ryland poked a quarter across the shelf and grabbed his bag.

In less than an hour, Ryland sat in Mr. Donleigh's parlor explaining his errand to the lawyer.

"Ah, so you've had one success in this effort already." Donleigh sipped his brandy.

He'd offered Ryland a glass, but since his employer was a strict teetotaler, Ryland had thought it best to decline. He could just imagine what Mr. Turner would say if his friend wrote to him that Ryland had shared a glass of brandy with him. Instead, he sipped coffee, which was surprisingly good in light of the recent shortages, and hoped it wouldn't keep him awake once he was installed in the comfortable room Mr. Donleigh had promised him.

"Yes, sir. I was able to locate one child, and he was in Maine last month to see his grandmother. But the next one, well, this promises to be a difficult task."

"You may have to wait until this infernal war is over."

"Yes, sir." Ryland frowned. When hostilities opened, nobody thought the war would go on this long.

"I'm surprised a man your age hasn't been conscripted yet," Mr. Donleigh said.

Ryland felt a flush creep up past his collar. "Well, you see, sir, Maine provided a large number of volunteers from the start. We've been able to meet the quotas without having to conscript."

"Ah."

Ryland cleared his throat. "I talked to Mr. Turner about it, and he let me know he'd be pleased if I didn't go."

"Hmm, yes. Jeremiah is getting on. Has he taken another partner in his practice?"

"No, sir."

"He should have someone. You're not inclined to read law yourself?"

Ryland blinked. Studying dusty old law books was the last thing he felt inclined to do, but he couldn't say that. "No, sir. I'm happy as Mr. Turner's investigator. I enjoy the travel—well, most of the time. This trip has been a bit of a disappointment."

"I'm surprised you got through on you mission last spring. I suppose things were easier west of the Mississippi?"

"Oh, no, sir. The railroads aren't finished, and when the war started the construction was interrupted. I went hundreds of miles in stagecoaches, which was no treat, I assure you."

For another hour, Ryland amused his host with tales of his travels. He was glad Mr. Donleigh didn't bring up the topic of enlistment again.

Ryland had considered volunteering, but to be honest, the thought terrified him. His widowed mother had begged him not to go, and it gave him some relief to know he had a family member who was dependent on him.

Mr. Turner had brought up the subject only once, when Ryland returned from his jaunt west.

"They've passed an Enrollment Act," he said. "Did you hear about it?"

Ryland had somehow missed that while traveling. His pulse raced. Would he need to register?

"Men aged twenty to forty-five are eligible for conscription," Mr. turner said, "but Mainers are exempt."

"Oh?"

"The newspaper said we raised more volunteers proportionate to our population than any other state."

"Really? That's impressive."

"Yes, so I hope you haven't any notions of joining up, Atkins."

"I—no, sir."

"Good. I need you."

And that was the end of the discussion. If Mr. Donleigh or anyone else questioned his patriotism, he had at least two reasons for staying out of uniform—his mother needed him, and he was doing important legal work.

But when he thought of men like Matthew Anderson, Mrs. Rose's grandson who'd been wounded at the Battle of Glorieta Pass, he still felt guilty.

"So you can't get through to where this missing person lives?" Donleigh's words jerked Ryland back to the present.

"That's right, sir. My plan was to travel all the way to Emmaus, Pennsylvania—"

"Where's that?"

"Near Allentown. But I was told it may be weeks before I can get through."

"Hmm. Could you send a message?"

"I tried that, sir. I addressed a letter to Mr. Charles Miller, Emmaus, Pennsylvania, but it came back."

"So he doesn't live there?"

"I don't know. It was the only clue I had to his whereabouts. I thought I'd ask around in the area."

"Yes, I see."

"But now they tell me the telegraph lines aren't functional there at this time. I expect I'll have to go back to Maine for now and wait until spring."

"Once you get home, you could write to the mayor, if they have one."

"That's a thought." Ryland had no idea whether or not Emmaus had a mayor. He would have to put his brain to work on this one. Maybe Mrs. Rose or Mr. Turner would have some insight he lacked.

Another thought struck him. "I've wondered if the man I'm looking for has gone into the military, but I don't know who to ask."

"Hmm. Find out if you can what regiment the boys in that neck of the woods would be likely to join. Then you might be able to find out if they have any Millers on their rolls."

"Thank you, sir. I'll try that."

October 19, 1863
Emmaus, Pennsylvania

RYLAND PUSHED his way through the crowd on the depot platform. Apparently he'd arrived the same day a company of soldiers was leaving. His pulse surged as made his way toward the street exit carrying his valise and cane, trying not to catch anyone's eye.

Being the only man not in uniform rattled him, though he tried not to let it. Even the porter had eyed him askance as Ryland fumbled for a tip. He gave the man twice as much as he normally would and grabbed his luggage.

Once he'd left the railroad station, he found it easier to breathe. Emmaus was a small town, but close enough to Allentown to be a busy one. He figured his best chance of finding the Millers was through the post office. Even though his letter had been returned earlier, surely someone knew something about the family. If not here, he would go to surrounding towns and inquire. His inquiries to the army had so far not been answered.

He stood in line behind four other customers at the post office and tried to keep his patience. On one side of the large room, a small room was walled off, with a metal grille over a window-like space. A sign above the opening said, "Telegraph." Intermittent clicking came from there, and a couple of men came in and spoke to the man behind the grille.

At last he was next in line.

"May I help you, sir?" asked a man of about forty.

"I hope so. I'm looking for a man named Charles Miller and his son. I have some urgent news for them. Can you help me locate them?"

"Miller ... Miller." The man frowned. "I've only been the postmaster here for about four months. Let me just check ... " Behind the counter, he opened a large ledger and skimmed through several pages. "Hmm, we have a Danforth Miller on Oak Street, and there seems to be a farmer named Miller on the Bog Road."

Ryland's heart leaped.

"James Miller," the postmaster said.

"Not Charles?"

"I'm afraid not. But those two might be able to help you."

"Yes, thank you." Ryland copied down the addresses in his pocket notebook. He was glad the postmaster wasn't snooty like the one in Portland, who sometimes refused to give out addresses. For the residents' protection, he argued.

The door behind Ryland opened, and a middle-aged woman came in.

"Wait just a second," the postmaster told him. He called to the woman, "Mrs. Lane, can you help this gentleman? He's looking for a Charles Miller." He said to Ryland, "Her husband is one of our mail carriers."

"Charles Miller? Why yes, I knew him," Mrs. Lane said.

"Knew him?" Ryland's hopes dove once more. Was the man dead?

"He moved away. But he used to work here." She waved toward the telegraph booth. "He was one of the telegraph men. Worked here for years in this very room."

"Of course," the postmaster said. "I thought I'd heard the name before, but he left before I took over the post office here. Came from Bethlehem, I did."

"Do you have a new address?" Ryland asked eagerly.

"Hmm, let me check."

The man rummaged about for several minutes, until Ryland began to feel guilty for delaying Mrs. Lane from completing her business.

At last he returned to the counter emptyhanded. "I'm sorry, sir. I can't seem to find a forwarding address in any of the usual places."

Ryland let his shoulders slump.

Mrs. Lane touched his sleeve. "Ask Mr. Gooley," she said. "The man at the telegraph."

Of course! "That's a good idea. Thank you so much." Ryland walked over to the telegraph window and looked in at the man clicking away. He waited for a pause. The man wrote something on a form and finally looked up.

"Hello. Help you?"

"I hope so. I understand Charles Miller used to work this job."

"Yep, he did. His son used to for a while too, and then his daughter."

"Really?" Ryland's pulse sped up again. "What was the son's name?"

"Uh, Jack. Yes, that was it, Jack."

"Jack Miller."

"Yes. But Charles had six or eight kids. I'm sure one of their boys died in the war, shortly after he enlisted. Ned, that was, I think. It was one of them."

"Oh." Was one of these boys the young man he was seeking? Ryland wrote down the names Jack and Ned Miller. "Well, the postmaster said the family moved away."

"That's right." The telegraph receiver began clicking again, and the man grabbed a pencil and turned his attention to it.

"Do you know where they are now?" Ryland asked quickly.

The telegrapher shook his head. "Connecticut, maybe?"

He was engrossed in his message now, and Ryland didn't like to bother him again. He frowned, thinking of his options. Go and talk to the other Millers, he decided. They might be relatives of Charles, Jack, and Ned. Maybe he could stop back here tomorrow and see if the telegraph operator had remembered anything else.

14

November 3, 1863
Washington, D.C.

J ack stretched his brain trying to figure out how the Confederates had encrypted their message. They were using a new method, one he hadn't seen before. In fact, this message seemed to use at least four different ciphers, changing with each line.

He leafed through the notebook he'd started during training, glancing at every cipher variation he'd ever studied.

The Confederates used several substitution ciphers throughout the war. In 1862, they'd tried a dictionary code and then moved on to Vigenère ciphers, where a multi-alphabetic table was used to encrypt and decrypt the messages.

With persistence, Jack and his colleagues had managed to solve nearly all of them, even though some were ridiculously convoluted. The Confederates probably spent as much time preparing the ciphers and encoding their messages as the Union cryptographers took to crack them.

"A very complicated cipher isn't practical," Mr. Strouse had told him, and Jack believed him. Getting a message off quickly and knowing the recipient would understand it immediately took priority over devising some clever device that would keep enemy spies from decoding it. Delivery to the right person in a timely manner was paramount. What good was it if your urgent message got through to a general in combat and he couldn't read it?

Besides, Mr. Strouse had heard from a reliable source that Rebel telegraphers were much better at making ciphers than they were at breaking them. So the Union mostly stuck with their route codes.

Not the Rebs.

Jack poked at the cipher for nearly three hours. Suddenly he had a breakthrough with a pattern word using odd shapes instead of letters. He was sure it signified "river." From there he was quickly able to decipher the rest of the line. "Will cross the river at Istanbul." Istanbul, of course, was a code word. It must be. Still, he'd rarely seen the Confederates mixing ciphers with codes.

Wishing they'd go back to their messages created with Vigenère tables and cipher wheels, which he could readily crack, Jack lumbered on, and by brute force had the entire message in plaintext after nearly five hours' work.

He got up and strode to the supervisor's desk.

"Here, sir. Took a while, but I'm pretty sure this is right."

The captain took his message and read it, his frown deepening. After a moment, he tossed the paper to his desktop.

"It's almost identical to a message Phifer cracked this morning."

Surprised anyone else had solved it quicker than he had, Jack asked, "Was it in this weird code?" He held out the original.

The captain grunted. "It was a Vigenère. What on earth is that? It looks like something two boys would contrive."

"I thought so too," Jack said. "Maybe they tried sending it in different ciphers, to see which method was better."

"How could this be better? We solved them both, and

anyway, how would they ever know which was better?" The captain shook his head. "Get some dinner, Miller. I'm sorry you wasted half a day on that."

"Yes, sir." Disappointed, Jack went to the room where the men were allowed to eat their lunch. It was empty, and the lack of companionship only added to his dark mood. He quickly ate the sandwich and apple Mrs. Grayson had packed for him, supplementing it with a cup of very weak coffee. The square of cake wasn't sweet and could almost pass for flavorless cornbread.

He'd only been back at his desk in the workroom for a few minutes when a uniformed private dashed in and went straight to the supervisor with a message.

The captain rose and rapped on his desk.

"Gentlemen, it seems we've had a breach in Maryland, inside our lines. The telegraph station in Hagerstown was briefly captured, but our troops have secured it. However, after using it to intercept messages for approximately six hours, the Rebels destroyed the equipment there and tore down the lines for several hundred yards. We'll send out a crew to repair things immediately."

Jack's heart pounded as the captain looked around the room, his eyes resting on a man here, then another.

"We need to send a top-notch operator out there to replace the one they injured."

Jack clenched his teeth. If the captain called his name, he'd go, but he kept seeing Nash lying in the telegrapher's wagon, his blood soaking the floorboards. He'd since learned that Nash had died of his wounds.

Still, the danger was past in Hagerstown. Whoever went there now would probably be safe. Safer than out with a regiment, stringing new lines, at any rate.

"Clifton, I'm sending you with them." The captain locked eyes with a young man from New Jersey who had been with the unit more than a year.

Jack let out his pent-up breath. Not yet. He knew he'd be sent to the field someday, but not now.

November 4, 1863
Emmaus, Pennsylvania

FINALLY. Ryland sat in a cramped parlor opposite Miss Ava Mulland and her mother. He'd nearly given up on the door-to-door search for someone—anyone—who knew the Millers well.

Miss Mulland had been away when he'd first arrived in town, visiting her cousins in the country. Last week, her mother had told Ryland that she'd been to school with the Miller children and was a close friend of the daughter Caroline. Waiting for Ava's return was the biggest reason Ryland had lingered in Emmaus. He needed to settle, once and for all, which of Charles Miller's sons had begun his life as Elijah Cooper.

"So, you knew Miss Miller well? Miss Caroline Miller, that is?"

"She was a grade behind me at school," Ava said.

"And you knew her brothers?"

"Yes. Jack was older than me, and Ned was younger." Her cheeks flushed. "The little boys—I don't know them very well."

Ryland nodded, suddenly hesitant to ask her the defining question. His worst fear was that the dead boy, Ned, was Mrs. Rose's grandson.

Last summer everyone in New England read reports of seven thousand men killed and another forty thousand wounded at the drawn-out, bloody battle in Gettysburg, Pennsylvania, less than a hundred and fifty miles from Emmaus. If Elijah Cooper had been engaged in that battle, or any other of this horrible war, Ryland's quest could end today in heartbreak for Mrs. Rose.

For weeks, he had pored over the printed casualty lists with her and Abby, but they'd been unable to find any word of Elijah

Cooper's fate. Of course, they didn't know his new name then. All they had was his adoptive father's name, Charles Miller, but neither had turned up on the lists.

His ill-fated trip as far as Boston in August had ended in disappointment, but now he hoped to take a major step in his quest. Just from the ages of the Miller sons, he thought he knew which boy was Elijah, but he had to be certain.

"I believe one of the boys was adopted," Ryland said, watching her face carefully.

She nodded. "That was Jack. They made no secret of it. Got him when he was quite young."

Ryland puffed out a breath. He was right. Jack, the teenager who'd worked in the telegraph office, was the one he sought. He'd be twenty-four now, Ryland reminded himself.

"And do you know where Jack is now?"

Her features tensed. Ava wasn't pretty to begin with, so when she scrunched up her mouth like that she lost all traces of beauty.

"No, but I hope he's safe. I do know he was with Ned when —" She broke off with a sob and clutched a handkerchief to her lips.

"I'm sorry," Ryland said. "I heard Ned was killed in action."

She sniffed and dabbed at her nose.

While he spoke to Ava, her mother had been pouring out cups of tea, and she passed him one now.

"Thank you, ma'am." He took an automatic sip. It was very hot, so he set the cup and saucer down on the side table. "Miss Mulland, do you know what regiment the brothers were with?"

"Forty-seventh Pennsylvania. All the boys around here joined up with them."

Ryland nodded. He'd been fairly certain after talking to others in the town. The Forty-seventh was one of the regiments to whose commander he'd written, to no avail.

"They went south, of course," Mrs. Mulland murmured.

"Of course." Ryland picked up his cup and saucer and sipped

once more. The tea was abominable. How did they get better tea in Maine than the people here, not far from the huge city of Philadelphia? Of course, Mrs. Rose had contacts in the shipping community, and money helped, he was sure. She always had a stash of excellent tea.

"Did you know the older daughters?" He looked at the mother, as Ava surreptitiously wiped her nose.

"There were a couple of older girls," Mrs. Mulland mused.

"They're both married," Ava said.

"But the older girl," her mother prompted. "Elizabeth, wasn't that her name?"

Ava nodded. "She moved away somewhere when she got married. I'm not sure where."

"I understand the entire Charles Miller family moved away recently." Ryland arched his eyebrows at Ava.

"Last spring," Mrs. Mulland said.

"End of February." Ava threw her mother a glance that, to Ryland, seemed to hold a tinge of superiority.

"Where did they go?" he asked.

Ava sighed. "I'm not sure."

He tried not to show his disappointment. "Caroline didn't tell you?"

At this, Ava's expression fell into decidedly unhappy lines. "No. It was quite sudden."

"I see." Ryland drew the conclusion that Ava wasn't quite as close to the Miller children—especially the girls—as she had implied. He said nothing of the faint hint he'd received from Mr. Gooley at the post office that the family had moved to Connecticut. Perhaps Jack and the rest of the Millers didn't really want Ava to know where they were. If they did, she'd have a way to contact them.

"What about Jenny?" her mother asked.

"She's gone too. Went with her folks, I expect. Her husband's a soldier. She wouldn't want to stay here alone when her parents moved."

Ryland sensed that his time in Emmaus was coming to an end. He'd verified Elijah Cooper's new identity, Jack Miller. But for all his digging, he hadn't come up with anything solid that would help him find Elijah. The few remaining Millers in town had no idea where the family had gone and insisted they were not related to Charles—one of the pitfalls of searching for a person with a common surname.

No one other than the man now holding Charles's old job at the telegraph station seemed to know where they'd moved to, even those who had known the Miller family personally. If only someone could tell him where the eldest daughter lived, he might find them that way.

But he had only the unconfirmed lead pointing to Connecticut. Charles had moved his family away from the worst of the war, a neighbor had said. Their boy Ned had died, and Charles wanted to keep the rest of his brood safe. Nobody had been able to pinpoint it further than that.

Ryland went straight from the Mullands' house to the train station and bought a ticket for New York. Connecticut was too large an area for him to strike out blindly. Once he got home, he could start a methodical search. Charles Miller was an expert telegrapher. Chances were, he'd continued in his profession after the move. Ryland was confident he could eventually track him down.

Ava Mulland had assured him Jack enlisted with his brother. As far as she knew, Jack was still alive—at least, he had been when the family moved away. But she had no idea where he was now.

With a sigh, Ryland boarded the train the next morning, headed for New York in hopes of learning something about the baby girl, Jane Cooper.

15

April 11, 1864
Portland, Maine

The snow was nearly gone when Ryland paid a visit to Edith Rose.

"I'm leaving tomorrow," he told her and Abigail. Since the widow was Mr. Turner's client in his quest for the Cooper children, Ryland always tried to keep her up to date. "I should be able to get to the Philadelphia area, and I'll try to get a line on Elijah's regiment. After that, if I can't go directly to him, I propose moving on to Hartford, Connecticut. If the Miller family isn't there, I'll sniff around until I find out where they are."

"How will you do that?" Abigail asked.

Ryland gazed at her wide, blue eyes, so typical of the family. Her fair hair was pulled up on the back of her head, and he would love to see it hanging free one day, rippling in the wind.

He gulped. "I, uh, will search for Mr. Miller as a telegrapher. I doubt he would give up his calling, when by all accounts he was good at it. Telegraph operators are much in demand these days. I even learned that the War Department tried to recruit him, but he turned them down."

"You said that Elijah enlisted in the army," Mrs. Rose said.

"Yes. I hope to find his adoptive parents and learn from them where he is now." Ryland pressed his lips together for a moment. The possibility that Jack Miller, the soldier, had become a casualty of war still chilled him. Elijah Cooper was of prime age to be in uniform. The war had dragged on for three years now. A bright young man like him had most likely been promoted. Ryland refused to think that Elijah was lost and they were too late in their search.

While waiting out the winter, he'd studied up on how to contact regimental officers and sent more than twenty letters of inquiry. He'd finally heard from a clerk in eastern Pennsylvania that the 47th had been in Florida for several months, then South Carolina, and back to Florida. Ryland had no idea where they were now, and he hadn't been able to get any specific information on Jack Miller.

As a result, he'd spent several very boring months. All through the fall and the harsh Maine winter, he'd bided his time, trying not to be discouraged. Between his bouts of correspondence, Mr. Turner kept him busy with errands and investigations within the state. He'd located a missing heir and tracked down a man who'd abandoned his family in Skowhegan. But he was eager to get back on the Cooper case, and he was determined not to give up this time.

Now spring had arrived. Daffodils would soon bloom in his mother's yard. Already robins and phoebes were building nests, and the maples were showing red blossoms that would fall and be replaced by delicate green leaflets. Ryland was tired of keeping busy with errands for Mr. Turner and correspondence with county and town officials in Connecticut. He was ready to go on the road again. His biggest regret would be leaving Abigail Benson behind.

"So he enlisted under his new name?"

Mrs. Rose's question jerked Ryland back to the task at hand. "Yes, I believe Elijah enlisted under the name Jack Miller."

"Or John Miller?" Mrs. Rose liked to have every detail spelled out for her.

"I haven't found any evidence that he uses the name John. Of course, people might assume it's his real name, and it may be his legal name, but so far all I've gotten from the folks in Pennsylvania is Jack. I'll continue checking for both, though, as well as Elijah Cooper. But I don't believe he's used the Cooper name since his adoption."

The old woman sighed. "That's probably true. Elijah was only five when his mother died. I do hope he had a happy childhood after the Millers took him."

"From what I've heard, I think they had a house full of lively children. They all seem to be clever, normal children, and most are grown up. I believe the youngest would be ten or eleven now. It's a shame he lost one of his new brothers."

"Yes, so sad."

Abigail's eyes swam with tears, and Ryland hastened to change the subject.

"I'll do everything in my power to trace him. His new family should be able to tell me where he's stationed now. Depending on his assignment, I might not be able to actually contact him yet, but I'll do my best, Mrs. Rose."

The old woman nodded. "Do what you can, Mr. Atkins. My prayers will be with you."

Ryland felt he was dismissed, but he hesitated. "There's one other thing you should know."

Mrs. Rose peered at him, her faded blue eyes sharpening. "What is that?"

Ryland cleared his throat and shot a glance at Abby, who listened avidly. "It's about your son-in-law, Ben Cooper. We may have a line on him."

Abby gasped. The old woman sat stone-faced for a moment then met Ryland's gaze. "I am not interested in Benjamin

Cooper at this point. I just want to find my grandchildren. And I wouldn't want your activities to hint to him that we've found one of them or that we're looking for the rest."

"I understand," Ryland said. "I will not pursue that avenue, but I will go in search of Elijah, and if opportunity presents itself, I'll also make more inquiries about Jane."

It was one of those inquiries that had brought Ben Cooper's name to his attention. A former neighbor in New York recalled Cooper returning briefly and asking if anyone knew what became of his children. Ryland was glad Jane was the one he'd focus his search on last. Maybe by the time he looked for her in earnest, Cooper would have given up his interest in the children.

"I'll see you out, Mr. Atkins." Abby rose and walked with him to the front door. She had lived with her grandmother for several years, and she seemed as eager as Mrs. Rose for Ryland to complete his job of finding her lost cousins.

The reunion with her eldest cousin, Zephaniah Cooper, or, as he was now called, Matthew Anderson, last summer had delighted her and her grandmother. The family prayed that his sister and brother could be located and reunited with Matt, Mrs. Rose, and Abby.

The elderly grandmother was not robust, and Ryland had feared she would not last through the war. Yet she seemed no weaker now than she had when she'd begun the quest a year ago and funded his trip west. No end to the war was in sight, and he hoped she would hang on to what health and strength she had.

"I hope you have a safe journey." Abby's smooth forehead wrinkled. "I'm glad you're staying in New England this time. I'm told that south of New York, travel is quite an adventure these days."

Even closer than that, Ryland thought. Boston could be quite a hubbub, but no need to mention that. "I hope I'll have no trouble getting to Hartford and moving about in Connecticut if that's called for. Of course, if I find out where Elijah's regiment is right now, I may take a southerly course."

"We'll pray for you," Abby said. "We want you to find him, of course, but we don't want you to endanger yourself."

"Oh, don't worry about me," Ryland said with what he hoped was a jaunty smile, though he felt apprehensive himself.

Abby reached out to him, and he grasped her hand, catching his breath at the pleasant shock of her touch.

"God can smooth the way for you," she said. "We'll pray that He will."

Abby's faith and Mrs. Rose's were much stronger than his own, but Ryland wouldn't mind knowing people prayed for him.

She opened the door and they stepped outside.

Ryland didn't want to leave her, but he really had no excuse to delay. Even so, he paused on the steps. "Your grandmother seems quite well."

Abby's smile was dazzling, and his heart flipped. "Her health was much better this winter than last year. Having Zeph—I mean Matt—and Rachel visit last summer brought her such joy. She was a little let down after they left, but they've promised to come see her again as soon as the war ends. And if you can find either Elijah or Jane, she'll be ever so pleased."

"Well, as I told her, I'll do my best."

"I know you will." She extended her hand once more, and Ryland clasped it for a moment. He felt like carrying it to his lips, but that would be presumptuous—or downright silly.

"Good-bye, Miss Benson. I appreciate your thoughts and prayers."

April 26, 1864
Philadelphia, Pennsylvania

Dear Mrs. Rose and Miss Benson,

I've sent a telegram to Mr. Turner, and I trust he's shared the contents with you. I knew you would want more details.

Today, at last, I learned that the 47th Pennsylvania is currently posted to Louisiana, under General Nathaniel Banks. They joined his Red River Campaign in March. I am not certain yet of which company Jack Miller is a part, but several soldiers of his regiment were captured after a battle at a place called Pleasant Hill on April 9. Those men are being sent to a Confederate prison camp in Texas.

My dear lady, do not lose hope. Be assured that your grandson may not be among the casualties of battle, or among the prisoners. I am only getting partial reports at this point. I do not know for certain that young Elijah is even with this group at all, though it seems the entire 47th is now part of this western campaign in Louisiana. As soon as I learn more definite news, I will pass it on to you.

RYLAND CHEWED the end of his fountain pen and frowned at his letter. He didn't like telling Mrs. Rose such discouraging news. But she would want to know.

He sighed. No, he should wait—except that Mr. Turner would already have told her the 47th had been posted to Banks's command. That was all he'd said in the telegram. And paper was so hard to come by now, he couldn't just tear up the letter and start over.

He wished he could get to Louisiana and find out Jack Miller's true whereabouts and condition. But the captain he'd spent an hour with had told him the railroads were a mess in the South. Half of them were torn up, and the rest were held by the Confederate army. There was no way he'd get through by rail, even if he tried. And he certainly couldn't ride a horse that far. Sea travel was very risky at best and, for the most part, forbidden.

Connecticut. He'd sent dozens of telegrams to the Nutmeg State over the winter without success, but he wasn't giving up. If he could find the Miller family, maybe they would have some news of Jack. He didn't trust the captain he'd talked to. It had taken three days to get access to the man, and Ryland was sure he knew more about Jack's regiment than he had revealed.

He gritted his teeth and added a line to his letter.

I plan to go to Connecticut next and follow up on a lead that came in just before I set out on this journey. I hope to be able to track down Charles Miller there.

In as neat script as he could produce, he wrote *Sincerely yours,* and signed his name.

16

May 28, 1864
Washington, D.C.

J ack hesitated in the hallway. He rarely entered the upper levels of the War Department building, but he'd been summoned that morning to the office of Thomas A. Scott, Assistant Secretary of War. Jack had never met the gentleman, but he'd seen him at a meeting where the telegraphers had received a blanket welcome, and he knew Scott was influential in the establishment of the Military Telegraph Corps.

He pulled in a deep breath and knocked.

"Enter."

He went in and realized the man he was facing was an underling, probably Scott's personal secretary. An open door behind led into another room.

"Jack Miller," he told the minion.

"Oh, yes. Mr. Scott will see you. Go right in."

Jack followed the direction of his sweeping hand and walked over to the doorway of the inner office. Behind a desk strewn with piles of paper sat Scott. Jack gulped.

"Jack Miller, sir."

Scott looked up with a paper in his hand. "Come in, Miller. Take a seat."

Jack complied and tried not to let his nerves show. He breathed slowly through his nose and met Scott's gaze.

"New orders, I'm afraid, Miller. You've done well here, and we'll miss you."

Jack swallowed hard. He'd expected this, but it still made his pulse race. "Thank you, sir."

Scott sighed and tossed the paper he'd held onto one of the piles. "Unfortunately, one of our key field telegraphers is unable to continue his work. You've no doubt taken messages from him —Grice."

"I—yes, sir. That is, I believe I have. Isn't he ..." Jack didn't want to finish the sentence, because the implication scared him a little.

"Yes, he was with General Sherman. The general needs a quick-thinking, resourceful man, Miller. Mr. Strouse decided you're the best one for the job."

Jack nodded, not sure he agreed. He'd heard lots of things about the general—West Point grad, brilliant and insightful, but melancholic. Wounded at Bull Run, a bit sloppy, somewhat of a complainer, and known to bend the rules. After his stint as commander of the Department of the Cumberland, there'd been rumors of a nervous breakdown and even insanity.

But he'd come back at the end of '61 and proven his worth. Lincoln believed in Sherman, and now the general was head of the Military Division of the Mississippi.

"He's been facing off with Johnston all month," Scott said. "He continually outflanks the Confederate army. His job is to break them up and inflict massive damage. His goal right now is Atlanta."

Jack nodded, knowing he'd be thrust into the thick of it.

Scott eyed him keenly. "Sherman needs a telegraph operator at his side constantly, to receive new orders quickly and get his reports out securely and concisely. We think you're the man, Miller."

"I'll do my best, sir."

"I'm sure you will." Scott picked a sheet of paper off another pile and handed it to him. "Be at the train station tomorrow at 7:15 a.m. Pick up your ticket when you get there. You'll get as far as the railroad can take you, and a cavalry detachment will meet you and get you the rest of the way, to wherever the general is by that time."

"Is there a telegraph construction crew out there?" Jack asked.

"Yes, a very good one. I fear Sherman is tiring them out with his constant movement, but they've served him well. Since Grice became ill, however, he's had to make do with a mediocre operator. He's screaming for one with more skill. That's you."

Jack's face warmed. "Thank you, Mr. Scott. I'll try to justify your confidence in me."

May 31, 1864
Bridgeport, Connecticut

AFTER A HALF-HOUR WAIT, Ryland stepped up to the telegraph desk at the depot in Bridgeport. The large man sitting behind the desk that held the transmitter looked exhausted, but his placid expression and the crow's-feet at the corners of his eyes gave the impression of an amiable personality.

"Mr. Miller?" Ryland asked. "Mr. Charles Miller?"

"Yes, sir. How can I help you?"

The tight knot in Ryland's chest began to loosen.

"You can have no idea how pleased I am to find you, Mr. Miller."

"Oh?"

"Yes! I've been looking for you—well, seven weeks or more

on this trip alone, but it's been months. I've been to Pennsylvania, and—never mind. I've found you."

"You have, indeed, sir. May I know the reason for your diligent quest?"

Ryland curbed his smile. He was sure this was the right man, but until he had absolute proof—

"Do you have a son called Jack Miller, sir?"

Charles's face fell. He looked at once confused and apprehensive. "Yes. Is something wrong?"

"No, sir. At least, not that I know of. My errand is, I hope, a joyful one."

Ryland was aware of several people forming a queue behind him, and he didn't want to rush this interview. He was feeling a little unsteady on his feet, having forgone lunch in order to follow up on his latest clue. A severe bout of influenza had laid him low for nearly two weeks at a boardinghouse in New York, and he knew overdoing it could be disastrous now.

"Mr. Miller, is there a place where we could talk privately? When your shift is over, of course."

Miller eyed him closely. "Well, I was going to take a late luncheon at two. Would that suit you? Have you eaten?"

"I have not."

"Good. We can get something at the diner near the ticket office, if that's agreeable."

Ryland took out his pocket watch. Two o'clock was only twenty-two minutes away.

"Excellent. I'll see you then."

He killed ten minutes by wandering about the station and reading notices on the walls. Someone had left a newspaper on a bench. He picked it up and walked to the diner, where he claimed a table and unfolded his find. Though small and consisting of only four pages, the newspaper was a daily, so he hoped the news would be fresh.

Above the fold, the top headline screamed, *Ewell faces Grant in Virginia*. Farther down was an article titled *Sherman strikes*

Johnston's supply line in Ga. Ryland sighed. He couldn't find anything about Louisiana. He assumed the 47th Pennsylvania was still somewhere over near the Mississippi.

"Anything worth repeating?"

He looked up to find Charles Miller smiling at him as he pulled out the chair opposite.

"Not really, at least as far as my mission goes."

"Which is?"

All right, he wanted frankness. Ryland squared his shoulders.

"I believe your son Jack is the young man I'm searching for at the request of his grandmother, Edith Rose."

Miller might have been a statue, he sat so still. After a long moment, he huffed out a breath.

"Well."

"You son is adopted, I believe?"

"Yes, but—" Miller shook his head. "We didn't expect anyone to come looking for him, not after all this time."

"His grandparents tried to find him shortly after Jack's mother died," Ryland said. "The grandfather was out to sea—"

"Jack told me he was a ship captain. I didn't know whether to believe it or not, but the boy isn't one to spin tales."

"Oh, Captain Rose was very real. Unfortunately, by the time he returned home from his voyage and got to New York, the three Cooper children had all been adopted."

"Cooper, yes. That was Jack's name."

"Elijah Cooper."

A woman in a long white apron came to the table, and both men ordered coffee and a sandwich. When she left, Ryland turned back to Miller.

"Jack's a grown man now." Miller's face looked paler than it had, and his smile had disappeared.

"I know. And his grandfather is deceased. But his grandmother is still living, and she would like very much to see him."

"Huh. So would I."

Ryland smiled apologetically. "I understand Jack enlisted in the army. Forty-seventh Pennsylvania?"

"That's right. How did you—" Miller shook his head. "Can we back up just a minute. I don't know who you are or where you sprang from."

"Sorry. Ryland Atkins. I'm an investigator for an attorney named Jeremiah Turner, Esquire, in Portland, Maine." He extended his hand, and Miller shook it across the table.

"And this lawyer is trying to find my Jack for his grandmother?"

"That's right. She is Mr. Turner's client, and she hopes to find all of the Cooper children."

Miller let out a soft whistle. After a moment he chuckled. "Jack's wanted that all his life—well, ever since we got him, anyway. He told me how his baby sister was taken away first, and then his big brother. I think he kind of gave up on ever seeing them again."

"Well, when I find Elijah—that is, Jack—one of the first things I intend to tell him is that we've located Zephaniah. He's alive and well, and he'd love to see his brother again."

"He'll be so happy. What about the girl?"

"Not yet. She's next on my list. We've learned she was adopted by a couple in Brooklyn, New York, but they've left the area. So far, I haven't been able to trace them." Ryland smiled. "If they're as hard to track down as you were, it may take some time."

"Oh. We moved about a year ago," Miller said.

"So I learned. I found it odd that a man who worked in a post office left no forwarding address."

"I didn't have one when we left. After that, it never occurred to me. Our older daughter, Elizabeth, has the address. Is that how you found us?"

"No, I never got to meet her," Ryland said. "That route might have been quicker. But the old postmaster in Emmaus died, and the new fellow—"

"Ed Heinz died?"

Ryland nodded.

"That's a shame."

"I found you through Western Union, actually. But what matters now is communicating with Jack. Do you write him letters?"

"We do, and we hear from him regularly. Once in a while, he even gets to send me a telegram."

"Really? Isn't that unusual for soldiers?"

Miller grinned. "Jack's not a soldier anymore. He's in Washington, D.C."

Dumbfounded, Ryland stared at him. "How long?"

"A year and a half, maybe?"

"But ... I thought he was with Banks in Louisiana. That's where his regiment is, or was, the last I heard."

"Jack's a telegraph operator, like me. He spent time in the army—went all kinds of outlandish places—but then they mustered him out so he could do telegraphy for the government. He's got a desk job in the capital."

"Well, I'll be." Ryland laughed. "Can I send him a telegraph there?"

"Now?"

"Yes, today."

Miller shrugged. "I guess so. If you're paying, that is."

"Oh, I'll pay for it."

"Fine. Come back to the office with me when we're done and write out your message."

Fifteen minutes later, Ryland watched in satisfaction as Charles Miller tapped out his message to his son Jack.

HAVE INFORMATION ABOUT YOUR GRANDMOTHER ROSE AND
BROTHER Z COOPER. NOW WITH YOUR FATHER IN CONN.
SEND REPLY BRIDGEPORT.
RYLAND ATKINS

It seemed too easy, after all the hours he'd put in, the uncomfortable travel he'd endured, and the many disappointments he'd faced. He could picture Abigail's face when she read the news to her grandmother. What a triumph!

"Now we wait," Charles said.

A line was forming again to make use of his services, and Ryland nodded. "I'll come back in an hour."

He left the depot and walked along the streets, toward the harbor. He wanted to send word right away to Mr. Turner and Jack's family, but it would be best to wait. When he heard back from Jack, that would be the time.

The sun beat down on him, and he turned his face upward. Summer was nearly here, Jack Miller was found, and all was well.

"Dear Lord," he whispered, almost shyly. He and God had only been on speaking terms since his encounter with outlaws in Colorado last summer. At that time, Ryland had begun praying in earnest, but it still seemed odd. "Thank you for bringing me to Charles Miller at last. Please let me bring Elijah home to his grandmother. Amen."

He pulled in a deep breath, his chest swelling with satisfaction. One more to go.

Back at the telegraph office, Charles caught his eye when Ryland was still two people back in line and shook his head.

Crestfallen, Ryland kept his spot and inched up to the window.

"No word yet," Charles said. "Do you want to go to your hotel, and I'll send you a note when we hear?"

"I'm not sure. How long—"

"Impossible to say. I had to send it to his boardinghouse. Can't send it to the War Department, where he works. But he takes different shifts, and I hoped he'd be at the boardinghouse today. I'm sorry."

"No, that's all right. I guess I'll go to the hotel, as you say."

Ryland's fatigue had caught up with him by the time he reached his room. The flu had taken a lot of starch out of him.

He lay down on the bed, but his mind raced. He jerked awake later, surprised to see dusk gathering outside.

He freshened up and went down to the front desk.

"If a Mr. Miller comes looking for me, I'll be at the restaurant next door," he told the clerk, and then he went in search of supper. Minutes ticked by, and his elation deflated until depression began to settle in.

At half past nine, a knock came on his hotel room door. Still fully clothed, Ryland leaped up and opened it.

"Mr. Miller! Come in."

"Sorry to come by so late, Atkins. I stuck around the office in case something came in tonight, and we just heard." He held out a telegram form, a bleak frown sending Ryland's heart plummeting.

He opened the message. It was headed with Ryland Atkins, Bridgeport, Conn.

J MILLER REASSIGNED MAY 28.
MRS. L. GRAYSON

Baffled, Ryland sought Charles's gaze.

"What does it mean? Who's this Mrs. Grayson?"

"She's his landlady. Jack mentioned her in some of his letters. I'm not sure exactly, but it sounds as though Jack was posted to a new location three days ago."

Ryland nodded slowly, pondering the unhelpful words. "Yes, but where?"

"She probably doesn't know. Jack led me to believe his work was a bit secret. I think he handled telegrams from army officers in the field, but he never said as much. I don't think he was allowed to discuss it."

"So ..."

"He could be anywhere," Charles said.

"Why wouldn't he send you a message before he left?"

"There probably wasn't time. Or maybe he wasn't allowed

to." Charles shook his head helplessly. "He wouldn't have been able to tell us where he was headed, anyway."

"But you can't even write to him!"

"We'll have to wait for him to write to us."

Ryland scowled. "Can we contact the War Department? You said he worked there."

"I doubt they'll tell us anything."

"But it's worth a try."

"I don't know." His voice was heavy with skepticism.

"My employer will pay."

Charles shrugged. "If you want to try, come to the office first thing in the morning. I'm working from eight to five tomorrow."

"I'll be there."

As Miller put his hand on the doorknob, Ryland snatched at one positive note.

"He was alive three days ago. At least we know that. He's been safe in Washington all this time, and he was there just three days ago."

"Yes, there is that."

"Can you wire money to someone?"

Charles's eyebrows shot up. "To Jack?"

"I was thinking of Mrs. Grayson. I only count eight words she'd have to pay for, but still, that's a lot for some people."

June 7, 1864
River Lea Plantation

MARILLA PAUSED in the doorway to Uncle Hamilton's study. He was kneeling with his back to her, before his open safe. No doubt getting out some cash for the ammunition Zeke Vernon said he needed. The overseer had appeared, conveniently for him, at breakfast, and her great-uncle had invited him to join them at the table.

Because of Vernon's sly smiles at her and his open leers when Uncle Hamilton wasn't looking, Marilla had soon excused herself, but not before she heard him tell his boss they needed to replenish their stockpile of rifle cartridges if they could find them. The Yankees were headed for Atlanta and no mistake. They'd taken Altoona Pass and the railroad line there. If Atlanta fell, the surrounding communities would suffer.

She gave a quiet cough, and Uncle Hamilton's head jerked toward her. *Nothing wrong with his hearing, more's the pity.*

"I'm sorry to bother you, Uncle, but I wondered if you were going into town today. We're nearly out of coffee again."

He scowled and lumbered to his feet. For a moment, he stood with one hand on the open safe door, catching his breath. Despite the shortages, Buckley managed to continue eating vast quantities of food, and his large frame was, if anything, bulkier than when she'd first met him.

"Zeke is going in. See if—never mind, I'll send Lazarus."

He strode past her, and Marilla shrank back against the doorjamb. She glanced at the safe he'd left wide open, and the flicker of a thought crossed her mind. She tried to ignore it, but she couldn't.

Uncle Hamilton plodded to the front hall. "Lazarus!"

Marilla found it hard to breathe. She may never have this opportunity again. She took two faltering steps into the study and looked over her shoulder. Her jewelry was in that safe. She'd seen a small, carved wooden box in there once, and she had an inkling the trinkets were in that. She took another step.

"What are you doing?"

At his harsh voice, she turned and faced Uncle Hamilton.

"I—I wasn't sure you'd be right back, and I knew you wouldn't want to leave the safe open. I thought I'd shut the door."

He eyed her with suspicion. "Well, I'm sending Lazarus to catch Zeke and tell him you need coffee, if he can get it. But he'll need more cash." He pushed past her toward the safe. "Go on, now. I'm seeing to it."

"Yes, Uncle. Thank you."

Marilla swallowed her disappointment and tiptoed out of the room.

17

Ryland entered the law offices of Jeremiah Turner, Esquire, with a bit of apprehension. The message said he had news in the Cooper case, and that could mean anything.

Mr. Turner kept a very spare office, with functional furnishings and few decorations. Some lawyers believed in a show of opulence, but not this one. He'd never had any partners in his business, though he was now past his sixty-seventh birthday. He didn't even employ a secretary.

Ryland opened the door and stepped into the outer room. One other, smaller room lay behind it, and unlike other professional men, Mr. Turner preferred to have his desk in the first room, using the other as his library and filing room.

"Come right in, Atkins," Mr. Turner said. He wore one of his three suits and a spotless white shirt. Ryland had never seen him wear anything else. Boring.

"You've had some word, sir? Is it Jack Miller?" He half hoped it was about Jane, whose name was now Molly Weaver. At least she wasn't in danger on the battlefield.

"Yes. I received a telegram from his adoptive father."

Ryland seated himself in one of the stiff, rather uncomfortable client chairs. He speculated that Mr. Turner could charge higher fees if he just offered his clients a few amenities. But that wasn't the way his boss worked. He preferred to invest money in good legal services, not plump cushions and silver tea sets.

"It seems the family had a letter from Jack," Mr. Turner said. "He's now in Georgia."

"Georgia?" Ryland's heart tripped. He'd read the papers. He knew what was going on in Georgia. General Sherman was harrying Confederate General Johnston, hoping to cut off his supply train and take Atlanta. If that city fell, it would be a huge blow for the South's morale.

"Mm. Of course, details are few, but apparently when young Jack was sent into the field, he was assigned to that area. I expect he's stringing wires for General Sherman now."

More likely sending and receiving Sherman's reports to and from Washington, Ryland thought, but still. Jack Miller was in the thick of it now, there was no doubt.

"Mr. Miller—Charles Miller, that is—says he will write us in more detail."

"He knew we'd want to know right away," Ryland said. Already his mind was whirling. Traveling into Georgia would be impossible right now, even if he wanted to.

Mr. Turner seemed to read his thoughts.

"Of course, it's too dangerous to go looking for him down there. We'll have to wait until hostilities cease."

"But, sir, it's been three years now, and we don't know how long this war will go on. Mrs. Rose might not last another three years."

Mr. Turner sighed. "Actually, she seems in better health than when she asked me to take on the search for her grandchildren. Better spirits too."

"I agree with you there. Seeing Matthew last summer gave her a real boost. Miss Benson says her grandmother didn't have the low period last winter that she normally sinks to in the cold months."

"Yes." Mr. Turner met his gaze. The old man's eyes were still sharp, but he looked tired. "Anything positive we can tell her will keep on encouraging her, I'm sure. I just hope we don't lose Elijah, now that we're this close to finding him."

"Did Mr. Miller give you an address, where we can write to Jack?"

"No. I await his letter, to see if it gives us more information. But it may take two or three weeks for that letter to get here. The mails have been horribly slow of late." Mr. Turner blinked. "I say, Atkins, I'm thinking of taking on a young man to help with the workload. It's that or stop taking new clients."

"Sir?" Immediately, Jack wondered how this would affect his role in the business.

"Yes, the nephew of a friend is interested. He's had two years of law school but can't afford to go back. He could read law here with me and get into practice. Name's Joshua Wicker."

"I see. When will he begin?"

"I've got to find him lodgings. I thought maybe you could look into that for me, since we're at a standstill right now on the Cooper children."

"All right." It wasn't exactly Ryland's idea of investigative duties, but it was something to do.

Mr. Turner's eyes narrowed. "You haven't changed your mind on that score have you? Because I'd rather take on a man I know ..."

"No. I'm sorry, sir, but books were never my first love, especially big, thick ones."

"Mm. Well, you've done well for me, Atkins. But, as Mrs. Turner keeps reminding me, I have to face the truth: I am getting older. If I don't train someone now, I'll find myself at the place where I have to retire but have no one to take over the practice."

Ryland had never seen such a bleak expression on his employer's face. The Turners had no sons, only daughters, and all of their sons-in-law were immersed in careers that had nothing to do with studying law books or representing clients in court. It must be disheartening to reach an advanced age and have no one to keep your life's work going, no one who appreciated all you'd done and wanted to see it continued.

"I hope it goes well for you." Ryland stood. "If there's nothing else, sir, I'll make some inquiries about lodgings."

August 15, 1864
Near Atlanta, Georgia

THE SWELTERING HEAT was almost more than Jack could bear. In the early morning and after sunset, he could walk about outside, so long as he stayed within the picket lines. The temperatures were more bearable then. But in the middle of the day, when they were at their worst, he was stuck inside.

They were close to Atlanta, only a few miles outside the beleaguered city. General Sherman, or "Uncle Billy," as the soldiers called him, was confident they would soon prevail. The Confederates couldn't hold out much longer without provisions.

For weeks, Jack worked out of a tent as they drew closer and closer to Atlanta. Captain Nason, his commanding officer, had commandeered a small house for the telegraph team, less than a quarter mile down the road from the house Sherman had made his temporary headquarters.

Though abandoned, the house looked as though its occupants had left in a hurry. Their dishes and furniture were still inside, and a few articles of clothing. A few tools were scattered about, and a shelf in the parlor held books. But there was no food, and no fuel for a cooking fire. Jack was just as happy to eat cold food in this miserable weather.

The private who prepared their food had tried cooking over a fire outside, in the middle of the night, but found it wasn't that much cooler than the daytime. The crew ate whatever he managed to scare up.

Before noon every day, Jack's shirt was soaked with sweat. How did people stand living here? Maybe it was nice in winter, but in the middle of August it was an inferno.

Captain Nason took over the small desk in a room down the hall from the parlor, probably the original owner's study. His aide, Lieutenant Peterson, had a small table in the parlor.

They'd set up the telegraph apparatus in an upstairs bedroom, where Jack had slung his bedroll. This limited workspace was far better than working out of a tent or the back of a wagon. But even with the windows wide open, the place was like an oven.

Captain Nason came upstairs and stood in the doorway. "Anything for the general yet?"

"Not yet, sir," Jack said.

"He told his man to wait. He really needs to hear from Chattanooga."

Jack nodded. Now that they'd severed the Confederates' supply line, the Union army was dependent on a similar arrangement. So far so good, but if the Rebels managed to cut off their connection with Tennessee, the massive army would be without provisions. Jack wished he could make the receiver start clicking, but that was beyond his power.

Footsteps thudded up the stairs.

"Captain."

Jack recognized Lt. Peterson's voice, and Captain Nason turned in the doorway.

"What is it?"

"One of the guards just brought this in. That fellow the pickets caught," Peterson said, "the one who was snooping around our armory—"

"Yes, what is it?" Captain Nason asked.

"He had this on him." Peterson held out a crumpled paper

and shook his head. "I expect it's nothing, sir, but I thought you should see it."

The captain took it and frowned. "Strange."

Peterson shook his head. "It's just a scribble, sir."

"Then why did he have it on him?" The captain turned and looked at Jack, who had been listening from his makeshift desk. "Miller, take a look at this, won't you?" He walked over and handed the paper to Jack.

On the sheet was a zigzag line that indeed looked like a scribble at first glance. Jack squinted at it, noting a few crucial details. Something he'd studied during his training flitted through his mind.

"It's a cipher, sir."

Peterson laughed outright. "Come on, that's nothing."

Jack swallowed hard and looked at the captain. "Actually, sir, it's a very old method of disguising a short message. These lines connect dots that are placed in different columns as you go down the page. I might be able to decipher it. Would you like me to try?"

"Please," said the captain.

Jack turned around and went to work. He prepared a grid that would allow all the letters of the alphabet to appear, evenly spaced, across the top of a sheet of paper the same size as the one the guard had brought in. Was it possible the Confederates had used a new method, much less complicated than their usual cipher? Perhaps the person sending it wasn't familiar with the Vigenère tables used by the Southern army.

"He won't be able to make anything out of that," Peterson said derisively.

"See if you can get me some coffee, Peterson—or whatever passes for coffee these days."

The lieutenant scowled and strode down the hall to the stairway. Jack hid his smile. The errand was far beneath Peterson's usual duties. Jack heard him barking an order at a hapless soldier in the hall below.

"Well, Miller? Think it's something?" the captain asked.

"I do, sir, and I've got their method. It will just take a few more minutes."

"Take all the time you need." The captain strolled over and peered over his shoulder. Jack tried to ignore his hovering.

Five minutes later, Peterson came in carrying a steaming mug.

The captain sniffed the brew suspiciously. "Chickory?"

"No, sir, something from beans of what they call a Kentucky coffee tree."

Nason frowned but took an experimental sip and made a face. "Hmm. Could be worse. Do we have any sweetening?"

"No, sir. Sorry."

Jack checked his work and wrote his solution at the bottom of the paper. He hesitated, hoping Peterson would leave, but the lieutenant sat down on the edge of Jack's bed, took out his pocketknife, and began to clean his fingernails.

Jack stood and walked over to the captain. "Sir."

"Yes, Miller?"

"It says, 'Two companies at Covington.'"

The captain's eyebrows twitched. "Two companies at Covington? That's all?"

"Yes, sir. This type of cipher is for short messages only. Unless there were other sheets, of course."

"I see."

Jack cleared his throat. "Covington is a little town east of Atlanta sir. More of a village."

"I'm aware." The captain drummed his fingers on the top of a walnut dresser for a moment. "They may be gathering raiders to strike against us." He looked at Jack. "Prepare a message to General Sherman, Miller. I'll send a runner with it immediately. Tell him about this, but stress that we haven't verified it. And stand by. He may want to send some messages out immediately."

"Yes, sir."

Peterson sat scowling until the captain handed him the paper Jack had prepared.

"Tell the messenger to put it in the general's hands," Nason told him. "No one else."

"Yes, sir." Peterson hurried out.

Nason turned to Jack. "I've told the construction crew to string more lines. We have to be closer to General Sherman's headquarters. It will take Peterson at least ten minutes to get that message to him. You need to be under the same roof with the general."

"Should I pack up now, Captain?"

Nason sighed. "Not until the new line is in place. They're having to cannibalize the lines we tore down a couple of weeks ago."

Jack nodded. Cutting off communication into the city had been as high a priority as stopping the food supply. But it was getting harder and harder for Sherman's army to support their own need for provisions and contact with the outside world. Small bands of Georgian civilians kept showing up to inflict damage, and it was impossible to predict where they would strike next.

"I'll post a wagon outside," Nason said decisively. "That way, whenever we need to move, all you'll have to do is disconnect your lines and get the equipment into the wagon."

August 31, 1864
Outside Atlanta, Georgia

THEY'D MOVED AGAIN and were just outside the city. Jack was relegated to a tent once more, in the back yard of the house where General Sherman was billeted. He didn't mind. It wouldn't be for many nights, and Captain Nason had hinted that General

Hood would evacuate Atlanta soon, and Sherman's force would move in.

"Sir," said the guard outside his tent, and Jack heard footsteps and shifting of feet and guns.

He barely had time to stand, sending his stool tumbling backward. As he straightened it, Sherman himself ducked under the tent flap and stepped inside, squinting in the comparative gloom.

"Anything, Miller?"

"Not since that last note, sir, but I expect word any minute." Jack reached for the folding stool. "Would you like to sit down, sir?"

"No, I'm fine." Somehow, Sherman managed to pace in the four feet of space between Jack's bedroll and his makeshift desk.

The general made him a little nervous, but Jack busied himself by sorting the messages he'd received in the past two days and consulting his cipher book so he'd know exactly what words to substitute for locations if he had to send a message to Washington.

The apparatus began to click, and he grabbed his pencil. Sherman's footsteps halted, and Jack knew he was standing right behind him. He pushed the officer's presence from his mind and concentrated on the code.

"Schofield's done it, sir. He's cut their last supply line at the town of Rough and Ready." Jack quickly transcribed the rest of the message and turned to hand it to Sherman with a grin.

"Well done, Schofield," the general murmured. "Now, if we'd just hear from Howard." He met Jack's gaze with a nod. "I'll be at my lodgings working on logistics for the occupation, Miller. Notify me as soon as you hear anything about Howard's army. I hope he's giving Hood a good whipping."

He strode from the tent, and Jack sighed with relief.

Not two hours later, the message Sherman wanted so badly came in. He sent the young private who was his usual runner with the initial, short message. Sherman arrived five minutes later.

"Details, Miller?"

Jack was used to his terse conversation and lack of polite greetings.

"Here you go, sir. They've pushed back Hood's army at Jonesboro."

Sherman frowned and read the half-page message in silence, his frown deepening. "A hundred and seventy casualties among our boys."

"Yes, sir. But ten times that from the Army of the Tennessee."

Sherman nodded decisively. "Miller, you be ready to move. We'll enter the city tomorrow and see if we can't find a proper telegraph office for you to work out of. Of course, we'll have to get the lines connected and all that, but I want you in business as soon as possible."

"Yes, sir."

"They might take the equipment with them, or destroy it so we can't use it, so you be ready to set up from scratch."

"I will, sir."

Without another word, Sherman turned on his heel and hurried from the tent.

September 2, 1864
River Lea Plantation

"ATLANTA HAS FALLEN," Zeke Vernon said grimly from the parlor doorway.

Hamilton Buckley's face turned crimson. Marilla feared he might have a fit of apoplexy.

His bourbon glass thudded on the table beside his chair. "Don't tell me that!"

"But it's true, sir." Vernon held out a folded newspaper and wisely took a step back. "Hood abandoned the city and destroyed the arsenal and stocks of provisions that his men couldn't take with them. That dog Sherman has Atlanta now."

Uncle Hamilton swore and snatched the newspaper, which was only one sheet, printed on both sides and folded over. His jaw tightened as he skimmed the front. With a roar, he crumpled it and threw it into the fireplace, which hadn't held a blaze for months because of the heat.

"There's something else, Mr. Buckley."

Uncle Hamilton glared at Vernon. "Something not in that blasted rag?"

"Four more of the remaining field hands have legged it, sir."

Marilla caught her breath and tried to shrink smaller in her chair. Zeke was between her and the main doorway, but she wondered if she could slip out through the dining room and escape the hurricane of anger that would come next.

The master stood very still for a moment then said through clenched teeth, "And where were you and your men, Vernon?"

"I had two men posted all night, as customary, sir, but they seem to have slipped through. When I went out this morning to set their work, they were gone."

"What do the ones who are left say?"

"Nothing. They claim they didn't know."

"Oh, that's likely."

"Pretty much, Mr. Buckley."

"And the house slaves?"

"All here that was here yesterday, except for Thomas."

Marilla's mind whirled. Thomas was Buckley's personal slave and served as his valet. The master must be livid.

Provisions were already scarce, but it sounded like things would get worse. She and Reenie would have to go out and glean what they could from the kitchen garden tomorrow. A lot of the plants had died because of the extended heat, but there were still a few vegetables, and she planned to put in a few seeds soon for a fall garden.

Uncle Hamilton hurled curses at Vernon. "Get out of my sight!"

Zeke turned toward the door. Marilla got up and ran for the dining room before her great-uncle could turn around and rant at her.

18

October 10, 1864
River Lea Plantation

Hamilton Buckley held up the newspaper and read it in a thundering voice as he paced the verandah. "Would you see the fair daughters of the land given over to the brutality of the Yankees?"

Marilla squirmed but didn't dare leave her seat on the wicker settee. Uncle Hamilton erupted in rage the last time she skipped out on one of his tirades.

"You see what Davis is saying?" He glared at her until she nodded helplessly.

"He doesn't want the Yankees to overwhelm us."

"That's right. Listen to this. 'We are fighting for existence, and by fighting alone can independence be gained.' He got that part right. You know I don't have much use for Jefferson Davis, but he's right on the money there."

"Yes, Uncle."

He walked back and forth with measured steps, muttering as he read on.

Marilla cleared her throat. The latest news of Sherman's men sending away nearly all the residents of Atlanta and stealing food from outlying farms and plantations alarmed her.

"Do you think they'll come here?"

"If they dare set foot on River Lea, my men will hold them back."

She took a shaky breath, wondering what his ragtag band of twelve men could do if a force of any size came against them. Besides, she knew Zeke Vernon and the others were having a hard time finding enough food for themselves. She'd heard Sadie and Reenie muttering. Though she had no proof, Marilla feared they'd commandeered whatever supplies the slaves had set aside for the coming winter.

"Where was the president when he made that speech?" she asked.

"Augusta—a week ago. Who knows where he is now? He's keeping on the move."

Marilla found it hard to draw a full breath. A stark emptiness overcame her as Buckley continued to read snatches from Davis's speech aloud, alternated with invectives against him.

If Yankee soldiers came here, what would she do? She didn't think Buckley and his men would protect her. Maybe if she told them she was living here against her will—

She settled back in her chair, outwardly calm but in inward turmoil. Maybe the coming of the Yankees was the best thing that could happen to her.

***

October 17, 1864
Atlanta, Georgia

JACK COULD TELL the previous telegrapher had taken care of his new workstation. The padded chair was actually comfortable, and the desk had a broad top at just the right height. He even found a supply of blank telegram forms, and the walls held several posters of instructions on preparing a message for the operator. Most of the time, Jack had the place to himself. He was glad the telegraph office had been spared in the Southern army's rampage before they abandoned the city.

But he didn't like the way Lieutenant Peterson, Nason's aide, haunted the place. For the past few days he'd claimed to be waiting for an urgent message for the general, but Jack had his runners for that. They took messages to the general, or if Sherman was out tending to business, which was often, they took them to Nason or one of the other captains.

Peterson probably wanted to see the sensitive messages before his superior officers did, and that was highly unethical. The runners knew they were not, under any circumstances, to open and read the messages Jack entrusted to them. He doubted Peterson would comply.

They wouldn't be here much longer, though. Already he was shuttling messages back and forth between General Sherman and the Secretary of War, and he was reasonably sure the general's next objective was Savannah. Getting twenty thousand soldiers ready to march took time, though, and planning. Supplies, provisions, ammunition.

The tables were turned now. The Confederates were attacking the rail line used to bring in food, medicine and other supplies, just as the Union army had when Hood held the city. Over and over they raided and initiated skirmishes along the line, trying to disrupt the flow of needed provisions.

The telegraph wire was busy today. Jack translated as he wrote. Sometimes the operator on the other end would make a mistake, and he had to take his best guess at the meaning of a sequence.

On top of that, the arbitraries, or words they substituted as code names for some people, places, and actions, had recently been changed. Jack had to consult his new cipher book often until he had them all memorized.

The receiver clicked away for a couple of minutes, and he could feel Peterson's impatience.

"What you got?" The lieutenant demanded.

"Working on it."

Peterson's heavy breathing and restless movements distracted Jack, but he kept on, doggedly writing out the English words for the Morse Code message.

He almost laughed when the word "monkeys" sprang from his pencil. That must be a null word that the operator had added at random to even out a column when he rearranged the message in a grid.

When the signal stopped, Jack quit writing and puffed out a deep breath.

"Message ended?" Peterson said.

"Yes. Now I have to decrypt it."

Peterson paced back and forth a few minutes, while Jack carefully rewrote the words on a lined paper he'd ruled into squares.

"You done?"

"Not yet," Jack replied. He still had to rewrite it, following the routing instructions indicated by the guide word at the top, but he had no intention of revealing that to Peterson. Mentally, he mapped it out. Column three up, column four down, column one up, column six down ...

At last he had the words in the order they were intended. Now to translate the arbitraries. He reached for the little cipher book.

"*China set angels Moon roads*—That doesn't even make sense," Peterson said loudly in his ear.

Jack's back stiffened. "I'm not finished, Lieutenant. Give me a few minutes, please."

Peterson came around to the side of the desk, where Jack could see his face. "Is that the codebook?" The lieutenant held out his hand eagerly. "Let me see it."

Instinctively, Jack lowered the leather-bound cipher book

below the edge of the desk. "Why?" If he were still in uniform, he'd have added "sir," but he was a civilian now, and he didn't like Peterson's attitude.

"I want to see how you do it. And maybe I could send out messages for Captain Nason when we're in the field."

"I can't do that."

"That's an order, Miller."

Jack swallowed hard. "I'm sorry, Lieutenant. My orders come from the Secretary of War. I took an oath not to give my cipher book to anyone else, not even military officers."

Peterson's face reddened. "Indeed?"

"Yes." Jack stared straight ahead.

"I'll see about that. Finish it up and give it here."

"Begging your pardon, but I'm required to give it to the runner or the person to whom it's addressed." And right now, Jack was inclined to deliver the message himself, fearing Peterson would waylay the runner and take it from him.

To his relief, Peterson stalked out of the room, muttering under his breath.

Jack inhaled deeply and translated the code words as quickly as he could. He rewrote the plaintext message, discarding the meaningless null words, sealed it, and went to the door.

"Smitty! Come quick."

The private trotted to him, and Jack put the message in his hands. "To headquarters, as fast as you can. And do not give it up to anyone except the general, or if he's not there, Captain Shibles."

"Yes, sir. I mean, Mr. Miller."

Jack chuckled. "It's all right. Now, go."

The receiver was clicking again, and he hurried back to his desk to write out the incoming message.

He heard no more about the unpleasant matter. A relief operator had joined them after they gained access to the city, and he sat by the telegraph station each night, so Jack could catch some sleep. The young man would transcribe the Morse, but he wasn't privy to the cipher book, so if a coded message came in, he had to wake Jack to decrypt it. That happened two or three times a night, but somehow Jack managed to get his sleep in.

General Sherman walked into the office unannounced one afternoon. The receiver was silent at the moment, and Jack jumped to his feet.

"At ease, Miller," the general said. "I'm told a message was taken off a captured Rebel scout."

"Sir?"

"Did someone deliver such a message to you?"

"No, sir." Jack hesitated. "You mean, today?"

"That's right."

"No. Definitely not."

Sherman scowled and turned on his heel. As he stepped through the doorway, Jack heard him bark, "Have you got a message for me?"

"Uh, well, sir, I was going to give it to the telegraph operator, in hopes he could translate it for you."

"This is the one taken off a captured scout?"

"Uh, I believe so, sir."

"Give it here."

Sherman stormed back into Jack's office and tossed a rumpled paper on the desk. "What do you make of that?"

Jack picked it up and studied it carefully. The message was in code, but letters had been penciled in beneath some of the words.

"It seems someone's had a try at deciphering it, sir."

Sherman strode to the door. "Lieutenant!"

A moment later, Peterson slunk inside, not looking at either of them.

"As I understand it," Sherman said, "we've had that message for at least three hours. Where has it been?"

Peterson gulped. "I—uh—"

"You thought you'd try cracking it?"

Peterson said nothing but stared at the floor, his upper lip quivering.

The general whirled on Jack. "Miller, are you allowed to share enemy messages with army officers?"

"Only you or one of the captains in your absence," Jack replied.

Sherman nodded. "How long will it take you to solve that?"

"Perhaps twenty minutes, sir."

"Good. I'll be in the house. Send it by approved courier."

"Yes, sir."

The general stalked out, and Peterson pulled in a cautious breath.

"I was coming to ask you about some of the words, Miller. The codes used for—"

"Please leave now," Jack said with his back to the lieutenant. As he sharpened his pencil, he heard muffled footsteps as Peterson slunk out the door.

Fifteen minutes later, he had the message in order. He ran his eyes over the lines once more for a quick reassurance that he had it correct. He swallowed hard. The troops might have a bit of trouble because of the delay. They needed to get to the water tower down the rail line immediately. He ran to the door. The telegraph receiver began to click.

"Smitty!"

When the runner hurried in, Jack was already taking down a new message. He nodded at the solved one. "Get that to the general at once—and nobody else. Then get back here for this one."

Smitty snatched up the paper and ran out the door.

November 14, 1864
East of Atlanta

JACK'S HORSE plodded behind the wagon carrying his telegraph apparatus. The construction crew of fifty men from the Military Telegraph Corps was accompanied by a dozen uniformed soldiers—enough to make Jack feel fairly secure, since many of the crewmen were armed as well. He had a revolver himself.

When they'd left Atlanta two days before, Sherman's troops were destroying anything they left behind that the Confederates might find useful. They tore up railroad track and burned train depots and other important buildings. Sherman planned to split his forces into three columns, cutting a wider swath as they headed east and south and giving them more opportunity to scavenge for food. Jack shuddered to think what the people of Georgia would face in the coming weeks.

He and the construction crew were to go to a point the general had indicated would be his next stopping place and string telegraph wires as quickly as possible. Close to Atlanta, some of the old poles were still in place but stripped of their wires. Away from the city, the crew had to set new ones. They'd used more than half of the poles they'd brought in long wagons. When they ran out, they'd have to cut and limb trees as substitutes.

Jack helped dig the holes and hoist new poles. The soldiers couldn't help them—their job was to keep watch while the civilians worked.

One of the privates rode ahead to scout and returned to the caravan.

"There's at least six poles in place up ahead, maybe more. It's less than half a mile from here."

"Great," said Jim Clarkson, the leader of the construction crew. "Hear that, boys? We can make that far by lunch time. After we set two more poles, I'll send one of you ahead with Cookie to fix our dinner."

Jack was the lucky one to draw the short straw. He tried not to feel too guilty as he rode ahead with the chuck wagon and two of the soldiers. His horse trotted along, and Jack kept his rifle resting on his thigh, just in case. Clarkson's crew was still in sight when they stopped beneath the first of the poles left standing beside the road.

"Let's get a fire going and fix some coffee," the designated cook for the unit, "Cookie" Randall, said. He jumped down from the wagon and fetched some feed for the mules.

Meanwhile, Jack looked around to see if any likely firewood lay in sight. No such luck—troops passing through had apparently picked clean whatever might have been available. He went to the back of the wagon to see how much fuel Cookie had left.

"You cooking much?" he asked.

Randall shook his head. "Just coffee, and I wouldn't do that except the men have worked hard all morning and need a little cheering up. Cold biscuit, cheese, and one slice of bacon each. I cooked extra this morning."

Jack removed the gloves from his blistered hands and set about building a small but, he hoped, efficient fire.

He'd just set a match to it when a shot rang out and he jumped, almost pitching forward onto his fire ring.

Catching himself, Jack looked around. One of the two guards was slumped in his saddle.

"Get down," the second soldier yelled. Jack dove under the wagon, wondering he if he could reach his horse and the rifle in his saddle scabbard. He heard hoofbeats—the rest of the detachment? Who would guard the rest of the telegraph crew?

He pulled his revolver but couldn't see any Rebels. Several shots rang out, and he covered his head, praying he would make it out alive.

Someone grasped his ankles and pulled him out onto the dirt road. Jack clamped his mouth shut and grabbed a wheel as he was dragged past it.

"Let go, Billy Yank," said a harsh, deep voice. "You wanna come with us or lie here in your own blood?"

Jack gasped and rolled, his gun in his free hand, but three

men were waiting. One instantly pinned Jack's arm to the ground with a heavy boot and wrenched the revolver from him.

"Up!"

Jack stumbled to his feet. Two of the armed men tugged him up while the third kept his own revolver trained on him. They shoved him off the far side of the road, into a neglected field that hadn't been planted that year.

From farther down the road, more gunshots sounded. Bile rose in his throat. How many of his friends were being slaughtered?

"Hold him still, Frank," the smaller man said.

His captor held Jack upright while his pal patted him down and took his knife. Then he slid the small book out of Jack's shirt pocket.

"What's this?"

"Nothing," Jack said quickly. "My expense record."

The man frowned and opened it. "I don't see no money amounts. What's this? Davis, Pollard. Lincoln, Adrian. Richmond, Moon Meadow. Atlanta, fireside. What the dickens? Look, Frank." He shoved the cipher book toward the big man's face.

"Huh." Frank frowned. "Some of 'em's printed and some of 'em's written in with pencil." He looked at his friend, his eyes widening. "That there's a codebook, Hughey, or I'll eat my belt."

A smile spread slowly across Hughey's face. "That right, boy?"

Jack clenched his teeth and said nothing.

"I think the colonel will be interested in this," Frank said.

"By jiminy, I think you're right." Hughey pocketed the cipher book, and a lump of stone formed in Jack's chest.

"Come on, buddy boy." Hughey tugged at his arm.

"Where are you taking me?" Jack asked.

"Just down the rud a piece," Frank said.

They marched him back to the dusty road, where several disreputable-looking men were bent over forms lying on the ground. One was climbing onto the driver's seat of the cook wagon. Jack turned his face away.

They led him about a quarter mile down the road, to a clearing under a cluster of oak trees. Frank shoved him to the ground then tied him to the bole of a tree. Jack fought nausea as he sat leaning against the rough bark. A breeze stirred, and acorns plopped to the ground around him. He winced as one hit him on the head.

Soon he learned that the raiders took four horses, including the bay gelding Jack had been riding, along with the cook wagon and the four mules pulling it. Two other mules trailing cut straps were tied to the back.

"What about the other wagons?" Jack asked.

"What them ones with the telegraph poles? We got no use for them,"

Jack gulped. "What about the men?"

The big man who'd pulled him from his hiding place said gruffly, "Most of the others we let go, but with orders to keep marching west or we'd shoot 'em the second they turned our way."

Sorting it out in his mind, Jack decided that meant the soldiers were likely all dead, or at least disarmed, and maybe some of the construction crew, but at least a few were on foot, heading back toward Sherman's approaching force.

The raiders gathered, a surprisingly large group. Jack counted more than twenty men but noticed no other prisoners.

"What now?" one man asked Hughey.

"We head east."

"What you going to do with him?" asked a man in tattered clothes, nodding toward Jack.

"I think Colonel Buckley will want to see this man."

"Who is he?" a couple of the others asked.

Hughey turned to Jack, frowning. "What's your name, son?"

"Miller."

"You Federal army?"

"No. I'm a civilian."

"What are you doing with that bunch of blue bellies?"

Hughey laid his hand on Frank's sleeve. "I think that's obvious from what he was carrying. Come on. We need to get him to River Lea. This could be important." He patted his own pocket, where the cipher book now peeked out at the top.

19

River Lea Plantation

Marilla sat reading in the small sitting room that evening, or trying to read. She'd heard Uncle Hamilton tell Zeke Vernon to go out and look for Betty, a field slave who'd managed to run off with her young sons.

"I want them back here," Buckley had screeched.

Marilla understood his fury, though she didn't feel it. If things continued this way, pretty soon she and Uncle Hamilton would be left to their own devices with no one to tend to the plantation, no one to keep the house for them, and no one to cook.

Well, Marilla could get by in the kitchen if Sadie left, and she wouldn't blame the cook. But if Marilla had to haul all the water and firewood as well, not to mention scrounging up the food and butchering any meat they were lucky enough to come by, well, they might be in trouble. Even worse, they'd heard the Union army was on the move, and a large force was headed in their direction.

The house was quiet with Zeke out on his mission. After supper, Uncle Hamilton had retreated to his study. What he was doing, she had no idea. Probably writing angry letters to the newspapers, Jefferson Davis, and their congressmen. She had decided to hide out in the small sitting room, not the big parlor. Her great-uncle was less likely to find her here than in the bigger room or up in her chamber.

She had only completed two pages when a hammering came on the front door. She started then sat listening and trying to calm her pulse. Hearing no stir from Buckley's study or from the house slaves, she rose and went out into the grand entrance hall. As she approached the door, another loud knock shook it.

Cautiously, she tried to see out the sidelight, but darkness had fallen and the lamplight inside made it impossible to see who was on the verandah.

"Who is it?" she called, hoping the visitor couldn't hear the tremor in her voice.

"Zeke Vernon."

She opened the door.

"I need to see Mr. Buckley."

"He's in his study."

"Thank you." Zeke strode past her.

Marilla shut the door and headed back toward the sitting room, but Uncle Hamilton had come out into the hall to greet Zeke.

"What's the word, Vernon?"

"Well, sir, the band of men you sent out last week to try to bring back those field hands is back."

"Did they catch them?"

"No, but they'd joined up with a bunch of scouts, and they got their hands on something interesting. They thought you'd want to see their prisoner."

"Prisoner?"

Marilla's ears pricked up too, and she lingered just inside the sitting room doorway, hoping Zeke would keep speaking loudly.

"Yes, sir. They were out to disrupt the Feds' progress any way they could, and they stumbled on a telegraph crew stringing lines. They figured that meant Northern troops were headed this way. They killed their guards and cut down the poles they'd set. The civilians were sent off westward on foot, except for one. He's apparently the telegraph operator, and he had some kind of codebook, so they took him prisoner. My men brought him back here, and some of that scout group came too. I've got 'em waitin' out near the springhouse."

"Bring in their leader and this prisoner fellow."

"Right." Zeke ambled out the door.

Uncle Hamilton swung around and impaled Marilla with his gaze before she could duck out of sight.

"You heard?"

She nodded.

"Is Sadie in the kitchen?"

"I don't think so," she said. "All the house servants have gone to the quarters."

He scowled, and she knew he was still fuming about his personal man, Thomas, running away. Uncle Hamilton did not like having to dress himself or having an inexperienced and untrained person tend to his wardrobe. The shouts from his suite each morning testified to how trying he found it.

"Do you think you could fix some coffee?"

"Why, yes, I can do that." She was a bit surprised, because usually when her great-uncle entertained visiting men in the evening, he reached for the bourbon.

She hurried past him to the kitchen, where she lit a lantern and checked the fire in the stove. Sadie had banked it for the night, and Marilla quickly raked up the coals and piled on more wood then filled the coffeepot.

By the time the coffee was ready, no one remained in the entrance hall, but she could hear men's voices coming from her great-uncle's study. She tiptoed forward and peeked around the doorjamb, then drew back, her pulse rocketing.

Her uncle and Zeke hadn't noticed her, nor the man in gray who must be the leader of the company of soldiers, but the prisoner glanced her way. His clear blue eyes had met hers just for an instant, but she'd felt a jolt of recognition. Somehow she felt she knew this man, but that was ridiculous. Wasn't it?

She flattened her spine against the wall outside the room, trying to breathe silently.

"And what's this here book you were carryin'?" Uncle Hamilton asked.

For a moment, no one spoke. Then Zeke yelled, "Speak up, boy, if you know what's good for you."

Knowing Zeke and how he treated their field hands, Marilla was afraid he would strike the young man. She hauled in a deep breath and stepped into the doorway, trying hard not to look at the prisoner, for fear her eyes or a blush might give her away if he really was an acquaintance.

"Excuse me, Uncle. Do you wish the coffee to be served in here?"

Uncle Hamilton's lips curled as he looked over at her. She thought he would send her away, but the man who purportedly led the group of soldiers—if they were, indeed, soldiers —spoke up.

"I can smell that coffee, missy, and it sure has me hankerin' for some."

"Bring it in here," Uncle Hamilton said.

As Marilla stepped into the hall, she heard her great-uncle say, "Now, Miller, you be straight with us, boy. Is this some kind of key for a code?"

Miller!

Her stomach plunged, and Marilla almost stumbled. Of course. He was one of the Miller boys. She hadn't seen any of them for more than eight years, but with a flash of certainty, she knew the prisoner was Jack Miller. Not Ned or one of the younger boys. This one was a grown man.

And besides, he had blue eyes. He was the only one of the Millers with blue eyes. She'd always thought it odd. Mrs. Miller, Jenny, and Ruthie's eyes were hazel. Charles Miller and the other children had rich brown eyes. But Jack's were a vivid blue. She would never forget those eyes.

He used to have blond hair, she remembered. It was a little darker now, but she'd glimpsed a glint of gold. She was sure he was Jack, and her heart pounded as she balanced the heavy tray. She'd put four cups on it with the coffeepot, hoping they would give the prisoner some coffee, but maybe not.

As almost an afterthought, she took a can of pecan cookies from the cupboard. She'd planned to serve them at lunch tomorrow, but the men would be pleased if she offered some now, and the treat might serve as enough of a distraction to allow her to get a closer look at Jack.

When she reentered the study, her great-uncle was examining a small booklet. It looked like a leather-covered pocket diary.

"This might be of value to our cause," he mused.

When the men noticed her carrying the laden tray, Jack and the ragged soldier were the only two who moved to stand. Zeke Vernon put a hand on the prisoner's shoulder and shoved him back down in his chair. Only then did Marilla realize Jack's hands were bound.

"Let me help you with that, missy." The soldier was at her elbow now, and she forced herself not to cringe at the body odor wafting off him. "Sergeant Manfred Hinkley, at your service." He took the tray from her.

"Thank you." Marilla pushed aside a candlestick and newspaper on a side table and nodded. Hinkley set down the tray. "I'll pour," she said quickly, before her uncle could send her away.

Her hands trembled a little. The first cup she carried to the desk and placed in front of Uncle Hamilton.

"Do you think we should send it on to Jeff Davis, Colonel?" Hinkley asked.

Her great-uncle shook his head. "Let me hold on to it for a while. I may be able to make some sense of this."

Zeke accepted the next cup of coffee. "You think we could

use it to garble up their messages? Maybe send some of our own that look like their field commanders sent 'em?"

"Maybe." Uncle Hamilton sipped his coffee and turned a page in the little book.

Marilla set a full cup before Hinkley and poured one more. With a sidelong glance at Hamilton, who seemed preoccupied with the book, she took it over to the prisoner.

"Coffee, sir?"

Jack looked up into her eyes and inhaled carefully. "I—" Helplessly, he held up his tied hands.

"Perhaps ..." She eased the cup between his fingers and he clasped it then cautiously raised it to his mouth.

Hinkley, who seemed to have charge of the prisoner, said nothing, but eyed the tray wistfully. Marilla hurried to it and brought the plate of cookies to him.

"Fresh today, sir."

"Why, thank you, miss." Hinkley grinned at her and helped himself to two.

She hesitated then held out the plate to Jack. "Maybe if I take your cup for a moment, sir?"

"Here, Marilla, what are you doing?" Uncle Hamilton snarled. "Don't feed that scum."

Stricken, she stepped back. Jack's eyes flickered at the sound of her name, and he focused on her for a moment before lowering his gaze.

Zeke was only too happy to grab the plate from her hands. "Here, us good Confederates will take care of them."

She threw Jack an apologetic glance, but he was staring down at his coffee cup, no doubt wondering how long before that was snatched away too.

"You'll have to excuse my great-niece," the colonel said. "She's used to offering hospitality to all and sundry that walk through the door."

Hinkley and Vernon laughed a bit nervously.

"Forgive me, Uncle," she said.

"They're good, Miss Buckley." Hinkley gave her a sly smile. "Good coffee too. Haven't had real coffee in a dog's age."

"We don't get much anymore," Buckley said a bit defensively. "Happened to get a small packet that came through the blockade last week." He eyed the prisoner, who kept his gaze lowered and frowned.

Jack's cup was half empty. Marilla figured he'd decided to gulp it down as fast as he could, before they took it away. She hoped he hadn't scalded his mouth with it.

Hoping to learn more about the prisoner, she passed the plate of cookies again, careful not to offer it to Jack. With his awkwardly bound hands, he tipped his cup up again at his mouth. As she was about to pass behind him, he turned slightly and held out the cup.

"Thank you, miss."

Their eyes locked, and she found it hard to breathe. She nodded and took the cup from him.

"What about Miller?" Zeke looked over at Hinkley. "Where you reckon to take him?"

"I was thinking we'd pass him along to a company out of Macon," Hinkley replied. "I'm not sure where General Hood is now."

"Hood's long gone," Uncle Hamilton said. "I think we'll keep this fellow right here for a while, until I sort out this code business."

Jack's mouth set in a hard, thin line, but he didn't look up.

"But, Colonel," Hinkley said, "I ought to notify my superiors."

"You go ahead and do that. Tell them Colonel Buckley will board the prisoner for the time being, at no charge to the Confederate Army." Uncle Hamilton wasn't in the army anymore, but he'd served in the Mexican War, reportedly with distinction, and he never let that be forgotten.

Hinkley hesitated. "I guess that will be all right."

"You tell them," Buckley said. "If they don't like it and they want to take charge of the prisoner, they can come get him anytime."

Marilla's mind raced. What was Uncle up to? Where would he put Jack? Surely he wouldn't house him in the slave quarters. She'd seen one of the recaptured field hands led down there in shackles and grieved over her helplessness to change things. Would Jack be chained up? She couldn't bear the thought.

"Here, take these things away," Uncle Hamilton said gruffly, waving a hand toward the cups and the empty plate.

Marilla gathered the dishes onto the tray quickly and carried it to the kitchen. She wanted to go back and listen, but if the colonel thought she had too marked an interest in the prisoner, he'd be suspicious. She took a wet cloth and scrubbed the sideboard nearest the door.

A few minutes later she heard the men in the hall. She blew out the lamp and stood in darkness, listening.

"You know where to put him, Zeke," Uncle Hamilton said.

"Yes, sir, Mr. Buckley. You want me to untie him?"

"You can, once he's secure."

Marilla heard footsteps, and she ducked below the worktable. A door opened, but not the front door. She puzzled over it for a moment, trying to place the unaccustomed sounds she was hearing.

The cellar. They're going to lock Jack in the cellar. Probably the room where they stored potatoes, carrots, turnips, and other root vegetables. It was the only place in the cellar that she knew had a lock.

Poor Jack.

"I know, I know," her great-uncle was saying in the hall. "Make your men comfortable for the night. Here, take a bottle of bourbon. They can camp down in the stable. I've only got a few horses now. They can sleep in the hay. Just don't let them scatter it all over."

"But, sir, we could get in a lot of trouble."

"Did you tell anyone else about the prisoner yet?"

"No, sir, but—"

"But nothing. Stay here for a minute. Your boots look like they've seen better days. I'll get you a pair my son left behind, and I'll have Zeke bring you a sack of potatoes."

"Thank you, Colonel Buckley."

To Marilla, it sounded as though Hinkley had given in. He would take his bounty—or his bribes, more like it—and keep his mouth shut about Jack. For some reason Uncle Hamilton wanted to keep him here and study his notebook. She remembered Jack's love of Morse Code. Likely that little book was a copy of Morse Code, or held some encoded messages.

She heard her great-uncle's heavy tread on the stairs.

"Here, take those, Hinkley. Has Zeke come up yet? No?"

He walked closer and opened the cellar door. "Zeke! Bring up a sack of potatoes and a few turnips for the soldiers' supper."

Marilla decided she'd better scurry up the back stairs before Uncle Hamilton came into the kitchen for some other present to give Hinkley and his men. She hoped he wouldn't give away the rest of the good coffee or the white sugar.

JACK SETTLED down on a heap of burlap sacks once Vernon had left and locked him in. It was dark outside, but at least there was a tiny window high on the wall, probably at ground level on the house. If he stood in just the right spot he could make out a few stars.

All sorts of thoughts darted through his mind, and he tried to calm himself. Think rationally, that's what Pa Miller had taught him. Take things one step at a time.

So, he was now in the hands of a pompous plantation owner who had the markings of a despot. He was a man who flourished on having authority and wielding it. The band of Confederates—whether soldiers, irregulars, or civilian resisters he hadn't been able to discern—had turned in at the lane leading to the big house for a reason. They knew this man, Colonel Buckley, or at least knew of him.

Hinkley, the leader of the company, had seemed sure Buckley would let them bed down on his property for the night and perhaps even give them something to eat. But there was more. Something political. What gave Buckley the right to incarcerate him here, in his root cellar, rather than send him on to Confederate authorities?

This odd situation might be to his advantage, Jack thought. Surely this place would be easier to escape from than a regulation prison.

And then there was Marilla.

What was she doing here?

She'd taken pains not to reveal that she recognized Jack, but he was sure she had.

At first he hadn't known who she was, only that she looked familiar. When Colonel Buckley called her Marilla, it hit him with a jolt. But she couldn't be—could she? Several surreptitious glances had clinched the matter. The young woman living in this house was the same girl he'd known eight years ago in Emmaus.

"Lord, You work in strange ways," he whispered. "I don't know how or why she's here, but I can't help thinking Your hand is in this."

She'd been a schoolgirl the last time he saw her. Jack knew from their few encounters that she was bright. Good at math, if he remembered correctly, and she'd taken to Morse Code that one time, like a crow to a cornfield. He recalled that she'd said she wanted to be a telegrapher one day.

And now she was here, in war-torn Georgia. "Uncle," she'd called the colonel, and their last name was the same. Was he Marilla's father's brother then? He seemed quite old for that relationship, but then, Jack had never seen Marilla's father.

Marilla's mother was widowed when they moved to Emmaus, he was sure of that. She and Marilla were living with a relative. Mrs. Clayton, that was it. But Marilla and her mother had moved away when Mrs. Clayton died. Jack had no idea where they'd gone. To Georgia, it seemed. Was Mrs. Buckley here too?

He stayed awake a long time in the damp, chilly cellar, pondering the intricacies of the Buckley family. Was Buckley really a colonel? He wasn't in uniform. Maybe in the last war. But many of the men who'd served in Mexico had been called back to duty.

Maybe Buckley was too old, though he was certainly younger than General Winfield Scott, who had served in the War of 1812, the Mexican War, and even in the early stages of this war for the Union. Or maybe Buckley had old wounds or other health problems that kept him from serving now. He was certainly running to fat, which would be a drawback to an active military man.

Enough thoughts of Buckley for now. Jack rearranged the sacks so that two were between him and the dirt floor, which seemed to be getting colder by the minute. The rest he pulled over him, but there weren't enough to really keep him warm.

20

W hen Marilla entered the dining room the next morning, Uncle Hamilton appeared to be just finishing his breakfast. Sadie poured him a fresh cup of the blockade-run coffee.

"Good morning, Uncle." Marilla slid into her chair and looked at Sadie. "Are there any eggs, Sadie?"

"Yes'm. You want one poached on toast?"

"That sounds perfect. And tea with that. Thank you."

Uncle Hamilton frowned. Marilla wasn't sure if it was because she'd thanked the slave or because she didn't usually eat breakfast with him. She either ate alone after he'd left the house or gone into his study, or she ate in the kitchen in the midst of helping Sadie and Reenie with their morning's work.

She smiled at him. "How is everything going this morning, Uncle?"

"Seems all right, for this time of year."

Marilla nodded. Harvest was done, and the depleted group of field hands would be put to chores that weren't so urgent as when there were fields to plant or cotton to pick.

Sadie brought her tea first, casting her a baffled glance, but Marilla accepted it and sipped the hot brew while she waited for her egg, as if this were her normal routine. Uncle Hamilton hunched over a newspaper, and she wondered if Zeke had somehow got hold of a new one. It grew harder every day to find one with fresh reports of the war. The local papers and some of those in Atlanta had stopped printing since the evacuation, at least for the time being.

"Have the soldiers who were here last night left?" She asked, with as innocent a tone as she could muster.

The colonel grunted and turned to the back page of the paper. "Pulled out at dawn."

"Well, good. I hope they get safely to their destination."

He reached for his coffee and took a swallow then smacked his lips.

Sadie brought in her toast and poached egg, and Marilla accepted it with a smile.

"Don't you go down in the cellar," Uncle Hamilton said.

Marilla arched her eyebrows. "Oh? Why not?"

"Just you mind what I say. If you need something in the kitchen, let Reenie or Sadie get it."

"All right." She cut into the egg and took a bite. After a moment, she said, "The hens are still laying. I'm pleased, aren't you?"

He scowled. "If Sherman's men come around here, the chickens'll disappear quick as a wink. I think I'll have Lazarus build them a pen down in the woods beyond the cowshed."

"Won't the foxes get them there? They'd have to have a proper coop."

He made a displeased sound in his throat and folded the newspaper. He emptied his coffee cup and stood. "I'll be outside for a bit. Mind what I said about the cellar."

"Yes, Uncle."

When he'd left the room, Marilla finished her breakfast quickly and carried her dishes and his to the kitchen. Sadie was preparing a tray with a bowl of porridge, two slices of toast, and a mug of tea.

"What's that for?" Marilla asked, though she knew.

Sadie rolled her eyes. "Seems they's a guest in the root cellar."

"Would you like me to take it?"

"Huh-uh. The colonel says only me and Reenie can take it, and Lazarus has to be with us."

"I see." Marilla took a steaming kettle from the stove and poured hot water into the dishpan. "Then I'll wash up these things."

"No need, Miss Marilla."

She smiled. "I know. But if I do this, you can do more of your marvelous cooking."

In a rare occurrence, Sadie returned her smile.

Marilla hummed as she washed and dried the dishes, thinking all the while about Jack Miller down in the root cellar. Was he restrained or able to move about? And how could she manage a word with him? She wouldn't go to the cellar, that was certain. In fact, she wouldn't do anything today to arouse suspicions. If she wanted to help that man, nobody could know she'd known him in her life up North.

JACK SCRATCHED a mark on the stone wall with a jagged pebble. How long would Buckley keep him here?

He no longer thought he was better off in this cellar than he would have been with Hinkley and his band. The door to his prison was solid, the window too small for him to squeeze through. He wouldn't attack one of the maids who brought him his meals—that wasn't in Jack's sphere of possibilities. Besides, a large man usually accompanied them when they brought him food and stood by until Jack was once again alone and the door locked.

Digging had entered his mind early on, but he had no tools. A slat broken from one of the vegetable bins was the best he could do, but the earthen floor was packed solid. He'd have to go down below the foundation wall, under it, then upward. It would take years at the rate he was able to progress, and he would have rubbed all the crates' pieces to splinters before he got a foot deep.

He heard footsteps outside. He could hear them when they came down the stairs if he was quiet, and over the past three days, he'd become attuned to the faint sounds.

The key turned in the lock, and the door swung open. A woman carried a tray, as usual, and behind her stood the big man they called Lazarus, carrying a lantern.

He opened his mouth to greet her but quickly closed it.

"Good morning, sir." Marilla sounded impersonal and didn't look into his eyes. She lowered the tray to the top of a crate of sand, in which carrots were buried, and eyed the dishes. "Oh, Lazarus, I forgot the gentleman's fork."

The huge black man snorted. "He a prisoner, Miss Marilla, not a gentleman."

"Well, now, we don't know what his life was like before this war, do we?" she said. "Will you please run up and fetch us a fork?"

"I'm not supposed to leave you down here with that man, Miss Marilla."

Jack held up his hands. "I'll stay back here in the corner, I swear. I wouldn't hurt your mistress for anything in the world."

"I dunno." Lazarus shook his head. "Mr. Buckley be mad if I do that."

"Oh, for pity's sake." Marilla flounced to the door. "I'll get it, but you'd better leave him alone while I'm gone."

"I'm not doin' anything, Miss Marilla." The slave must be near forty years old, but he sounded like a little boy trying to convince his mother of his innocence.

Marilla hiked up her skirt and ran up the stairs.

Jack sat still on the burlap sacks, eyeing Lazarus. He'd promised not to misbehave if Marilla was left alone with him, but did that extend to his behavior now? Sizing up Lazarus, he decided that even if he surprised the man with a swift tackle or a head butt and shove, he probably wouldn't get past him. Lazarus may not be quick, but he was huge. He also carried an oil lantern, which could start a fire if it was dropped. Jack didn't want that.

All he wanted was his freedom.

Lazarus met his gaze for only an instant then looked at the floor.

They wanted the same thing, Jack thought. He'd been a prisoner for three days and he was going stark, raving mad. But Lazarus had probably been enslaved all his life. What went on in that man's head?

Instead of thinking how to tackle the big man, Jack leaned sideways a little and tried to get a view of the main part of the cellar. He saw boxes and barrels, quite a lot of them, and a rack of bottles. Wine? Buckley might be a connoisseur. Rich people could afford luxuries like that, and he may have stocked his cellar decades ago, before the war interfered with trade.

Marilla's light tread came down the stairs, and he settled back against the wall.

"There you go," she said cheerfully. She stepped into the room and laid a fork on the tray. "My great-uncle had a young pig butchered yesterday, to save it from the Yankees, and we had a pork roast tonight. There was plenty left, so I managed to slip a bit onto your plate."

Jack hardly knew what to say, but he nodded. Did Lazarus and the other slaves get part of the pig? He'd bet they didn't.

"All right, then. I'll be back down later for your dishes." She started to turn but stopped. "Oh, Lazarus, leave him your lantern, so he can see to eat."

Lazarus's eyes went wide. "Oh, no, missy. Mr. Buckley says no fire here. No candle, not even that."

"Well, you can't expect him to eat his dinner in the pitch dark."

Jack gulped but said nothing. Eating in the dark was exactly what he'd done the past two nights, and in the gloom with just a bit of light from the tiny window for his other meals. He ate his suppers as if he were blind, feeling each bit of food and shoving it into his mouth, then licking his fingers clean.

"I ... I guess I stay while he eat, Miss Marilla."

She sighed heavily. "If that's all you can do, Lazarus. Look, why don't you fetch one of those empty barrels to sit on. I'll hold the lantern while you do it."

Lazarus hesitated then passed her the lantern. She held it up by the bale, and the slave lumbered out into the cellar. Marilla backed up a step and felt behind her, grazing the edge of the tray. Jack saw something white leave her hand and land beside the plate. His lungs tightened, but he didn't dare move.

Her delicate fingers probed while she kept her face toward the outer room. She managed to tuck the white bit—a folded piece of paper, Jack was sure—under the plate's edge.

Lazarus brought a large keg in and stood it bottom side up. Then he looked around and moved to hang the lantern on a peg high on the wall.

While he tended to the lantern, Marilla planted herself, billowing skirts and all, between the two men.

"Careful, Lazarus," she said.

Jack was sure she was blocking him, in case Lazarus looked his way. He scrambled to his feet and stepped quietly to the bin with the tray on top. Marilla fussed at the slave a little more, about the angle of the lantern, and Jack extracted the paper, folded into a square only an inch each way, and shoved it in his pocket.

When Lazarus turned, he glared at Jack. "You get back til Miss Marilla's gone!"

"Oh, don't growl," Marilla said, stepping toward the doorway. "He's fine, Lazarus, and I'm leaving anyway." She focused on Jack. "Now, you enjoy your meal, Mr. Miller."

"Thank you, ma'am." He didn't move again until she'd gone out and shut the door.

It wasn't until morning that he was able to open and read her message. He couldn't do it with Lazarus watching, and when the slave left, he took the only light. That was all right. Jack settled down for the night with the pleasure of having something to look forward to.

As soon as dawn sent a pale gleam through the window, he brought out the paper and unfolded it. Two words were on it, written in Morse Code.

Take hope. Jack smiled and settled back against the cold stone wall.

November 18, 1864
River Lea Plantation

THE SUNLIGHT STREAMING in through the windows was blinding, and Jack squeezed his eyes shut.

"In there." His keeper shoved him.

Jack stumbled and opened his eyes as he lurched forward. When he straightened, Colonel Buckley was eyeing him with distaste. He sat in a padded chair beside the fireplace in the room where they'd taken him before—a sort of library or study. The warmth of the blaze drew him, and Jack took another step toward it.

"Well, Miller, what do you have to say for yourself?"

"What do you want to know, sir?" Jack glanced over his shoulder. Lazarus had closed the door and taken up a post beside it. In stark daylight, the black man was as big as Jack had gathered in the dark cellar, and the sight of his bulging muscles gave Jack a dispiriting shudder. That was one man he would never beat in a fair fight.

"I've been looking at your book," Buckley said.

Jack swiveled his head to stare at him. Should he clam up, pretend to help him, or taunt him? He didn't want to take a beating, but he wasn't sure what to do. When he was in the army, he'd been instructed not to give much information if captured, and in training for the Telegraph Corps, their instructions were much the same. He kept his eyes on the cipher book and said nothing.

Buckley's voice lowered and became friendly—too friendly. "Now, son, if you want to go home, you need to help me out a little."

Jack raised his gaze to meet the colonel's but remained silent.

"I can see that you use some of these words to take the place of names in your messages, but that can't be the extent of your code work. Why, there was a notice in the paper last month where they printed a code message the Confederate Telegraph Corps had captured, asking any member of the public who could help solve it to come forward."

Keeping a straight face was difficult for Jack. He'd heard rumors of the Southern leaders appealing to the public to help crack the Union codes, but he hadn't been sure whether or not to believe it.

The head of the U.S. Army Signal Corps, Colonel Anson Stager, would no doubt change the arbitraries as soon as word got out that Jack and his cipher book might be in enemy hands. He'd seen them do that before. Overnight, all the operators in the Telegraph Corps were issued new cipher books, and they kept on with business as usual.

Stager was behind the routing ciphers they used, and he was a brilliant man. No doubt the little cipher book in Buckley's hands was already useless. Even so, Jack didn't like to leave it with the man. He didn't think Buckley was clever enough to solve a message encrypted using the Union method, but someone with a bit of experience might figure out the basics of the system. No, if he had a chance to escape he had to take the booklet with him.

"Are you hungry, Miller?" Buckley's eyes narrowed.

Jack swallowed hard. When Lazarus unlocked the door to

the root cellar, he'd expected his luncheon to arrive—an hour or so late, if his internal clock could be trusted. But instead, he'd been brought up here. Was Buckley planning to starve him if he didn't cooperate?

On the other hand, if he said no, the colonel would have a perfect reason not to feed him. Why waste good food on a man who wasn't hungry?

"Yes, sir," he said.

"Would you like your dinner?"

Jack hesitated but couldn't see any point to denying it. Maybe Buckley just wanted to crow over the fact that he could withhold sustenance from his prisoner.

"Yes, sir."

Buckley smiled. "Suppose we sit down and talk about this code of yours for a while, and I'll have the cook make you a plate?"

Jack took two breaths before replying. "As you please, sir."

"Good, good." Buckley got up and moved to his desk. He nodded to the slave, and Lazarus brought a chair—a wooden straight chair—over and placed it on the opposite side, facing the colonel.

"Sit, Miller," Buckley said as Lazarus retreated. "Now, see here." He leaned forward, holding out the open cipher book. "This page has a lot of words printed down the side, what I might call random words out of the dictionary. Bellows, brandy, bridle, budget, and so forth. And other words—names and places —are penciled in beside them. Is that your writing?"

Jack knew he was wading in dangerous waters.

"I'm not allowed to speak of it, sir."

"Oh, you're not allowed. But you want your dinner."

Miserable, Jack sat in silence, refusing to meet his gaze.

"Come now, Miller. I'm not asking you to translate a particular message for me."

No, Jack thought, you just want to unravel our method so that you and your friends can decrypt all our future messages.

He exhaled slowly, trying not to think about food. He could wait.

"These names," Buckley persisted. "Some are generals' last names, aren't they? And some are places I recognize. And the governor of South Carolina is listed here."

Jack clenched his teeth.

"Now, son, it's a reasonable assumption on my part that if you were going to send a message concerning one of these people or places, you'd substitute the word beside it for that name. Am I right?"

Was the man planning to use the codebook to send false messages, as a method of confusing the Union's officers? Maybe Buckley thought that would give him clout with Confederate bigwigs. Perhaps he hoped to gain a high seat in the new government if the Confederates won the war.

"So that's the way of it," Buckley snarled. "Lazarus, take him back to the cellar." He opened a drawer and took out a bottle of liquor. Whiskey, Jack guessed. Most likely the locals' favorite bourbon.

Lazarus grabbed Jack's arm and tugged him roughly from the chair. "Walk, mister."

Jack straightened and went out into the hall. He turned without pause toward the cellar stairway near the back of the house. The door to the kitchen was open, and tempting smells issued from it, causing his stomach to rumble. A black woman was standing over the cast iron stove, and—

He caught his breath. Marilla was washing dishes.

Lazarus gave him a shove toward the cellarway, and he nearly plunged down the stairs but caught himself on the railing. What was the mistress of the house doing in the kitchen, performing such a menial job? They had slaves for that. It didn't make sense.

With great care, he kept a couple of steps ahead of Lazarus and entered the root cellar, then turned to face the door. The slave was already closing it. He heard the key turn in the lock.

Stupid, he told himself. Instead of gawking at the women in

the kitchen, he should have been looking around for a weapon with which he could attack the big slave, or at least something he could use as a tool to escape his prison.

One thing seemed pretty certain, he wasn't getting any meal. Maybe tonight he'd get supper, but that wasn't a sure bet.

He'd pawed around in the room yesterday and discovered several large wooden bins containing root vegetables. One was full of sand, with raw carrots buried in it. Keeping them from the air would preserve them and also keep rodents from getting at them, he knew. Well, a few raw carrots would keep him from starving. He wondered if Buckley would think of that and have him tied up again or move him to another spot.

Grimly, he made his way to the carrot bin and plunged his hands in. He only had to dig down three or four inches to find a few of the roots. He pulled them out and wiped the sand off on his pants. Then he ate every bite, thanking the Lord for this provision.

MARILLA CREPT down the back stairs. Darkness had fallen hours ago, and it was well after ten o'clock by the little china clock Aunt Olive had given her on her fourteenth birthday. Usually she was asleep by now, but she'd sat up in her room, waiting to hear Uncle Hamilton retire.

Finally, she'd heard his heavy tread on the stairs. After five long minutes, she'd stealthily opened her door and crept out to the back stairway. On the last step she paused, listening. No light showed at the bottom of the door panel, and no sounds came from beyond.

Carefully, she lifted the latch and pushed the door outward. Its hinges creaked a little, as they always did. As she'd expected, the kitchen was dark except for a streak of moonlight coming in the window.

After listening at the doorway to the hall, she dared light a candle and tiptoed about. As was customary, Reenie and Sadie had eaten most of the leftovers from supper, but she found some cold meat and some biscuits and rye bread. She didn't dare cook anything, but she made Jack a substantial sandwich. She added some pickles to the plate and set a dish of applesauce on the tray.

The coffeepot was empty and cold. With a sigh, she poured out a glass of milk and one of water. The tray was getting heavy. She opened the cellar door first and set her candle on the tray.

Four steps from the bottom, her heel caught in the hem of her skirt. She wobbled, her stomach doing a flip. With all her concentration, she stayed upright, but the candle toppled over the edge of the tray and went down. She was plunged into darkness.

Her heart racing double time, she stood as still as she could. At least the glasses and food hadn't fallen. It was probably a good thing that the candle went out on the dirt floor too. At least she didn't have to worry about a fire. But how could she get off the stairs in pitch blackness without spilling anything?

Her hands were shaking. She stood still and took deep, slow breaths. Since she was nearer the cellar floor than the hall above, going down seemed her best option. She shifted one foot and lowered it cautiously over the edge of the step. The space below seemed endless.

The tread met her heel, and she lowered her foot. The dishes rattled on the tray, and her stomach roiled, but her toes met the next stair tread. She stood with one foot on the lower step and one on the upper, trying to draw courage to make the next move.

Light flickered above and behind her, and she froze.

"Who's down there?"

21

Marilla shivered, fearing she'd drop the tray. She'd been caught.

Felix. One of the few remaining house slaves, he'd taken over Thomas's duties as the colonel's personal servant.

"It's me, Felix."

"What you doing down there, Miss Marilla, poking around in the dark like that?"

"Oh, I had a candle, but I dropped it. Could you—could you just stay there a moment while I get down the rest of these stairs? Thank you so much!" Her legs trembled, but she managed the last three steps and set the tray down on top of a cider barrel.

She picked up the candle and went to a shelf where they always kept a few extra tapers and a box of matches. After setting the candle firmly back in its holder, she lit the wick.

"Thank you, Felix. I'm fine now."

Instead of retreating, he came halfway down the stairs and peered at her.

"Miss Marilla, the colonel say don't give him no extra."

Her lips quivered as she considered how to respond. At last

she said gently, "Felix, do you remember when Mr. Vernon whipped Olney so bad he couldn't stand?"

"Yes, ma'am." Felix's eyes flickered.

"The women in the quarters took care of him." Marilla's heart raced, and she watched him closely for signs he would try to stop her from feeding the prisoner.

"Yes, ma'am." Felix met her gaze. "I recollect how you came down there, missy. You brought him soup and a bit of the master's brandy."

"And did you tell Colonel Buckley?"

"No, ma'am."

"Why not?"

Felix pulled in a deep breath. "Because we all loved Olney, and we didn't want you to get in trouble or have him whipped worse."

Marilla nodded. "I loved Olney too. Maybe not in the same way you do, but he was a good man and a hard worker. And I despise seeing another human being mistreated."

She waited a long time for Felix to respond. Was it because she'd said they were all human beings? She doubted Uncle Hamilton believed that.

The field hand, Olney, who'd been beaten savagely for a minor infraction, had now left River Lea. A month after the beating—as soon as he was able to walk—the other hands had helped him escape to the nearest stop on the Underground Railroad. Marilla didn't know where it was, or who managed it, but that was all right. What she didn't know, she could never betray.

Finally, Felix gave a curt nod and turned to go back up the stairs.

They were all free now, she thought. *Why don't they all go away? That proclamation ...*

She thought she knew the answer. Many had left, but they had nowhere to go, nowhere they could feel safe and know they would be able to survive.

It was only a matter of time. Felix thought about it, she was certain. The four remaining house slaves were only waiting for the best time to go.

When the door at the top of the stairs closed, she lifted the tray and walked slowly to the root cellar door. She had to set down her burden to get the key, which hung on an iron ring from the spike driven into a bank of shelving. Once the door was open, she picked up the tray and walked in.

Grubby and smelling none too sweet, Jack shuffled to his feet.

"Marilla?"

"Yes, it's me." She set the tray carefully on top of a potato bin. "I brought you some supper."

"I'm guessing you weren't supposed to do that."

She nodded. "Did you hear my conversation with Felix?"

"No. I heard voices, but they were too low for me to make out anything through that door."

"He's Colonel Buckley's personal servant now. He caught me bringing this food down and told me that my great-uncle had forbidden it. We talked for a minute, and I think he saw reason. But be aware, the colonel or the overseer, either one could come storming down here at any minute. So I'd eat up if I were you, while you have the chance."

"Thank you. I don't want you to take risks for me, Marilla. I'm the enemy, after all."

She smiled as he picked up the glass of milk first and swallowed half of it.

"I will never think of you as the enemy, Jack. After all, you taught me Morse Code."

He laughed, and his whole face changed. How long since he'd smiled? A long time, Marilla thought, at least since before his capture.

She shivered and hugged herself. The damp cold of the cellar must drain Jack's energy. "I must go as soon as you finish. I can't leave the dishes."

"Right." He quickly downed the food.

"Sorry to make you eat in a hurry," she murmured.

He shook his head, chewing.

Marilla glanced around. "I suppose you could always eat raw vegetables."

The smile was back as he reached for the water glass. "Did that earlier. Carrots. They weren't bad."

"Well, I guess you wouldn't literally starve down here. But I'm afraid he'll do something vile to you if you won't do what he wants."

"It's a possibility. Is he prone to harsh discipline?"

Reluctantly, she said, "He's been known to give severe beatings—that is, he has his overseer do it, but under his orders. But I ... I have seen him strike the house servants before."

Jack grunted. "The overseer ... that would be Vernon?"

"Yes. That man has no soul." She let out a sigh. "Truthfully, I don't think Uncle Hamilton is much better." She looked over her shoulder, though the door was closed. "Jack, he treats his people like animals. I refuse to call them slaves. They're free now, but they don't seem to believe it. Some have run away, but there are still at least twenty of them on the plantation. And he's still sending his gang out to catch them when they try to leave."

"That's criminal."

"Not to Uncle Hamilton's way of thinking. Lincoln is the criminal—and all the men doing his bidding, including you."

Jack scooped the last bit of applesauce into his mouth and set down the dish. "You'd best go. What will he do to you if Felix tells him?"

She pressed her lips together. She'd seen her great-uncle backhand one of the female servants, and he'd pummeled Lazarus once, with the huge man cowering before him. Then he had Zeke administer ten lashes. They didn't fight back. The blacks knew they'd be hurt worse or even killed if they did.

"Has he said anything about me?" Jack asked.

"Not to me. But he takes out your little notebook every night and studies it. He had it in a locked cupboard, but I saw him put it in his safe this evening. He didn't know I saw him, but ... well, I think he's convinced it's important. Is it?"

"Probably not anymore."

She wondered what he meant by that.

Before she could ask, Jack picked up the tray and held it out. "Here. I'm sorry I can't carry it up for you."

"No worries." As she took it, she glanced at the pile of burlap sacks where he'd been sitting when she entered. "You have no blankets?"

He shrugged.

"Oh, Jack."

"Don't fret about it."

"I will." Squaring her shoulders, she said, "I'll see to it that you get something."

"Now, don't put yourself on the wrong side of the colonel."

Marilla knew that if she had a choice between ruffling Uncle Hamilton's feathers and keeping Jack from harm, Jack would win. On the other hand, she wasn't sure her great-uncle held her in very high esteem. He put up with her, but she doubted he'd tolerate disrespect or any undermining of his orders.

"I'll try to see you again soon, but I can't promise."

Jack's eyes were sorrowful. "I appreciate you coming down here tonight, but it's much more important that you keep safe."

"I will." She picked up the tray and carried it out to the big room and set it down. Then she went back and, with a pang of regret, locked the door and hung the key on its nail.

THE NEXT MORNING, Jack was surprised when the door to his prison opened a scant hour after dawn. One of the maids came in hesitantly, fear in her eyes. She was thin, and she moved like a skittish bird.

"Hello." Jack didn't move from where he sat, not wanting to traumatize her.

She put the tray gingerly on top of the potato bin.

"Thank you," Jack said.

The big man, Lazarus was waiting for her, holding up a lantern with one hand and a bundle of cloth in the other. The woman took the bundle from him and tossed it toward Jack. It landed on the dirt floor before him, and he realized it was a woolen blanket.

The woman ducked past Lazarus without a word.

"Thank you," Jack yelled, but her feet were already tapping quickly up the stairs. Lazarus scowled at him and closed the door with a thump.

Jack rose slowly. So, they weren't going to quit feeding him after all. And they'd brought him a blanket. Was that at Marilla's behest? Surely Colonel Buckley hadn't ordered it. Who would take the blame if the master found out?

Breakfast was scanty—a bowl of porridge and a small cup of milk, another with tea made from some minty plant, not real tea from the Orient.

To keep up his strength, Jack scraped the bowl clean and drained both cups.

Noon passed, and he marked the hours of the afternoon by watching the light from the tiny window above as it inched across the floor. He poked little marks in the dirt floor when he guessed it was noon and again at sunset. He considered breaking one of the cups to use as a digging tool, but that might bring consequences. He decided to wait and see what developed.

Finally, as twilight fell outside, one of the women came in again with a bowl of broth and a biscuit, along with tea.

Jack smiled and kept his seat as she placed the tray.

"Thank you, ma'am."

The woman threw him a startled glance.

"Do you have a name?" Jack asked.

She hesitated, and he could see her fingers tremble. "They call me Reenie," she said softly.

"Reenie." He nodded. "I'm Jack. I appreciate you bringing my meal."

Reenie picked up the tray of dirty breakfast dishes and scuttled out past Lazarus.

This went on for two more days. Reenie, another woman who he learned was named Sadie, or Lazarus brought him meager meals morning and evening. He saw nothing of Marilla, and he found himself waiting after darkness fell, hoping she would sneak down once more.

The next morning, after he ate his porridge, Lazarus returned.

"Colonel Buckley wants to see you."

Jack's heart sank. He'd hoped for a chance to get out of the cellar, into the daylight. An opportunity to talk to other people. But he had a bad feeling about this meeting.

Upstairs, he blinked in the strong light and shuffled along to the study door. Colonel Buckley sat behind his desk. He eyed Jack pensively as he entered.

"Well, Miller, are you ready to help me with this? My men have gotten hold of another message."

Jack swallowed hard. How could he appease the man without giving away government secrets? He certainly mustn't give any hints about the routing of the ciphers or the code words.

"Sit down."

Once Jack had taken a chair, Buckley passed him a crumpled piece of paper. The words on it didn't seem to make any sense, but Jack knew that with a little loving care they could be teased into a rational message. He recognized the formatting at once, but not the handwriting. He'd half expected a new key word, but it was too soon for them to have changed the keys and distributed them to all the field operators.

"Give me some background. Where did this come from?" His own words startled him. He hadn't intended to offer his assistance, but seeing a cipher message had triggered his long training.

"My men took it off a fellow who was rowing down the river in the dead of night. A stranger to the area, though his speech pegs him as a Virginia man."

Jack said nothing, but he drew plenty of conclusions. He frowned over the paper, hoping his features wouldn't give anything away. The first word told him at once how the communication was routed, and his eyes skimmed up column four, down five, up two, down one, up three. He skipped the null words that were only there to fill in gaps and mentally translated the arbitraries.

"Well?" Buckley asked.

"A message like this takes hours, sometimes days to decrypt."

"Really? It's not very long."

"Yes, but ..." Jack looked at the desktop but saw no sign of his cipher book. He didn't want to lie, but neither did he want to tell the truth. The message indicated that two Union ships would leave Savannah on Sunday, heading for Charleston. He wasn't positive, but he thought Sunday was tomorrow. Unless he'd lost track. And this message could be outdated. At any rate, he wasn't about to give Buckley the plaintext.

He cleared his throat. "Without a key, I'm afraid I'm floundering."

"A key? You mean your little book?" Buckley's lips formed into a sly smile. "Suppose you tell me what to look for?"

Jack sat still, staring down at the paper, trying to come up with an appropriate but discreet response.

"Zeke!" Buckley moved to the window and flung it open. "Zeke, get in here now."

The front door opened and Jack heard the overseer's hasty footsteps. His lungs squeezed as he tried not to imagine why the colonel had summoned Zeke Vernon.

"Stand up, Miller," Buckley said.

Jack pushed himself shakily to his feet. He felt Zeke's presence behind him.

"This man doesn't seem to want to cooperate." Buckley put a hand on Jack's shoulder and pushed to turn him around.

Reluctantly, Jack made a half turn so that he could see Zeke. The overseer looked eager and a bit self-satisfied.

"Is that right?"

Zeke's punch to his stomach took Jack completely off guard. He doubled over, nauseated and cradling his midsection. Pain radiated through his whole body. He gasped in a shallow breath but couldn't speak.

"Now, you got to learn to do what the colonel says," Zeke said affably.

Jack couldn't hold it in any longer. He spewed his meager breakfast all over the colonel's carpet and Zeke's boots.

Buckley's face went red and he leaped back a step, bumping into his desk.

"Get him out of here!"

Zeke stared down at his soiled boots, his fists clenching and unclenching.

Making a wide berth around them, Buckley marched to the door.

"Lazarus! Get in here!" When the big man came to the doorway, he shrieked, "Take the prisoner downstairs. And tell Reenie to come clean up this mess!"

Before Lazarus shut the cellar door firmly behind him and turned the key in the lock, Jack saw some changes. So much for emergency rations. In his absence, the smaller vegetable bins had been removed and the bigger ones had been emptied.

November 20, 1864
River Lea Plantation

"COLONEL!" Zeke Vernon strode across the verandah and into the entry hall.

"In here," Uncle Hamilton called.

Zeke came through the doorway of the parlor and stopped before his employer. "The Yankees are in Covington."

The colonel scowled up at him and took a quick sip from his glass. "Any chance they'll come near here?"

"They're already near," Zeke sputtered. "They're burning anything they think we'd find useful in town, and I hear they're raiding farms and plantations along the road for supplies.

Marilla shrank in her chair in the corner of the room, hoping Zeke wouldn't notice her. She ducked her head and went on with her sewing.

"They'd better not try to take our foodstuffs."

"No, sir. I'll have my men keep watch around the clock."

"That may not be enough, from what I've read about Sherman." Buckley sighed and stood up, his joints popping. "We'd better have the field hands move everything out of the smokehouse."

"Where will we put it, sir?"

Buckley frowned. "Maybe the old summer kitchen."

"They'd look there."

"Hmm. Isn't there an empty slave cabin?"

"Yes, but it's pretty run-down."

"Then they won't think we'd put anything of value in there. Come on."

The two men left the room, and Marilla breathed easier, despite the word of impending danger. If General Sherman or one of his men marched up to her door, she'd tell them she was from the North and wanted to go back there.

She hoped they didn't come, and yet ...

And what would this mean for Jack?

22

November 30, 1864

Marilla didn't dare sneak down to the cellar again for more than a week. A small contingent of Yankees had approached River Lea, but Zeke and his dozen men had forbidden them entrance to the grounds. Since only four men made up the band of intruders sent out to forage for victuals, Vernon's men were able to run them off with the threat of rifles.

Colonel Buckley had been on edge ever since, staying up late and haunting the hallways in the wee hours of the morning, fearing the enemy would return with a larger force. His worst nightmare, which he frequently related to Marilla, was that the Yankees would burn the plantation house. But the Union horde apparently bypassed River Lea, though the Buckleys heard tales of woe and destruction from all about the countryside.

Every day Marilla uttered prayers of thanks, but she couldn't help wondering if they would all—excepting her great-uncle and his band of thugs—be better off in the hands of the Yankees.

The colonel seemed to have forgotten about Jack, or at least, she didn't hear about him interacting with the man. Appalled that he was keeping Jack prisoner so long, she bided her time and pumped Reenie and Sadie for information.

Each morning she made sure a tray went down to Jack. If none was sent at noon, she did whatever it took to see that he was fed in the evening. She tried reasoning with the kitchen servants, then threatening, but that felt wrong and brought mediocre results. Finally she decided bribery was her best option.

"Reenie, I know you're a free woman now. You can leave any time you want."

Reenie's chin rose a fraction of an inch as she folded laundry. She pulled a clean sheet from the basket, and Marilla stepped up to take the bottom edge and help her fold it straight.

"I won't let the colonel starve that man."

Reenie eyed her with what might have been skepticism. Marilla hadn't revealed to the others that she had known Jack previously. She didn't want Reenie and Sadie to get the idea that she had improper notions about the young man.

"Look, I know you'll want to get away from here eventually." Marilla watched Reenie's face and saw bit of a gleam in her eyes. "So I was thinking, you'll need some money when you decide you're ready to leave."

"What you sayin', Miss Marilla?" Reenie eyed her with obvious interest.

"I'm saying—" Marilla threw a glance over her shoulder. Sadie was in the kitchen kneading bread dough, but no one else was within earshot. She leaned toward Reenie and whispered, "I know my great-uncle is a cruel man. He's taken steps to keep your people from leaving here. He thinks the South will win the war, and you'll remain slaves."

As she reached for a clean pillow slip, Reenie's jaw clenched.

"But I know better," Marilla said. "I've lived up north. They have much more in resources and manpower than the South. It's only a matter of time. And when the end comes, no one will be able to say you aren't free, and you can go make a new life for your family."

"How we do that, Miss Marilla? At least here, we get fed."

"Exactly. But when the war ends, Colonel Buckley will be forced to pay you if you stay on to work for him."

Reenie's eyes widened.

"I know you're not supposed to have money now." Marilla looked to make sure Sadie was still oblivious as she placed her dough on a shelf over the stove to rise.

"I won't let him starve that man, Reenie. It isn't right. No more than it would be right to starve your people when he's angry with you."

Reenie said nothing but nodded.

"I've been forbidden to go down there. But you can, Reenie. You can make sure he has good, nourishing food."

"Mr. Buckley say don't give him much. He made Lazarus take the carrots and taters away."

"I heard." Marilla frowned. "Listen to me. I don't just want to help him. I want to help you too. I don't have much, but I have a little money. I'll give you some if you make sure that man gets enough food. Good food, Reenie. I'll give you what I can, and you do what you can. Then when you finally decide it's your day to go, you'll at least have a little bit of a resource."

"What's that?"

"Something to lean on. To tide you over." She reached into her pocket and took out a half dime. "Here's a five-cent piece. You take it, Reenie. It's yours. But make sure the prisoner has a good dinner tonight."

Wide-eyed, Reenie examined the coin. "This be Yankee money?"

"Yes, but it's what we use," Marilla said. "I don't think they've made Confederate coins yet. Well, maybe, but these are still good anywhere, North or South. Any store will take it."

Reenie drew in a slow breath, and her chest puffed up. "I'll do my best to save him some chicken tonight."

Marilla smiled. "Perfect. And some of Sadie's bread if you can. Whatever you can manage. Give him as much as you'd give Lazarus if the plate was for him."

Reenie's eyes widened. "He not be as big as Lazarus."

"No, but Lazarus hasn't been starving. That man's been down there more than two weeks."

"Yes'm." Reenie frowned.

"What is it?" Marilla asked.

"He trying to keep clean, but it's hard."

"Yes, I'm sure it is. Someone is tending to his ... his basic needs?" She hadn't thought about chamber pots and such, and she was sure Jack wouldn't want her to.

"Yes'm. Lazarus don't like it, but he takes care of things."

"I see. And have his clothes been washed?"

"No'm."

"I'm sure Mr. Miller would like to have a bath and a clean change of clothes."

"The colonel don't think that way."

"Hmm." Marilla's mind raced. If she tried to smuggle extra clothing to Jack, and even a basin of hot water and a cake of soap, trouble could follow. If Uncle Hamilton had him brought up to talk to him or, heaven forbid, descended to the root cellar, he would notice if Jack was wearing clothes that didn't come with him when he arrived.

"I'll have to think about that," she said. "But you take care of his meals."

"All right, Miss Marilla. I'll try, but if I get caught ..."

"Blame me."

"Oh, no, miss. I couldn't do that." Reenie took quick, shallow breaths.

"Why not?" Marilla patted her shoulder. "I don't want you to get in trouble because I asked you to do something. Don't lie for me, Reenie. But be careful."

December 2, 1864

MARILLA ATE alone in the evening. Hamilton Buckley had gone to have dinner with his friend, Dr. Riley, and she had pleaded a headache. The doctor's office had been raided but not burned two weeks earlier. His home had been stripped of valuables, food stores, bedding, and winter clothing. Wisely, the widowed man had squirreled away some cash and buried an extra set of medical instruments in the yard behind his office.

He'd come through the ordeal all right, but now had no laudanum or ether, and only a small amount of morphine he'd cached. But he was alive, and his services were in demand, though his patients often couldn't pay him. Still, he'd apparently scrounged up enough food to invite his friend to share a meal. Uncle Hamilton left home with gifts—a bottle of wine and a small cake Sadie had baked with a scant amount of sweetening.

When she'd finished her solitary dinner, Marilla helped wash up in the kitchen then announced to Sadie and Reenie, "I'll take the prisoner's tray down."

They both stared at her.

"You mustn't Miss Marilla," Reenie said at last.

"My great-uncle's away for the evening. It will be fine if you two keep quiet about it."

"What about Lazarus?" Sadie asked.

Reenie glared at her. "I'll go with her and take the lantern. If Lazarus comes in, you tell him we've already fed him and he doesn't have to stay."

Sadie looked doubtful, but Marilla set about preparing the tray, her pulse fluttering. At last, she would get to see Jack again.

When Reenie opened the door for her, his gauntness shocked her. He sat on the burlap sacking with the wool blanket she'd ordered Reenie to provide wrapped around him, but she could tell he'd lost weight. His eyes appeared sunken and dull, his cheeks thin beneath the now full beard.

He gazed at her for a moment as though he didn't recognize her.

"Jack!"

She carefully positioned the tray on the corner of an empty wooden bin, making sure it was stable. Jack hadn't moved or spoken. She picked up the cup of hot tea—Buckley had somehow managed to get hold of a small amount of real Indian tea—and carried it to him.

"Here, Jack. Drink this."

The cellar was frigid and she shivered, wishing she'd worn a shawl. A foul smell hung in the air.

"Reenie, bring the lantern closer. This man is ill."

Reenie obeyed her and set the lantern on the floor. "You want me take out the pot, Miss Marilla?"

"Yes, please. And bring back another blanket and a pillow."

"Mr. Buckley not gon' like that, missy."

"Does he ever come down here?"

"He done once."

"Well, do as I say. If he finds out and objects, you can blame me."

"Yes'm. Where do I get a pillow from?"

"If there's not an extra in the linen closet, take one of the ones off my bed."

Reenie fixed her with a scandalized stare and opened her mouth.

"Go, Reenie."

With a gulp, Reenie went to remove the covered chamber pot, scrunching up her face at the smell.

When she and Jack were alone, Marilla leaned down and put a hand on his shoulder.

"Jack. Do you know I'm here? It's me, Marilla."

He looked up at her, and his vacant eyes glimmered.

"Marilla."

"Yes."

"You shouldn't be here."

"Well, I am." She gathered her skirts and sat down next to him on the sacks, arranging the folds of byzantine to cover her legs modestly. She reached for his hand and cradled it in both of hers. "Your hands are like ice."

"It's cold here."

She nodded. "I'm so sorry, Jack. What else is he doing to you?"

"Mostly they just leave me here."

"Doesn't my uncle talk to you?"

"He has a couple of times."

"Drink the tea, Jack. I put a spoonful of honey in it."

He sipped from the cup and let out a big sigh.

"I brought you some stew and biscuits." She'd put four of those on the tray, knowing it was more than the servants would have given him. "And there's some squash and a piece of spice cake Sadie made. It's not very sweet, but it's nourishment."

"Thank you."

She rose and brought the tray over. Awkwardly, she stooped and lowered it to the floor in front of him without spilling any of the soup or the glass of milk she'd added.

"Your cow's still fresh."

She smiled. Obviously Jack still had his wits about him. He knew fresh milk could be hard to come by in winter.

"Yes, two cows. We're lucky the Yankees didn't steal them. They'll go dry eventually, but Princess will calve in a couple of months."

He picked up the glass. "I haven't had milk since you were last here."

Marilla made a mental note to chastise Sadie and Reenie and order them to bring him milk at least once a day, as long as it held out.

"Jack, do they hurt you?"

"That man, Vernon, hit me once. Otherwise, they just leave

me here. I tried to dig my way out, but it's no use. I only had a couple of sticks to dig with, and a little nail I pried out of one of the boxes." He shook his head. "They took those away."

"Oh, Jack."

"I thought maybe I could get past them, but that man is so big."

"Lazarus."

Jack nodded. "And I'm not as strong as I was, nor as quick."

She could see that. "I wanted to come sooner, but I was afraid Uncle would find out. He's away tonight, so I took a chance."

"What if the servants tell him?"

"Then I'll have to deal with it. Eat some stew."

His hand shook as he raised a spoonful to his lips. After sucking in the broth, he poked the spoon in and chewed potato and carrot.

"It's good," he whispered.

"I'm glad. There's a bit of mutton in it. We're going easy on meat, because provisions are short, but we manage to get by. I suppose we've all lost flesh."

"You look fine, Marilla."

She smiled. Her visit was worth the risk. He needed company and sympathy as much as he needed food.

"I'll try to come every night," she said in sudden decision.

"Don't. He'll be angry."

"I'd rather face his tantrums than know you're in need."

Jack ate the rest of the stew and a biscuit and finished the milk.

"I can't eat any more. I'd be sick."

"Save it for later." She took the linen cloth she'd used to cover the tray and wrapped the cake and extra biscuits in it then tied it up so they wouldn't fall out. "Hide this in the burlap sacks."

"The rats will get it."

She stared at him. "There's rats in here?"

"Not so bad since they took out the vegetable bins."

"I see."

They sat in silence for a moment.

Jack said, "Why are you here, Marilla?"

"To see you."

"No, I mean ... in Georgia."

"I was sent here after my mother died."

"I'm sorry." He looked her full in the face, and a pang of sympathy and longing went through her. "Was she ill?"

She couldn't bear to think about it, and she looked away. "No. After we moved to Philadelphia ... there was a fire."

Jack's lips skewed. "I'm so very sorry. I lost my mother too. She was sick."

Marilla snapped her eyes to his. "Mrs. Miller died?"

"No. I meant my real mother. I ... The Millers adopted me, you know."

"I guess I didn't know that, but it makes sense. You don't look like the rest of them."

He gave a feeble smile. "Is that good or bad?"

Despite the tears welling in her eyes, Marilla chuckled. "I've never met a Miller who wasn't good-looking."

She heard Reenie's steps on the cellar stairs and squeezed his hand. It seemed warmer now than when she'd first touched him. "Hide the biscuits," she whispered as she rose and moved away.

Jack stuffed the bundle somewhere behind him, and the door swung open.

Marilla bent and situated the empty dishes on the tray. Reenie threw her a dark look and brought over a pillow in a plain cotton case and another woolen blanket. Marilla took them, and Reenie turned to put the chamber pot in a far corner.

"Thank you, Reenie," Marilla said.

"Yes, thank you," Jack added, his voice stronger than she'd heard it this evening.

Reenie turned and looked at him suspiciously.

"Here you go, Mr. Miller." Marilla handed him the blanket and pillow. "I hope you'll be a little more comfortable tonight. I'm sorry Mr. Buckley thinks it necessary to treat you so shabbily."

She didn't look at Reenie, but she could imagine the woman's dark eyes popping wide.

Jack cleared his throat. "I appreciate it, ma'am. And Miss Reenie ..." He looked at the servant. "Thank you for your kindness, ma'am."

Reenie looked so flustered at his courtesy that Marilla almost laughed. Did Jack speak to her each time she delivered his meals? Maybe the hot food and company had made him more garrulous than usual tonight.

JACK WASN'T sure how she managed it, but Marilla visited him more often after that. Somehow, she appeared at least every third night, usually after the rest of the household had retired. The servants still brought his supper, but she usually had some extra treat for him.

His spirits improved immeasurably, and he was sure it was because of her sporadic company. Marilla would sit and talk to him for a quarter of an hour. They spoke of old times, of family, of whether the war would end soon. She gave him hope.

One night she came stealthily, as usual, carrying a lantern and a dish of canned peaches.

"Hello, Jack."

He smiled, although it hurt to do so.

"Marilla."

She set down the lantern. "We don't have much fruit left, and I wanted to make sure you got some."

He took the dish she offered and slid a peach slice into his mouth. The flavor burst over him, and he smiled. "That's wonderful."

"Enjoy it. I probably won't be able to pilfer more for you."

He ate them slowly, savoring each bite, then drank the juice from the bowl.

"I heard Uncle Hamilton had you upstairs this afternoon," Marilla said. "What did they do to you?" She was eyeing his face, and he wondered how bad the bruises looked.

"You might say we had a disagreement."

"Oh, Jack."

"He wanted me to translate a message they'd got hold of. This time he wouldn't take no for an answer."

She reached toward his face then drew her hand back. He knew the bleeding had stopped, but his jaw and his head ached mercilessly. He'd barely been able to sip the broth and sham coffee they'd brought him for supper, but he'd made the effort, knowing he needed the nourishment and the warmth.

"What did you do?" she asked as she settled beside him.

"Finally I gave him a phony message. He wasn't sure he should accept it as true, but I acted as reluctant to give it as I could, without further consequences." He'd hoped his hair and beard would cover most of the evidence, but he suspected his cheek and eye socket were purple.

"Why is he holding you?"

Her voice held a forlorn pleading that he couldn't answer. He shook his head. "I can't claim to know what he's thinking."

"Well, they've let you keep the extra blanket and pillow."

"Lazarus was going to take them, but I told him you'd be upset, and he left them."

"I believe Lazarus is a good man." Marilla sighed. "Honestly, I don't know why he's still here."

"Do they know they're free now?"

"They've heard it—not from the colonel, but all of the black folk know. Some of them have left. Some of the men have joined the Union army. And Sadie, in the kitchen, told me some of the planters are paying their former slaves now. But most of the owners don't admit it's true or that the proclamation will stand. If the Confederacy wins the war, the South will be independent, and you know they'll continue with slaveholding if that happens."

"It won't happen," Jack said.

"How do you know? Because my great-uncle insists the South will prevail."

"He's deluded."

She nodded gravely. "I fear you're right—in more ways than one. Has he told you he ought to have been president of the Confederacy, not Davis?"

Jack gave a little chuckle. "No, I wasn't aware of that. But he does have an attitude of self-aggrandization."

"This thing with the messages he wants you to translate. Those ought to be sent to the nearest military commander. But he has his own little army that goes out and tries to capture Union sympathizers and—well, people like you. He thinks he can learn something that will help him advance himself and gain him more power. So he hides these messages and keeps them to himself."

"I don't like to speak against your benefactor—"

"Don't call him that," she said quickly.

Jack eyed her, thinking about her words. "All right. I was going to say that he's only helping the Union cause in stealing the messages."

"Isn't he keeping them from getting to the Yankees in authority?"

"Well, yes, but he's also keeping the contents from the Southern commanders, who could in theory make use of that information."

"Yes."

Jack wondered briefly if he'd said too much, but he was confident Marilla would not repeat their conversation to Buckley.

"I could bring you a newspaper next time," she said. "You could see what they're saying. But I couldn't leave it here, of course. Someone might find it, or Uncle might miss it."

"Don't bother. I'm sure everything is slanted to what the Southerners want the people to think."

She was quiet, her brow wrinkled.

"Has he said anything about me?" he asked.

"No. It's as if he wants me to forget you're here—or think he's sent you somewhere else."

Jack stared down at his worn boots. "Without you, I'd have frozen or starved to death."

Marilla shivered. She wore her warm woolen coat whenever she came down here now, and gloves and a hat, but it was still cold. Very cold. She'd brought him a third blanket, so now he slept each night with one folded beneath him and two covering him. It was enough to get him through.

"What day is it, anyway?" He glanced up at the small window, where he could see a few stars.

"It's Thursday. December fifteenth."

"Almost Christmas, then." He shook his head. "I never imagined I'd be here this long."

"I'm sorry. I wish I could get you out of here."

He held her gaze. "Why can't you?"

Marilla caught her breath. Hadn't she thought of that before? If she could sneak down here at midnight, why couldn't she guide him up and out of the house? Or just leave the door unlocked one night and leave him on his own?

He didn't want to suggest it, but he'd decided planting the idea in her mind was his best hope of escape.

"I don't know." Her voice shook. "I couldn't—Oh, Jack, he'd kill me."

"Surely not."

She clamped her lips together, and they sat in silence for a long moment.

"You could say I overpowered you," he said at last.

"But then he'd know I'd been helping you. Reenie and Sadie would have to tell him I've been coming down here."

"Do they know you come late at night like this?"

"I'm sure they suspect. Sadie's commented on missing food a few times, and Reenie looks at me sometimes with such accusation, I—" She broke off. "I don't know, Jack. Uncle Hamilton is capable of violence."

"Himself? Or just Vernon?"

She frowned. "Sometimes he uses Lazarus to intimidate people, and when the slaves displease him, he has Zeke punish them. But I know he's been in altercations himself. He beat a field hand half to death once. That was before Zeke Vernon came to work here. He had a different overseer, and I think he found the man lacking in giving out discipline."

After a moment's silence, Jack said, "I'm sorry." Before the war, he wouldn't have imagined the reality of life for the people working on a plantation like this. He'd heard bits of rhetoric, and he'd even seen a few slaves in the keeping of Northern owners, but they'd seemed well-treated.

But in his travels over the last three years he'd had a closer view.

"We had a dozen black men on the construction crew for the telegraph lines going into Atlanta," he said.

"Slaves?"

"No, freedmen. The army paid them."

"The same as they paid the whites?"

"I don't know. I doubt it, but they were glad for the work."

She nodded. "Down here, they're not considered human."

"That's ridiculous. I talked to some of those men, and they were very human indeed." Jack rubbed a hand through his beard. "I reckon I need a shave and a haircut."

"I could give you one."

"No. People would see and maybe tell the colonel."

"Mmm."

"Of course, a bath would be nice too." He grinned. "Wonder if I'll ever get another."

She eyed him sharply. "Do you think you'll die here, Jack Miller?"

After a long pause, he said, "Pray, Marilla. I don't want you or the others to be punished on my account. But I don't want to die in this root cellar."

23

December 18, 1864

As he gained strength, Jack began to think more and more of escape. He would be no match for Lazarus, but sometimes one of the women came down alone with his meal. He could overpower Reenie, he was sure. Still, the thought of hurting her, or even shoving her aside roughly didn't sit well with him. And if he didn't silence her, she'd raise the household at once with her screaming.

He waited, impatient but knowing he'd be at a disadvantage if he fled. Buckley would hunt him down like one of his runaway slaves.

Marilla came downstairs alone, late in the evening. She wore a cape over her dress against the cold, and as usual, she brought him a hot drink and extra food.

A few nights earlier, she'd brought him a tattered coat. Grateful beyond her understanding, he'd donned it and slept feeling warm for the first time since his capture. But he feared the slaves would take it from him if they saw it, or that Vernon or Buckley would show up unannounced and do even worse.

During the day, the cold wasn't usually as bad as at night, and he hid the coat under his blankets. He put it on only after the house was quiet at night, or on an exceptionally cold day, after they'd served his breakfast and gone away. Hardly ever did they visit his cell more than twice a day.

"Thank you very much," he said when he'd finished the fried sweet potatoes and tea she'd brought him.

"You're welcome. What's that?" Marilla pointed toward his throat, and Jack quickly put his hand up to his neck.

"Nothing. Well, it's a keepsake."

"A necklace?" She frowned.

"No, it's a coin." Jack held it out so she could see it better.

"It has a hole in the middle."

"That's right. My grandfather was a ship's captain, and he brought it home from the Orient. He gave one to my brother too, and our little sister. He said in a letter that he was giving one to our cousin Abby in Maine. We call them cousin coins. We all have one, and if we ever meet up, it will be a way we can know each other."

"Wouldn't you know each other anyway?"

Jack hesitated. "Well, I don't remember that I've seen Abby. If I did, I was very small. And ... to tell the truth, I don't know where my brother and sister are now. We were all adopted by different families."

"Oh, how sad. You told me the Millers adopted you, but I didn't know you had siblings. You were orphans like me?"

"Sort of." Jack hardly ever talked about his first family, but somehow he felt Marilla would understand. "My mother died, and then my father ... well, he left us. We were at an orphanage for a while, but then we got separated."

"I'm so sorry."

Jack pressed his lips together and nodded.

"It's hard," she said softly. "My father died first, and my mother took me to live with her family up North. That's where I met your family—in Pennsylvania. But then her cousin died, and we had to move. Things were hard in Philadelphia, but we were getting along at first. Then, after Mama died, my great-uncle sent money for me to come down here and live with him."

"What about the rest of your family?" Jack asked.

"I was an only child. We'd been living with Mama's Cousin Anne. After she died, her house went to someone in her dead husband's family. As far as I know, there weren't any other relatives on our side, at least none that wanted a couple of poor relations living with them. We only had a week to move out, and we didn't have any money. Mama decided she had the best chance of earning a living in Philadelphia."

"What about Colonel Buckley? Doesn't he have children?" Jack asked.

She sighed. "His son, William, was killed three years ago, at Ball's Bluff."

Jack nodded. He was aware of the fighting close to Washington, right around the time Ned died.

"He's got a couple of daughters, but one's moved west with her husband. The other one lives about a hundred miles away, but she won't have anything to do with him."

Jack studied her face. "Why not?"

"I'm not sure, but she never visits or writes to him anymore. She did come for her mother's funeral in '58. I was pretty young, and but even so, I could tell there was tension between them."

They sat in silence for a moment. "What happens to you if your uncle dies?"

She let out a long, slow sigh. "I don't know. I think I'd go back north. But I don't know of any relatives."

"And what would happen to River Lea?"

"I have no idea. Maybe his daughters would get it." She shook her head, frowning. "Some lawyer would have to figure it out, I guess. But it's not my worry. Anyway, it's been challenging, staying here this long."

"I'll bet."

She must realize that Buckley wasn't completely sane. Jack

couldn't imagine how frightened she must have been when she discovered that.

"At least when your mother died, you got a nice family," she said.

Jack smiled. "Very nice. I was terrified at first. Ma Miller wasn't sure she wanted me. But Pa talked her into keeping me, and they have seven children of their own, so I had lots of brothers and sisters to do things with. I guess it kept me from being too lonesome without Zeph and Janie." He fingered the coin on the cord.

"And your new pa taught you to do telegraphing?"

"Yeah, he taught me Morse Code and let me practice with him. His boss was impressed at how good I'd gotten, and he hired me on part time when I was sixteen."

"I remember." At a noise from overhead, Marilla jumped. "Oh, no! Somebody's in the kitchen." She jumped up.

"It might just be one of the maids getting a drink of water," Jack whispered.

"And it might be the colonel." She hesitated. "I won't go up yet, but I've got to get out of here and lock your door."

Jack stood and picked up the tray. Marilla grabbed the lantern and took it out to the big room then turned back for the tray. Jack shut the door and heard the key turn in the lock. His heart pounding, he felt his way back to his bedding and sat down, his back against the wall.

More footsteps creaked above him. Beneath the door to the root cellar, the strip of light went out.

He breathed slowly, wondering if Marilla was cowering behind barrels in the next room. She was a nice girl, he thought. She'd risked much to help him. He smiled to himself. She reminded him in some ways of his sister Caroline. From the first night Pa had brought him home from Albany, Caroline had been his little shadow. In similar circumstances, she'd have helped the captive too.

But Pa Miller would never dream of holding a man prisoner in his home.

His heart ached as he thought of the Millers. They were farther away from him, now that they'd moved to Connecticut, but he was glad they'd gone. They were less likely to be caught up in the savagery of the war up there.

Quiet footsteps came above him, and he tried to picture where exactly in the house they were, but he couldn't. He didn't know the layout well enough.

When all went silent, he sat unmoving. Where was Marilla?

After another ten minutes, he heard faint rustling beyond his door. The light appeared at the crack beneath it. A door opened and closed softly, and the light was gone.

IN SPITE OF THE WAR, Marilla's great-uncle insisted they hold a Christmas celebration and invite friends from the town. When the invitations went out, both were appalled to learn how many were no longer in their family homes.

Though River Lea had been spared, most in the area had not. Instead of the forty people Colonel Buckley had hoped to gather, only seventeen, including him and Marilla, met in his parlor. Still, it was the largest gathering they'd had in a long time.

Marilla dressed in one of Aunt Olive's gowns at Uncle Hamilton's request. She'd worn it once before, to a ball before the war began. The bright green velvet seemed out of place in the bleak atmosphere, but she was relieved to find the other six women present had also dressed well. Marilla couldn't quite work up the nerve to ask about her emerald necklace.

Some of their gowns were obviously as outdated as hers, which was a small relief. Mrs. Chandler and her daughter wore plain dresses, and the mother explained that they'd been ousted from their home a month earlier without a chance to pack their wardrobes.

One couple and Dr. Riley stayed overnight, and Marilla didn't feel safe leaving her room that night. She'd warned Jack that she might not appear for several days.

She was surprised when Uncle Hamilton announced they'd been invited to spend a few days at another friend's house. After two excuses were rejected, Marilla reluctantly gave in. He was growing irritable about it, and he would become suspicious if she didn't go along peacefully.

To be sure Jack would be safe until they returned, she cornered Lazarus the night before their departure.

"You make sure Reenie and Sadie feed Mr. Miller, won't you, Lazarus?"

"Yes'm. Colonel Buckley say to keep him healthy."

"Good. I'm glad. We wouldn't want to come home and find he was ill."

"No, ma'am."

It was all she could do. Marilla went up to her room to oversee Reenie's packing of her clothes.

While staying at their friend's home, they were invited to a New Year's Eve gathering at another house. Marilla tried not to show her chagrin. Why were these people celebrating? She wondered if they sensed that it was the last time they'd mark the holidays as part of an independent Confederacy, though no one voiced such thoughts.

While other people were suffering horribly, Marilla found attending parties and chattering gaily obscene. When the guests talked about the war effort, they seemed to cling to Davis's recent assertions that the Cause would prevail.

Finally Felix drove them home January second. Zeke met them in the yard with the news that all of the remaining field hands had left. His band had tried to stop them, but Lazarus had joined them, and the slaves had outnumbered his men.

"I'd have shot the big devil, but they'd stolen all our ammunition," Zeke told the colonel. "Our pistols were empty! I don't see how they did it, but they must have."

Uncle Hamilton launched into a torrent of cursing.

Marilla closed her eyes for a moment then walked into the house and on back to the kitchen.

"Sadie, is it true? All your people have left?"

Sadie rolled her eyes. "Ain't no one here but me and Reenie, Miss Marilla. We keepin' on."

Marilla eyed her thoughtfully. "Why did you stay?"

Sadie shrugged. "I knew you'd be all alone when you came back. Thought I'd stay a while and see if Mr. Buckley will pay us now. If he won't, well, I s'pose us and Felix can find our way to where our friends are at. But at least you'll be warned. I couldn't just go without sayin' nothin'."

Marilla walked over and squeezed her wrist gently. "Thank you, Sadie. I've heard some of what's been happening. At the last house where we stayed, the men of the family were hauling in water and firewood. Most of the ... the free people had left. There were only a few house servants remaining. I don't know why the Michaelsons imagined they wanted to host a house party.

"Well, some people think if they close their eyes, things will be the same as the old days when they open 'em," Sadie said.

"I think you're right. Reenie's still here, then?"

"Yes'm. She be turning out the bedrooms now."

"I'm glad she stayed. Felix is bringing in the bags."

"I expect he'll have to put the horse away too," Sadie said. "They's nobody in the stable now."

Marilla asked softly, almost dreading the answer, "What about Mr. Miller? How is he faring?"

Sadie swallowed hard. "Mr. Vernon, he took him down to the quarters yesterday and put him in one of the empty cabins."

"What? Why on earth did he do that?"

"He say if none of our people live there, the prisoner can have one."

Marilla tried to process that. "Aren't they afraid he'll run away?"

"I don't expect he will." Sadie turned to open the oven door and slid a baking dish inside. "Mr. Vernon, he chained him up."

At her words, Marilla stood very still. "He put Jack Miller in chains?"

Sadie straightened and cocked her head to one side. "You take a mighty strong interest in that there Yankee, Miss Marilla. Colonel Buckley ain't gonna like that."

Marilla found it hard to breathe. "Is Mr. Miller all right?"

"I seen him out the window. He looked poorly to me."

Reaching for an apron, Marilla said briskly, "What do you have on hand that he can eat?"

"Got some biscuits and turnip and pie—but it's sour. Didn't have any sugar left for them dried apples."

"Did he have breakfast this morning?"

"I sent his usual porridge and tea down. Reenie took it."

"So Lazarus is really gone then?"

Sadie nodded. "I don't think Mr. Vernon woulda moved that man if Lazarus was still here. He spoke of it once before, and Lazarus told him he couldn't do it without Mr. Buckley's say-so." She shrugged. "But then Lazarus left."

"Well, I'm taking him some food, and I mean right now. Fix a tray, Sadie, and don't skimp. Give him some milk too."

"Them cows done dried up."

Marilla heaved out a sigh. "Coffee?"

"Just enough left for the colonel to have a cup tonight."

"All right then, water it is. Fix it while I get some dressings. I'll wager Mr. Miller was beaten."

"That's right, ma'am."

Furious, Marilla ran up the front stairs and strode to the linen closet. She gathered several soft cloths she could use for bandages and a container of ointment.

Reenie came from her uncle's bedroom with an armful of dirty linen.

"Well, Reenie, I'm glad to see you're still here," Marilla said. "Thank you for staying."

"Yes'm." Reenie wouldn't make eye contact.

"You should have changed the beds the day we left." Marilla immediately wished she hadn't criticized the maid first thing.

"Yes'm," Reenie said. "Been wild here."

"What do you mean, wild?"

"People meeting in the quarters every night, tryin' to decide if they gonna leave, and when to do it, and how they can get the best of that Vernon and his men."

"I heard him tell Colonel Buckley they stole the ammunition."

Reenie swallowed hard. "Yes'm, it's true. The only way they thought they could get away without bein' kilt."

Marilla nodded slowly. "I don't blame Lazarus or any of the rest of them."

Reenie raised her chin and shot Marilla a glance before looking away. "Lazarus say he'll come back for me when the fightin' stops."

A smile crept across Marilla's face. "I'm glad, Reenie."

She nodded, a glimmer lighting her eyes. "He didn't want to leave me, but I told him to find someplace safe, and then I'll go. He said he snuck into town three nights ago and heard men talkin'. They said that butcher Sherman went all the way to Savannah."

"It's true." Marilla glanced toward the stairs then said quietly, "I don't see how the South can hold out much longer, Reenie."

"You right. Mr. Buckley's lucky this house still standin', from all I hear."

"Yes. I've heard some awful tales, and I'm sure the worst of it wasn't told when ladies were present." Marilla's face heated at the memory of some things she'd overheard. She was ashamed of the Union army, and yet, in some perverse way she wanted to think the South deserved what they got. "It's very confusing."

"What you got there?" Reenie nodded at the ointment can.

"I'm going to check on Mr. Miller. You saw him this morning?"

Reenie grimaced. "He in a bad way, missy."

"What did Zeke do to him?"

"I think he beat him pretty hard, or maybe he let his men whomp him. He was hardly walkin' when they took him out of the house."

Marilla's legs quaked as she went slowly down the stairs.

24

January 2, 1865

Cruel sunlight and a cold wind hit Jack. He squinted his eyes, but that hurt, so he tried to roll over, away from the light and the cold, but that hurt too, so he lay still, panting and waiting for another blow.

"Jack?"

The gentle voice reached through his fear and pain, and he relaxed his muscles.

"Marilla?"

"Yes, it's me."

He turned toward her, wincing at the needles that pricked his knee and the soreness in his ribs.

She'd left the door of the shanty open, and her voluminous skirts blocked some of the searing light. She came to his side and crouched, setting a tray on the floor. Jack blinked until he could look at her without pain in his eyes.

"You're back."

"Yes, and sorry I ever left. Why did they move you?"

"I don't know. All I can figure is, Vernon was furious when

most of the black people left. His gang is dwindling too, and they couldn't stop the slaves from going. I had an idea he'd kill me before Colonel Buckley returned and make some excuse, like I'd tried to escape or something."

She looked with distaste at the shackles that bound him. "He put these chains in the floor to hold you?"

"Reenie said they were already here. Apparently they used this place to punish slaves who'd done something wrong."

Marilla's eyebrows drew together in a frown. She hadn't known, Jack thought. She never knew the extent of what her great-uncle did to his people—probably she deliberately didn't investigate. Until now.

"Here, drink this."

She held a cup of something warm to his lips.

Jack took a sip and winced, then drank again. Broth. Chicken, he thought, but his taste buds were off lately. It was salty, whatever it was, and it made the sores around his mouth and the raw spot inside his cheek where a tooth had tried to pierce it scream with pain.

"Now let me wash your face."

He tried not to cringe away. Her touch was tender but persistent, and as she worked the water in the bowl grew redder with each rinsing. She got the cut near his mouth and the one on his cheekbone, then started on the wound near his hairline.

"Zeke did this?" she asked tersely.

"He lined up his men and let them each have a kick." His words sounded slurred.

She stared at him for a moment. "What else is hurt?"

Jack hesitated. His manacled hands wouldn't let him touch most of his wounds.

"My ribs. My side. Right knee."

With a twitch of her skirts, she sank to the dirt floor beside him. Her fingers gingerly probed his side and he grimaced, which hurt his mouth.

"Here?" she asked.

"Some. The other side's worse."

"I'm sending for Dr. Riley."

She stood up in a rush, and Jack grasped the hem of her skirt before she could dash away.

"Don't make the colonel angry."

She hesitated. "I'll have to have it out with him sooner or later."

"Then make it later."

Tears filled her eyes as she gazed down at him. "Jack, I can't leave you here like this." She gently pried his fingers from her skirt. "I'll be back soon. I promise."

As Marilla walked toward the house, she heard hoofbeats. She paused on the path between the quarters and the back garden and peered between the leafless mulberry bushes. A band of horsemen rode from the stable area toward the main road. Colonel Buckley led Zeke Vernon and six of his rough men.

When they were gone, she hurried to the back door of the house and entered the kitchen. Sadie stood at the stove while Reenie sat peeling vegetables at the table. Marilla sensed that she'd interrupted a conversation.

"Where has my uncle gone?"

Reenie looked up from her task. "Mr. Crane sent for him, wantin' help to round up his field hands. He and Mr. Vernon and his men went."

That meant Uncle Hamilton wouldn't likely be back for hours. Marilla bit her lip, thinking hard. "Where's Felix?"

"He gone to the stable to get the horses ready," Sadie said.

Marilla ran through the kitchen and down the hall to her great-uncle's study. She opened his top desk drawer, and a blast of hope pierced her. He hadn't taken his wad of housekeys. She pulled out the bunch and fanned them, squinting at the different shapes and sizes. There had to be at least twenty keys.

Overwhelmed, she hurried into the hall and out the front door. As she crossed the verandah, she spotted Felix coming along the path from the stable and ran toward him.

"Felix! Do you know which of these keys fits the chains on Mr. Miller?"

His eyes widened, and he stopped in his tracks.

"What you doin', Miss Marilla?"

"I've just seen Mr. Miller, and he needs medical attention. Reenie told me Colonel Buckley has gone, and I'm guessing he won't be home before nightfall. I can't wait that long. Show me the key to the shackles."

Felix shook his head. "Ain't none of them."

"Then where is it?"

"Mr. Vernon, he have a key on his ring."

Of course. Zeke did this while she and her great-uncle were away, so he must be in possession of the keys.

"Isn't there more than one?"

Felix hesitated. "I don' know, Miss Marilla. Ain't nothin' they'd tell me."

Marilla huffed out a breath. "Are there any horses left in the stable?"

"Yes'm. That old mare you used to ride sometimes."

"Yes, take Star. Ride to Dr. Riley's house, and if he's not there, ask Mrs. Riley where you can find him."

It seemed to take Felix a moment to process what she'd said, but then he nodded. "Yes'm. And, Miss Marilla?"

Something in his tone caught her attention. "Yes, Felix?"

"They might be some keys in the master's bedroom."

She nodded slowly. Felix tended to Uncle Hamilton's clothing. He would know what was in his room.

"Any special place?"

"Might look in the chifforobe."

"Thank you, Felix. And thank you for staying."

"Is not for long, missy."

"I thought not. But thank you for all you've done."

He nodded without meeting her eyes and turned back toward the stable.

She hurried back to the house. Blast this corset! Without it, she was sure she could have run a mile, but the constricting garment kept her from pulling in a deep breath. She hurried up the main staircase and paused on the landing, panting.

Entering her great-uncle's room felt wrong. She shivered but walked steadily to the large, free-standing cabinet. She opened the side where clothes hung first. Trousers, jackets, shirts. Beyond them, at the end of the row, hung an old blue uniform. Pulling it out, she eyed it for a moment. Uncle Hamilton had worn it in Mexico, she was sure. She was also certain he would never fit into it now.

Quickly, she turned to the other garments and squeezed the trouser pockets and thrust a hand into those on the jackets. All were empty. As an afterthought, she went back to the uniform and gently probed the pockets. Inside the tunic, a small patch pocket had been carefully sewn, so that the stitches didn't show on the outside. She poked two fingers in and drew out a pasteboard card.

She frowned as she gazed down at it. 12-20-7. It was hard to say for sure, but she thought the numbers were written in Uncle Hamilton's hand. But what did they mean? Could it be a birthdate, if the 7 represented the year 1807? Certainly not Hamilton's. He was older than that, and his birthday was in May. She slid the card back into the pocket and redid the buttons she'd unfastened.

She closed the wardrobe door and opened the drawers beside it one at a time, from top to bottom. Careful not to disturb his folded clothing, she felt stealthily beneath the neat piles.

Not until the last drawer was she rewarded.

Under a set of long underdrawers she found another key ring. It held four keys. No tag or other explanation was attached. She took the ring, closed the drawer, and dashed out to the staircase.

Gasping as she ran back to the quarters, she wished she'd taken time to remove her corset and hoops and put on a plain housedress. She didn't know how much time they'd have, but she was determined to set Jack free.

She tripped over her skirt and sprawled in the path. Wincing at pain from a scraped shin, she rose and limped onward. A new determination came through her and solidified. Jack was not the only one who needed his freedom.

Portland, Maine

"WHAT DOES IT MEAN?" Abby whispered, looking down at the paper Ryland showed her.

"This pass will get me through at least to Washington." He gazed down at her. He didn't really want to leave Abby again, but if there was any chance of finding her cousin, he would take it. Bringing this case to a close was his top priority now, and after that ...

"When will you leave?"

Her clear, blue eyes were so trusting. Ryland longed to fold her in his arms and assure her that he'd be back, and that all would be well.

"Day after tomorrow. It may take me several days to make the connections, but I'm told the tracks are all in good repair now as far as the capital. Below there it's still a mess, but I hope I can meet with Elijah's supervisor in Washington and get more precise information on his whereabouts."

"Are you sure it's safe? Isn't the war still raging down there?"

He chuckled. "I'm told Washington is well protected." The last hundred miles or so may not be so safe, but he wasn't about to offer her that information. "Getting from here to

Boston will probably be the most precarious part of the journey."

A frown puckered her adorable brow. The temptation to bend and kiss it nearly overwhelmed him.

"Will you be able to keep us informed?"

"I think so. I'll telegraph you from Washington if I'm able. If not, I'll send a letter. And maybe I can get you a postcard of the White House."

She smiled then. "Silly. I'm sure the poor people of Washington aren't worried about providing postcards for tourists right now."

"Maybe not." There, that was much better. When Abby smiled, Ryland's heart was easy. Memories of her consumed most of his thoughts nowadays. His friends would say he was besotted with her—and the best part was, he was beginning to think the feeling was mutual.

He folded the official paper and put it back in his wallet.

"Come." She took his hand. "Let's go tell Grandmother. She'll be so happy to know you're able to resume your search."

He held back. "On one condition."

"Oh?" Her eyebrows arched delicately and her lips twitched, another smile seemingly just waiting to burst over them.

"May I call on you when I return? You personally, I mean, not your grandmother, though I'm fond of Mrs. Rose."

She lowered her eyelashes. "I think that might be arranged, Mr. Atkins."

JACK TRIED NOT to lean too heavily on Marilla as they left the quarters. She walked on his right, so he could use her as a crutch to compensate for his throbbing knee. Pain stabbed his midsection with every step, and he wondered if one of his ribs was broken.

"Where is everyone?" he asked.

"A neighbor's blacks ran away. Uncle and his men have gone to help bring them back."

"What about the slaves here?"

"Gone, or so I'm told. All except Felix, Reenie, and Sadie."

"Even Lazarus?"

"Yes, he's gone."

They could see the stable, and Jack paused, gazing toward it. "I suppose all the horses are gone. I heard you tell Felix to take an old mare."

"From what he said, I think she was the last one left here when the men rode out earlier."

"So, where are we going?"

"To the house, and then I'm not sure."

Jack tilted his head but couldn't see her face. She tugged him onward.

"Come," she said. "We don't know how much time we have."

"How far to the nearest town?"

"Eight miles, more or less."

Jack grimaced. "I don't know as I'd make it that far."

"It's too far for you to walk. Maybe when Felix comes back, we could take the mare."

"We?"

"I want to go with you, Jack. If you won't take me, I'll go on my own."

He stopped and eyed her closely. He'd never imagined such a turn of events. Surely he'd go quicker and be safer on his own. One person could always hide more easily than two.

"I don't know, Marilla."

She looked anxiously toward the house. "Look, we have to hurry, no matter what."

"Right. So, what about that mare?" They started walking again toward the plantation house.

"She is pretty old." Marilla's face scrunched up. "But you could ride her, and I could walk alongside."

"You sent Felix to bring the doctor here. Will he have a wagon?"

"A buggy, probably. But I don't think he'd help a Yankee escape."

"Maybe he would, with the right persuasion."

Her eyes opened wide. "You mean, a weapon?"

"Let's think about it. In the meantime, you said my cipher book is in the colonel's safe?"

"I believe so."

"Can we open it?"

"I don't have the combination."

"Who does?" Jack resumed limping along, and she kept pace.

"Uncle Hamilton. I'm not sure about anyone else."

"How about Zeke Vernon?"

"I doubt it. I don't think Uncle Hamilton would trust him with it."

"Isn't Zeke the colonel's right-hand man?"

"Well, yes. That doesn't mean he'd be loyal under any circumstances."

"Only if he's well paid?"

She winced. "I'm sorry. I don't pretend to know what goes on in Uncle Hamilton's head, but he's a very suspicious man. He'll visit his friends in town and then come home and rant about them and how their commitment to the Cause isn't strong enough."

Jack took a few more steps, thinking. If the colonel didn't trust his friends, he'd be even more mistrustful of his employees. "Maybe his attorney has it? I mean, if the colonel dies, someone's got to be able to open that safe."

Marilla frowned. "I think his attorney fled to Knoxville when Atlanta fell. But we can search Uncle Hamilton's desk."

"You think we may find it there?"

She shrugged. "I was just in there when I was looking for the keys and, I didn't see—" She stopped five yards from the verandah steps. "Oh."

"What is it?" Jack asked softly.

"Upstairs in his room. That's where I finally found the keys to the chains. And while I was searching his wardrobe, I found something else. Numbers."

Jack's pulse picked up. "What were they?"

"I thought it might be a date, but I couldn't make any sense of it. They were written on a card, in the pocket of his old army uniform. December 20, 1807. That is, 12-20-7."

"Sounds like a combination to me."

"Come on."

When they reached the front steps, Jack's knee buckled and he sprawled on the first stairs.

"I'm sorry."

"Not your fault," she said. "Can you get up?"

"I think so." Using the railing and her arm for leverage, he managed to stand. Hobbling up the steps was torture.

"Maybe you should have waited down there," Marilla said when they gained the porch.

"Too late now."

He put his arm firmly around her shoulders, trying not to think about how soft and pliant she was. When her hand came up onto his back, he caught his breath.

"Did I hurt you?" she asked.

"No."

He pushed thoughts of romance firmly away and limped along the hall with her to Buckley's study. She was helping him, that was all, the same way she'd help anyone in his misfortune. Her tender heart would go out to a dying man or an injured dog without prejudice.

"Here, sit down."

Jack eased onto the chair nearest the safe.

"Have you ever opened a combination lock before?" he asked.

"No. Is there a trick to it?"

"Sort of." Many times he'd opened the one where they kept

money they accepted for telegrams in the old office in Emmaus. "Start by just twirling the dial to sort of clear it. Go around clockwise about three times."

She did it, her jaw set in concentration.

"Okay, now go clockwise all the way around and to the first number."

He walked her through the process, and Marilla stilled when she'd turned the dial to the seven that was the final digit.

"And pull," Jack said.

She grasped the handle and pulled the door toward her. It swung open.

"It worked! I can't believe it!"

Jack chuckled and peered into the safe. On the top shelf was a stack of paper money—Confederate bills.

"Should we take some of that cash?"

Marilla looked up at him, clearly startled. "Steal Uncle's money?"

"We may need some if we're really going to flee."

Her eyes narrowed to slits. "Does that mean you'll take me with you?"

He hesitated.

"I know the area," she said quickly. "We can do it, Jack."

"All right," he said at last, but his misgivings were stronger than ever. "We might need money."

"I have a bit upstairs."

"Enough for train tickets if we get the chance?"

Her mouth tightened. "Probably not. But if we take his money, we'll be criminals. He'll set the law on us for sure."

"You think he won't anyway?"

"I don't know. But there's your codebook."

Jack lifted the leatherbound book out and slid it into his pocket. "It's probably no good anymore, but I don't want to leave it here."

"What do you mean, no good? Uncle's puzzled over it for weeks."

"They change the codewords any time there's a chance the cipher has been compromised. That's surely happened since I was captured."

"Oh." She blinked.

Jack gazed into the dark cavity of the safe. "Do you know what's in that wooden box?"

Marilla caught her breath. "I think—It may be my jewelry."

25

"You have jewelry?" Somehow that seemed out of place in Jack's knowledge of Marilla.

"My father's mother supposedly left me some jewelry. I have a letter up in my room describing it. But Uncle wouldn't give it to me after I got here. He said, 'All in good time.' But it seems that 'good time' never came."

Jack lifted out the box. The lid and sides were carved with vines and blossoms.

"Do you know what kind of jewelry?"

"An emerald necklace and earrings." Her eyes went dreamy. "A sapphire ring and a jet-and-diamond brooch. That's what the letter said."

The box had no lock, and Jack lifted the lid. The inside was lined with black velvet, and a brooch twinkled up at him from beside a fabric pouch. "There's your diamond pin," he said.

Marilla drew in a deep breath. "I wonder what's in the bag."

He lifted the pouch and handed it to her. "Oh, look." Under it was a ring, and he picked it up. A blue stone was mounted in a gold band. He held it out between them. "Is that a sapphire?"

"It must be." She gulped and met his gaze. "I've never seen one before—not that I knew of."

He nodded. "Open the bag."

She loosened the silken cord that held the pouch's neck closed and shook the contents into her hand. They both stared at the glittering necklace. Carefully, Marilla picked out two earbobs set with green stones.

"The emerald necklace and earrings," she whispered.

"And those are yours for certain?"

"The letter from Uncle Hamilton came just after my mother died. It said my grandmother left them to me in her will."

"Can you get the letter?"

She nodded.

"You'll want a few clothes too. But hurry."

"Of course. And I'll bring what little money I have."

Jack hesitated and closed the safe door on Buckley's stash. "We'll pray for God's grace to get us through without the colonel's money."

Marilla hurried to the doorway. Jack rose and followed her, flexing his knee a couple of times, trying to ease the pain.

Instead of darting up the stairs, Marilla headed to the kitchen, and he followed her.

"Sadie, I need your help. Where's Reenie?"

The black woman standing at the worktable blinked at her. "What you say, Miss Marilla?"

Jack hung back and watched from the threshold as the second maid, Reenie, came in from the pantry.

"Oh, good," Marilla said. "Listen to me, both of you. My uncle has gone out, probably for some time. I am leaving here, and I ask you to help me and not give Colonel Buckley any details when he returns."

They both gaped at her. Sadie's eyes glanced past her and landed on Jack.

"Who's there?"

Marilla turned her head then looked back at the two women. "He's Jack Miller, the man the colonel's kept prisoner for the last six weeks."

"I know who he be," Reenie said.

Sadie frowned. "They took him out to the quarters."

"Yes, they did," Marilla said evenly, "and I set him free. Just as you were set free two years ago. Mr. Miller and I intend to leave here. He wants to return to his family in the North, and I'm going with him, at least until I can find friends of my own up there. I suggest you two and Felix leave as well."

Reenie jerked her head toward the back door. "Where is Felix?"

"I sent him to get the doctor for Mr. Miller, but we can't wait for him to get here. I'm going to change my clothes and pack a few things. Will you help me, Reenie?"

"Yes'm." Reenie stepped toward her.

"You trust that man?" Sadie nodded curtly toward Jack.

"Yes, I do."

Jack was afraid she would mention their previous acquaintance in Pennsylvania, but she didn't. He was glad. If the women knew, Buckley might find out, and he was sure that would enrage him even more than their leaving would.

He cleared his throat. "Miss Reenie, Miss Sadie, thank you for all your kindnesses to me. You fed me and took care of me, and I appreciate that. I only want the best for you and this family. I think I can serve Miss Marilla best by helping her get back to people who truly care about her."

Who was he thinking of? Marilla knew of no other close relatives. It struck him that he meant his own family. They already liked her, and they would help the young woman any way they could.

Sadie hesitated then said, "You two gonna need some vittles. Go get changed, Miss Marilla. I'll pack you a lunch."

"Thank you, Sadie." Marilla turned to Jack. "Wait here. If the men come back, you'll have to run out the back and hide. I can meet you in town tonight, behind the church, if you can make it there."

He nodded, and she strode into the hallway with Reenie on her heels.

Sadie became a whirlwind of activity. She pulled from cupboards a loaf of bread, a block of cheese, and a battered knapsack. Soon she was shaping sandwiches, to which she added slabs of cornbread wrapped in a napkin, several apples, and a cluster of raisins.

"You," she said sharply, and Jack sat up straighter. "They's flasks in that drawer." She nodded vaguely toward a chest with several drawers topped by a breadbox. "You can fill 'em from the bucket yonder."

"Yes, ma'am." Jack pried himself out of the chair and hobbled to the chest.

"You hurt bad?" Sadie asked almost grudgingly.

"A bit." He found the flasks and chose two. Water was heavy, but he knew from experience with the regiment that a few drops of water could be lifesaving. He limped to the bucket near the woodbox. Bending to retrieve the ladle sent excruciating pain through his side. He gritted his teeth and crouched, keeping his back straight.

Sadie came over and snatched the ladle from his hand. "What they do to you, anyway?"

"Nothing they haven't done to you and your people, I'm sure."

She focused on his wrist, which was raw from the chafing of the manacles. "They chain you up?"

"Yes, ma'am."

She frowned. "You don't call me ma'am."

"Why not?" Jack asked. "You treat me like a lady would."

"You know what I am."

"I know you're a free woman. All the slaves in the southern states are free now, and I wouldn't be surprised if the whole country abolished slavery, North and South, soon. I heard Mr. Lincoln speak once in Washington, and I believe he'll do it."

Sadie's eyes opened wide. "You seen the President."

"Yes, ma'am. I even got to shake his hand."

Sadie drew in a sharp breath.

"You don't have to stay here," Jack said softly. "I don't know if you have people to go to, but you don't need to stay on and keep house for the colonel."

"Miss Marilla needs us."

"You're staying for Marilla?" Jack smiled. "That's wonderful. But you don't have to now. I'm going to try to get her back to Pennsylvania, or wherever she wants to go."

Sadie said nothing for a moment but set the first full flask on the sideboard and opened the second.

"So, what about Colonel Buckley?" Jack asked. "Will you stay for him?"

Sadie grunted. "Ain't none of us will stay for his sake. If Miss Marilla's leavin', I reckon we'll go too." She poured water carefully from the ladle into the flask and returned the ladle to the pail. "How you think you gonna get away?"

"I don't know yet."

Her mouth twisted.

Jack reached for the flask. "I can do that." He took it from her and screwed on the top.

"Listen to me," Sadie said solemnly. "The colonel will tear this place apart when he finds out you and Miss Marilla is gone. How you think you'll outrun him and that Zeke Vernon and their pack of dogs?"

Jack swallowed hard. "I'm not sure. But we have to try."

Sadie held his gaze for a long moment, as though measuring him against an unseen yardstick.

"It was Marilla's idea to go with me," Jack said. "I tried to talk her out of it, but she's determined to leave this place."

"Well, all I got to say is, you'll need help."

"You're helping us now, and I thank you."

"No, I mean when you leave here." She hesitated then gave a firm nod. "We know somebody. They told us when we ready to go, we should come to them. You ought to go there today."

"Where do you mean?"

She pressed her lips together and went back to her worktable. "Can't tell you their names. But they can start you on the way."

Jack stood still. He'd heard rumors—they all had in Washington. People who helped slaves escape the South. Ordinary people who risked their lives, their goods, and their reputations to help the enslaved.

Reenie entered the kitchen carrying a carpetbag. Marilla, right behind her, had discarded her crinoline and put on a very plain dress of dark calico and a straw hat.

"I'm ready," she said to Jack, "but Felix is coming. We saw him from the upstairs window."

"What about the doctor?" Sadie asked.

"No sign of him," Marilla said. "Jack, you stay here. I'll go out and speak to him and find out what's going on. If it's safe, we'll take the mare, but if the doctor's on his way, I think we should wait."

"Sadie was just telling me she knows of some folks who will help us."

"Oh?" Marilla arched her eyebrows at Sadie.

"That's right," Sadie said, looking down at the packet of sandwiches she'd prepared. "Felix knows them. He'll tell you. You tell him I said so."

Marilla hiked up her skirt and dashed out into the hall.

"Well, don't just stand there!" Sadie marched over to Jack and gave him a canvas bag. "Get over near the back door and be ready to run."

Heart racing, Jack seized the bag, which was surprisingly heavy, and limped to the door she indicated.

Reenie had gone to the kitchen doorway, but she turned back. "Miss Marilla and Felix are coming in."

A moment later, the two were in the room with them. Felix darted Jack a curious glance as he talked.

"... but Mrs. Riley said he'd likely be out all day. He's got a woman in labor clear out near the bridge, and she said he had at least four other folks to call on."

Marilla nodded. "We'll have to take the mare, then. Is she all tuckered out?"

"Well, if you take it slow and easy, she can go for a while. But you don't want to take the main road, Miss Marilla. The colonel and his men, they could come back anytime."

"Sadie has a plan," Marilla said.

Jack stepped closer, and they discussed their options in hushed tones.

At first, Felix balked. "We can't show no white folks who's the helpers, Sadie."

"They won't tell no one." Sadie fixed him with a glare.

Marilla reached out a hand, almost touching his sleeve. "Colonel Buckley will kill Mr. Miller if he catches him, Felix. And I don't know what he'll do to me."

"Surely not, missy. You his kin."

"I'm not sure that matters now. I want to get away from here and go back to my friends up North. I'll feel safer there."

Reenie raised her chin. "You'd be safer anywhere than here."

Marilla looked closely at Reenie, and Jack noticed a large bruise on her cheek.

"Did something happen I don't know about?" Marilla asked.

"You just go," Reenie said.

Marilla nodded and reached for the carpetbag. "Thank you all."

THREE HOURS LATER, Felix led them to a tobacco barn set off by itself in a field. Marilla was exhausted, but she was thankful their stopping place was so far from River Lea—about ten miles, Felix reckoned.

Jack seemed nervous as they crossed the open ground.

"What is it?" Marilla asked.

"Anyone could see us coming in here."

"Ain't anyone around," Felix said. He halted the mare beside the door, and Jack slid to the ground. Marilla purposely didn't watch how stiffly he walked as they made their way inside.

In a corner, they found a wooden chest containing a couple of motheaten blankets and a jug of water.

"You stay here," Felix said. "I'll be back after a while."

Marilla sat down on the box, and Jack settled on the ground with her carpetbag and their food sack beside him. They could hear the mare's footsteps as she plodded away.

"I wish he'd left Star to rest," Marilla said.

"He doesn't want to draw attention to this place." Jack closed his eyes and leaned back against the board wall.

"Do you think we'll stay here all night?" she asked.

"Until dark anyway."

At least half an hour passed before Felix returned. They didn't hear him coming, which made Marilla suspect he'd left Star somewhere else. He slipped in and stood taking quick, shallow breaths.

Marilla jumped up, and Jack struggled to his feet.

"Is something wrong?" Marilla asked.

Felix shook his head. "No—well, he didn't like it when I told him you was white. I told him they was nothing could make you let on to anyone else who he is."

"We won't," Jack said firmly.

"'S awright then. He say you stay here til he come. Don't you even poke your nose out a crack."

Marilla nodded.

"You eat some of them vittles Sadie give you. You'll need your strength. Tonight you'll go a far piece." He paused and eyed her gravely. "Lawd bless you, Miss Marilla."

"Thank you, Felix. You too. I told Sadie you all should leave River Lea as well. She's probably making preparations."

"I best get back."

"Yes, and you tell Sadie and Reenie I said they can take any of my things they find useful—clothes and such."

Felix blinked and lowered his gaze as though unsure what to say.

Jack stepped forward and held out his hand. "Thank you, Felix."

Felix stared at his hand then raised baffled eyes to Jack's face.

"You're free, Felix, just like me," Jack said.

Slowly, Felix reached out and grasped his hand. "God bless you, Mr. Miller. I pray they don' catch you."

He was gone before Marilla could say anything else.

26

The man arrived wearing a handkerchief tied over the bottom half of his face. Marilla wondered if he feared she might recognize him. Perhaps he'd been a guest at River Lea, or maybe he did business regularly with Colonel Buckley.

"You ready?" was all he said after letting himself into the barn.

"Yes, sir," Jack said, and Marilla nodded.

"You plenty warm?" he asked.

The temperature had fallen after dusk. Marilla had a warm coat and gloves, but Jack had only the ragged shirt he'd been wearing when captured.

"It'll get colder the farther north you go," their guide said. "When we get to the wagon, there's an old barn frock in there. It'll smell like manure, but it'll give you an extra layer."

"Thank you," Jack said.

The man nodded. "Keep quiet on the way. Don't use names, ever. Not until you're safe. My wagon's hid about half a mile from here. When we get close, I'll go first and make sure there's nobody about. Then you follow and jump into the back. Lie down and pull the canvas in there over you."

Both his passengers nodded solemnly.

"Are we going to a town?" Jack asked.

"Not this time. Maybe tomorrow. I don't know exactly where you're going, to be honest. It's safer that way. I pass you to the next conductor, and he takes you to the next. But we don't know beyond the next stop. That way, if anyone asks us, we can't give away much."

"That's wise."

"All right, get your stuff. I'll go out and watch for a couple minutes. If it's clear, I'll hoot like an owl. Then you come. Go to the right when you come out the door. You should see me. There's enough moon tonight."

Jack picked up the carpetbag. They'd eaten enough of their provisions that they could fit the food sack and water flasks in with Marilla's clothing, so they had only one bag to worry about.

The ride seemed endless, but it was still dark when the wagon stopped. After a moment, their guide's voice came from beside the front wheel.

"You can come out."

A second man was standing nearby, holding a dark lantern. "Come with me."

Marilla couldn't tell anything about him, except that he was not quite so tall as Jack, and he wore dark clothing. He started to walk away, and the man who had brought them climbed to the wagon seat.

Marilla turned back toward him. "Thank you."

He nodded and slapped the reins on his mule's hindquarters.

Their new host took them toward a shed. The dark bulk of a farmhouse loomed nearby, but they didn't approach it. The shed's door didn't creak when the man opened it, and Marilla surmised he kept the hinges well oiled.

"There's another package inside." The man's tone was almost apologetic.

Marilla didn't understand what he meant until he opened a slit on the lantern and she saw a young black man—a boy, really, not more than fourteen or fifteen years old—huddled in a corner between some crates and tools.

"It's all right," the man said. "These people are going with you." He turned to Jack and Marilla. "We'll bring you something to eat just before sunrise and again at sunset. Sleep if you can during the day. We'll leave when it's full dark."

January 3, 1865

JACK'S KNEE felt somewhat better, and he was restless. He got up and paced the shed's floor. He could only get in two strides each way. Probably he was driving the others crazy.

He sat down again, near the black boy. "My name's Jack. Do you know where we're going?"

"North, suh," the boy said.

Jack nodded. He'd asked for it. He couldn't see the young man in the dark, but he sensed fear peeling off him by way of his strong body odor. But, Jack reflected, he probably didn't smell so good himself.

When they'd been in the shed a couple of hours, a woman opened the door cautiously. She was thin, of medium height, and had her hair caught up in a bun. The farmer's wife, no doubt.

She set a basket inside, on the floor, and Jack moved to retrieve it. When he was close to her, she held out something dark.

"My husband said you need a clean shirt. If you folks want wash water, I can fetch it."

"That would be nice," Jack said.

She nodded. "Eat up. I'll be back."

In the basket, they found cornbread, a few raisins, and three strips of dried meat.

"We must be off Sherman's path," Marilla whispered. "I heard all the farmsteads were cleaned out, for a hundred miles or so on each side."

Jack took one of the strips and held out the third to the boy. He hesitated, then took it without making eye contact.

A few minutes later the woman returned with a wash basin of clean water, a towel, and a pannikin of soft soap. The sky was turning light, and Jack glimpsed a blush of pink on the clouds to the east.

"Is there anywhere nearby that we could send a telegram?" he whispered.

The woman frowned at him. "Most of the lines have been down since Sherman went through a couple months ago."

"Oh, I thought maybe we were north of there."

"Well, we are, but still—" She looked over her shoulder. "There might be a place in Gainesville. I'm not sure."

"How far is that?"

She shrugged. "The way you're travelin', at least two more days."

"Thanks."

"Well, if you go to Toccoa, and I don't know if you will, there might be a station there."

Jack nodded. "I thank you."

They were headed north and maybe somewhat east, he judged the next night from the stars. He didn't ask the driver any questions. He wished he was able to pay these people, but he knew they'd probably need Marilla's small hoard before they were done.

DARK TREES LOOMED over them when the conductor called a soft whoa and the team halted in the roadway. The wagon swayed as the driver climbed down.

Marilla could hear the murmur of voices, but she couldn't make out their words.

The canvas rustled beside her. A moment later, their driver said, close to them, "Change of plans, folks."

Jack and Marilla folded back the canvas and sat up. The black boy, who huddled in a back corner of the wagon bed, leaned forward.

"What is it?" Jack asked.

"The next stop—the house has been burnt. They think someone spilled the beans on the owner, and he had to take his family and flee. I'm sorry. This fella's his neighbor. The conductor asked him to meet anyone headed for the station tonight and tell them."

"What does that mean?" Marilla asked.

"It means the chain is broken. Until we can figure out a new path, it ends here. I'm sorry. I don't know where the next stop is beyond the one that burnt."

"Are we near a town?" Jack asked.

"About five miles." The driver gave them directions. "I'm sorry, but if I take you any farther, I won't get home before daylight."

"It's all right," Jack said. He scrambled over the side of the wagon and held out a hand to Marilla. She gathered her skirts and followed, stumbling as she landed but quickly righting herself.

The boy had vaulted over the tailboard.

"I thank you, sir," he said softly.

The driver nodded. "God speed, young fella."

Before Marilla realized what was happening, the boy disappeared into the dark woods.

"But—shouldn't we stay together?" she whispered.

Jack shook his head. "Two will be safer than three. Besides, he doesn't trust us."

"You think so?"

"Marilla, we're white, and we don't know his name—even a false one."

She sighed. "All right. What now?" She felt stupid and sleepy, and her stomach rumbled.

"We get off the road." Jack turned to the driver. "Thank you very much."

The man had climbed to his seat again. He didn't look their way, but said, "I don't know what you're talking about." He snapped the reins and drove on to a clearing, where he turned the wagon around and drove back past them without looking their way.

Marilla looked around. The man who'd brought him the news had disappeared as well.

"Come on." Jack carried her bag and grasped her hand with his free one. "If we hear anyone coming, we'll have to get off the road and hide. Even if they aren't out to find runaways, they'll be suspicious."

"We could tell them we're eloping." She smiled, but Jack didn't seem amused.

"Two Yankees?"

She looked up at him and batted her eyelashes, though she doubted he could see that in the darkness. "Why, darlin'," she said in her best Georgia drawl, "Cain't you talk like a Southerner?"

Jack grunted and quickened his pace, pulling her onward.

The five miles felt like a hundred. Marilla's feet ached, then her ankles and shins. By the time they saw a light far ahead, she was sure she had blisters.

"Is that the town?" she asked.

"Well, it's a light." Jack squinted at the gray landscape before them. "It may just be another farmhouse where people are starting to get up and do chores."

A few minutes later, he jerked her arm, startling Marilla. He cocked his head to one side, listening. Then she heard what he heard—hoofbeats.

"Come on!" He dragged her across the road to a row of bushes.

When Jack dove through the hedge, Marilla had to follow. She kept quiet, despite the scratching of numerous branches and what felt like a thousand thorns. On the far side, he pushed her to the ground and held her there with a hand lying heavily on her back. Marilla tried to breathe silently while he crouched beside her, tense and watching through the leafless branches.

The hoofbeats became louder, and Jack flattened himself beside her. The ground was icy cold, but Marilla closed her eyes and tried not to move a muscle.

The sound of the wagon's wheels on the hard-packed road nearly deafened her. She could hear the animals pulling it breathing and huffing, the creaking of the harness and rattling from the wagon bed. Suddenly the noise lessened, and the wagon was past.

"Keep still another minute," Jack whispered, his breath tickling her ear. A rush of warmth swept over her, and she had the disconcerting vision of Jack holding her in his arms and whispering sweeter things.

Finally he removed his hand, and she felt colder.

"All right," he said. "We can move on, but we need to be more careful. I think we're getting close to the town, and more people will be moving about. We can't let them see us."

Marilla sat up, squinting toward the east, where a glow hovered at the horizon.

"If we didn't have the carpet bag, no one would suspect anything, would they?" she asked.

"Two strangers, this early in the morning ... I don't know." He gave her a crooked smile. "Let's just keep our wits about us and plan our next hiding spot as we go. We may have to leave the road altogether."

"I thought you wanted to go into the town."

"I'd like to know if they have a telegraph. It may be too small, and if it's not near the railroad ..."

Marilla stood and brushed off her skirt, feeling more awake

and rational. "If we stash my bag somewhere, maybe we can find a business opening up and ask them."

Jack nodded slowly, his eyes half closed.

"Or you could leave me someplace and go alone to make inquiries."

He smiled. "I don't think I could mimic the accent as well as you do." He picked up the bag. "Come on. The longer we stay here, the harder it will be to get into town without being noticed."

They made their way to the outskirts of town, dodging out of sight whenever they saw people coming their way. Jack scouted out a shed behind a house set back from the road.

"I think you'd be safe here for an hour," he said. "Or at least we could hide your bag inside."

Marilla didn't want to be left alone, but she could see both sides of the plan.

"What if we split up? If I took the bag, I could tell people I had to leave home and was trying to get to relatives in Tennessee."

"South Carolina," Jack said. "I think we're closer to South Carolina."

"But that's not where we want to go. Uncle Hamilton said Sherman's heading there, now that he's sacked Savannah."

He frowned. "Tell them Chattanooga then. I'll ask about Knoxville. We don't both want to approach people asking about the same place."

That made sense to her. "How will we find each other again?"

"There's got to be a post office," Jack said.

At that moment a bell rang out in the distance. Marilla held her breath and counted.

"That's a church bell. It's eight o'clock."

"Good. We should be able to find that. Meet me at the church as soon as you hear it strike nine."

He looked toward the street. "You go first. I'll come along

behind you for the first bit, and then I'll veer off when I see a farmer or a shopkeeper or something like that."

"All right."

"Just keep your wits about you, Marilla."

She nodded. "I'll try. You too, Jack."

He wasn't limping much now, but a bruise on his cheek still showed, and she knew his ribs pained him if he bent over.

She took the carpetbag from him. It was heavier than she remembered, but she didn't dare discard anything. Who knew what she would need or when? She pulled in a deep breath and headed toward the cluster of buildings that made up the town center, passing several houses and then a blacksmith's shop where the owner was just rolling open the door. Maybe Jack would stop and talk to him.

She hoped for a café or a hotel with a dining room, where she could spend one of her precious coins on a cup of tea, but she didn't pass one that was open. Probably eateries were having a hard time getting supplies these days.

In the town's heart, several retail shops weren't open yet, but she spotted a sign for a physician's office in front of a house, and she turned in there.

The front door was unlocked, and a small bell jangled as she swung it open. She entered and looked around. She was in a small anteroom with three chairs and a side table holding a lamp. A woman approached from a hallway and smiled at her.

"Are you here to see Dr. Stevens? I'm his wife."

"Actually, I wondered if I could get some directions." Marilla softened her I's into ahs the way her great-uncle did, and the woman didn't seem to think her speech odd.

"Oh? where are you going?"

"Well, Chattanooga eventually, but I hoped I'd find a telegraph office here."

Mrs. Stevens frowned. "We don't have one. There was one in the next town over, but I'm told it's closed now."

"The work of that awful Yankee general?"

"No, but the man who ran it left town. People suspect he was a Union sympathizer. No one's been there to operate it for several weeks."

"Pity," Marilla said. "Well, where is the nearest railway depot?"

"That's about ten miles from here." Mrs. Stevens gave her instructions on finding the nearest stop on the line.

"Do you know if trains are getting through now?"

"I believe so. They had some trouble earlier, but I heard the grocer say they were getting supplies in from Chattanooga once a week now."

Marilla smiled. "That sounds promising. Thank you very much."

As she turned, Mrs. Stevens said, "Oh, do you have a way to get there?"

"Well, actually, no."

"I ask because my husband is making a call out that way this morning. He could perhaps convey you the first five miles if that would help you out."

"That would be wonderful."

Marilla waited while Mrs. Stevens went to speak to the doctor farther back in the house. She returned with a smile.

"Dr. Stevens says he'd be happy to take you along the road as far as his patient's house. He'll be leaving at half past nine."

"Thank you so much," Marilla said. "I'll be here. Oh, I'd like to stop by the church first. Could you please tell me how to get there?"

She hurried out carrying her carpetbag and made her way to the little white church. After turning a corner, she could see the steeple, standing stalwart against the sky. The bell began to ring as she dashed into the churchyard panting.

Jack stood on the church steps, waiting for her.

"I have to hurry," she said between shallow breaths.

"Why?"

"I have a ride halfway to the next train station. Five out of ten miles in a doctor's buggy. But should I tell him about you? I didn't dare."

"No, no, that's good. Where is it?"

She gave him the name of the town and Mrs. Stevens's instructions.

"I'll start walking," Jack said. "You should pass me on the way."

"Are you sure? Your knee—"

"It's fine. Just you take the bag and ride as far as you can. Your feet will get a rest in the buggy. I'll likely catch up to you before you get to the depot."

"Yes." She was doubtful, but she could see the sense of this plan. Her sore feet surely wouldn't hold out for ten miles. "Jack, she said there had been a telegraph station in the next town west, but the operator has left and there's no one there now."

His brow furrowed. "Hmm. I don't think it's worth going that far out of our way to send a telegram, assuming I could somehow get into the office and the equipment's still there. Let's get to the railroad as quick as we can."

"I think the Union army controls it up here now."

"I hope they still do. I know Sherman was getting supplies through from Chattanooga when we were in Atlanta, and they were supposed to get more at Covington. But I have no idea what's happened to the rail lines since I was taken."

"It hasn't been good for the people of Georgia." Marilla shrugged. "We'll pray we meet up with a Union detachment and get over the border, eh?"

27

January 4, 1865

Jack didn't hurry as he ambled along the road. A few farm wagons passed him. He kept an eye out for anyone approaching from behind him, as he couldn't discount the notion that Hamilton Buckley would send his band of thugs this far, looking for him and Marilla.

At last he saw a buggy, pulled by a horse that looked well fed and moved smartly, coming up behind. That must be the doctor. Even if Sherman's men had cut this far north, they wouldn't take a medical man's means of transportation away, would they?

He didn't look back again until they were almost upon him. Then he halted at the edge of the road. His eyes skimmed over Marilla and landed on the driver, a man in a sack coat, wearing a clean shirt and tie. No one had new, fashionable clothes these days.

"Hello," he called with as easy a smile as he could muster. "I see you're headed my way. Any chance I could get a lift?"

The doctor eyed him closely. Jack was thankful he'd been able to exchange the filthy, tattered shirt he'd worn while imprisoned. Marilla looked wary, and she studiously avoided his gaze.

"I suppose so," the doctor said. "Climb on behind."

It was that simple. Jack boosted himself into the compartment behind the seat, next to Marilla's carpetbag and the doctor's satchel.

"Only going about three more miles," the driver said over his shoulder.

"I appreciate it," Jack said. "That's three miles I won't have to walk."

The sun was well past noon when they limped into the next town, having left the doctor's buggy a good five miles behind them. Jack insisted on carrying Marilla's bag the last mile. She looked as though she would object, but with a sigh handed it over. As he'd guessed, she was too tired to fight about it.

"If their telegraph office is open, do you have the funds to send a message?" he asked.

"I think so, but what about food?"

"Yes, we should eat."

They walked on in silence until he spotted a shop with a small sign in the window—Post Office.

"Wait here." He handed her the bag and went inside. Behind the post office counter stood a man sorting mail.

"Excuse me," Jack said. "Is there a telegraph office in town? I'm new here, and I'd like to send a message."

"Across the street, next to the dry goods."

"Thank you." Jack wondered if he should dash off a quick letter while he was there, but time was fleeting, and besides, Marilla hadn't given him any money yet. He couldn't even purchase a postage stamp.

She was leaning wearily against the wall outside when he emerged.

"Come on." He picked up her bag and set off across the street. Not many people were out and about. He supposed no one had money to spend. The dry goods store was closed, which didn't surprise him. What would they sell, the way things were right now?

He peered in the front window of an office the size of a cracker tin. There was barely enough room for the desk and chair of the telegraph operator and space for a customer between the door and the desk. What surprised him most was that the operator was using a Beardslee telegraph instead of the usual telegraph key.

"Can you give me what you have in money?"

"How much?"

"I don't know. Two dollars, maybe, if you have it."

She pulled a small purse out of a pocket and handed him a Confederate ten-dollar bill.

"I didn't think you had this much."

She shrugged. "Inflation."

"Right." He'd heard tales in Atlanta about the astronomical prices asked for everyday goods when Confederate bills were presented. U.S. dollars and coins had been accepted without question, and it seemed all the local people knew Confederate currency wasn't worth much.

"Do you want me to wait here?" she asked.

"Probably best."

Jack walked into the tiny office, and the operator looked up.

"Hello. I'd like to send a message."

The operator pushed a form across the desk to him. Jack bent over it. He obviously couldn't send a telegram to a Union officer. If he sent it to his supervisor in Washington, would the operator object? He'd given the matter some thought on the long walk into town and addressed the telegram to Mrs. Grayson.

PLEASE TELL MY EMPLOYER ON WAY CHATTANOOGA. JACK.

He passed the form to the man behind the desk. "How much?"

The operator frowned over the words. "That depends. You got silver?"

"Uh …" Jack held out the ten-dollar bill.

The man's frown became a scowl. "I suppose that'll cover it."

"How much if I had silver dollars?"

"Two."

Jack sighed. If he and Marilla got over the Mason-Dixon line, the Confederate money would do her no good.

"Keep that," he said.

"Can you cut a word?"

Jack huffed out a breath. "Are you serious?"

"I am."

He took back the form, crossed out "on way" and replaced it with "headed."

"You have an employer in D.C.?"

"Oh, my old job. A former employer."

"Why does he care if you're going to Chattanooga?"

"Why do you care?" Jack asked. "You've got your money."

The man frowned and turned to the apparatus.

Jack was tempted to comment on the Beardslee. The machine was one used in the military. Instead of a regular key, this one had an alphabet dial that allowed the operator to turn it to each letter in the message, rather than tapping out the Morse Code symbols. But the man was already suspicious. If he expressed interest in it, or even hinted that he knew it wasn't the standard equipment for commercial telegraph offices, the operator might sound an alarm.

Still, the Beardslee was notorious for having a short range. It operated on a magneto, not batteries. That meant it could only send to another station less than ten miles away.

"You waiting for a reply?" the operator asked.

"Yeah."

"Well, I'm due for my lunch hour. Come back in an hour."

Jack said nothing but went outside. Marilla stood beside the steps. He jerked his head down the street and walked quickly away. Marilla followed him. After half a block, he veered off the street and stopped under a large tree.

"What is it?" Marilla asked anxiously as she joined him.

"I don't like this. They've got a telegraph machine that's used by the Union army in a pinch as a battlefield apparatus. General Burnside used it at Fredericksburg. It only has a range of five or ten miles."

"So ... he's not really sending the message?"

"Oh, I think he did, but it has to be picked up by someone not too far away and resent to Washington. And he was suspicious that I was sending anything to Washington. I addressed it to my landlady there, but still ... No matter what I put, if I wanted to get word through to anyone who mattered, it would look fishy."

"I hadn't thought of that. What should we do?"

Jack gritted his teeth. More and more, he was convinced he'd made a mistake.

Marilla could hardly believe her eyes. Around the back of the building, Jack tried the small window and found that the sash slid up quite easily. He instructed her to keep watch for any passersby. She gulped and did as he said, but she couldn't help casting quick glances back at him as he hoisted himself—how that must hurt his ribs!—and disappeared through a space she'd have thought too small for him to negotiate.

After a couple of minutes, during which she saw only a farm wagon passing the end of the alley, she shrank up against the wall and hazarded a quick peek inside.

Jack was leaning over the desk, doing something to a machine that looked like a largish wooden box with some kind of engine inside. It had a wheel of some sort, and he was turning it, his mouth set in concentration, first one way then the other.

Muffled voices reached her, and she plastered herself against the rough plank wall, clutching her carpetbag. The voices, she realized, were in the alley beyond the small building. As they retreated, she thought perhaps she ought to stand a bit farther from the open window, so as not to draw attention to it if anyone did come into the alley.

Jack poked his head out and hissed, "All clear?"

She jumped and jerked her head around. Her entire body was trembling, but she managed a nod. He glanced left, then right, and tumbled out the window, doing a neat somersault and landing on his feet next to her. With a mischievous grin, he reached up and eased the window sash down then grabbed her bag.

"Let's go."

Marilla had neither the strength nor the wit in that moment to do anything but follow.

January 5, 1865
War Department Building, Washington, D.C.

RYLAND ATKINS SAT opposite Jack Miller's supervisor in his Washington D.C. office at last. He'd followed the chain of command as far as possible, short of the Secretary of War and President Lincoln. David Strouse was as near as he would get to the top, and he was glad to have come this far. But he was still frustrated.

"Captured? Are you certain?"

"Absolutely," Strouse said. "I'm sorry I can't give you more information. If we knew where he was, we'd make an effort to rescue the poor fellow. Last we knew, the telegraph team he was with was attacked. Several men were killed, and their equipment was destroyed. The rest of the detachment high-tailed it back to the regiment they were serving, but without Miller."

"But no one saw him actually captured? Could he have been killed?" Ryland's throat felt drier than the Mojave Desert—or so he assumed, having never ventured quite that far into the Southwest.

"One of the teamsters saw the raiders hustle him off. If they didn't execute him, they took him somewhere. I suspect they thought he'd be valuable to them." Strouse shook his head. "Our best men haven't been able to find a trace of him."

"And this was in Georgia," Ryland said, fingering the brim of his hat, which he held in his lap.

"Yes, a bit southeast of Covington." Strouse rubbed his droopy eyes. "He was only a few days out of Atlanta with the crew, setting up lines so General Sherman could communicate with us."

"Of course." Ryland studied Strouse's face. The man looked exhausted. But it was now nearly two months since Jack Miller had been taken. What were the odds that he was still alive? "Could they be forcing him to work for them?"

"It's entirely possible." Strouse sighed and leaned back in his chair. "Look, normally I wouldn't give out this information, but it won't matter now. Miller had his cipher book on him when he was captured."

Ryland straightened. "What's that exactly, sir?"

"It's a key to the codes we use when sending top secret information by telegram."

"So the enemy has the code now?"

"Yes, but you have to understand—as soon as we heard about the incident, we issued a new cipher key."

"So, even if the Rebs got hold of the old one, it won't work for them."

Strouse shrugged. "There are always delays in communication and updating our methods. But yes, we feel fairly confident that the cipher has not been compromised. Anyone receiving a message using the old code words now would immediately suspect that something was up."

"I see."

"You're good at tracking people?" Strouse asked.

"Well, that's my job, sir."

Strouse grunted. "We have good men in the army, but so far ..."

"Sir, do you think I could go to where Mr. Miller was captured? Perhaps I might find something."

Strouse picked up a pen from the desktop, shaking his head. "Not a good idea, Atkins. Things are still unstable in north Georgia."

"Surely the Rebels have been subdued there."

"There are rogue bands doing damage to our supply lines and communications channels. And the local people are very resentful. If a Yankee stranger showed up asking questions, who knows what they'd do to him? And their irregulars seem to be organizing."

A brief knock came at the open door, and Strouse looked up. "Yes, what is it?"

An aide came in and handed him a folded sheet of paper. "This just came in, sir. It was sent in plaintext from north Georgia, just below the Tennessee border."

Strouse unfolded the paper and frowned at it. "Plaintext, you say?"

"Yes, sir. And there's a Mrs. Grayson asking to see you. She's out in the hallway."

Ryland caught his breath.

"It's related to this matter?" Strouse's eyebrows rose.

"I believe so, sir. She runs a boardinghouse in the city, and she received a message from a former boarder of hers this morning from the same station where this was sent out."

Ryland's heart stuttered and then raced on. "She's Jack Miller's landlady, sir. She sent a message to his father when Charles Miller tried to contact him."

"Show her in," Strouse said. He tossed the paper on the desk in Ryland's direction, and he picked it up.

FOUND KEY, HEADED BACK PORCH.

He frowned at Strouse. It might be plaintext, but it was obviously coded.

A plump, middle-aged woman came in, her eyes casting glances about the room and settling on Strouse, who rose from his chair behind the desk.

"Mrs. Grayson?" Strouse said.

"Yes." She walked over to him, ignoring Ryland. "I received an odd telegraphic message this morning, and I thought you should know. You were Jack Miller's employer when he was here in the city, were you not?"

"I was his supervisor, yes."

She rummaged in a taffeta purse and pulled out a folded slip of paper, which she turned over to Strouse.

He opened it and read it silently, then raised his eyes to meet hers.

"And you're certain this came from Jack Miller?"

"He's the only man named Jack who's boarded with me, sir."

Strouse nodded. "May I keep this?"

"Yes. I figured if he wanted to tell me something I should know, he'd have said it. Seems to me he wanted you to know this bit about Chattanooga."

"I agree, and I thank you very much. Er ..." Strouse glanced at Ryland then back to Mrs. Grayson. "Did you incur any expense in getting this to me, ma'am?"

"No, just wear and tear on the shoe leather."

"I'm sorry. It would please me to hire a cab to take you home."

Mrs. Grayson shrugged and looked at the floor. "No need."

She didn't sound too convincing to Ryland.

"I insist." Strouse strode to the door and opened it. "Carter, please give Mrs. Grayson a dollar for cab fare home and escort her down to the street. Make sure she finds a ride."

"Of course." The aide came to the doorway and smiled at the woman. "Come with me, madam."

Strouse turned to Mrs. Grayson. "Again, thank you for your help in this."

"Do you think Jack's all right?" she asked.

Strouse hesitated just a moment. "That's impossible to say, but I hope so. He seems to indicate that he's heading back this way, so perhaps before long he'll show up on your doorstep."

"Where has he been?" Her voice was stronger now, as though she wanted some answers.

Strouse gave her a serene smile. "I'm sorry, that's government business, ma'am, and I'm not allowed to disclose anything about the matter. But this telegram is a good sign. A very good sign."

He watched her leave with the aide then closed the door. Turning back toward Ryland, he let out a deep breath. "Well, Atkins, you heard the lady. I don't suppose there's any harm in you seeing this."

Ryland was surprised that he held out the printed telegram. He read the terse message:

PLEASE TELL MY EMPLOYER HEADED CHATTANOOGA. JACK.

He raised his eyebrows. "You think he's escaped his captors?"

"It seems likely. Miller is a resourceful man. I'd about given up hope for him. I thought, at the least, he was languishing in one of their prisons. But it seems he's on the way back. I'm sure the key he mentions in the first message refers to his cipher key, and 'back porch' is an old code designation for Chattanooga. He probably sent the landlady's telegram first, in case he couldn't get off a secure message to me."

"Chattanooga, Tennessee? I want to go and try to find him."

With a frown, Strouse said, "You might miss him on the way."

"Or not. And if he was in Georgia and is headed to Chattanooga, that means he's not there yet. I could go to Chattanooga and wait for him. The city is in Union hands, is it not?"

"Yes, but ..." Strouse frowned.

"What is it?"

"Miller is one of our cryptographers. It seems odd he didn't encrypt this message further."

"Perhaps he thought that would draw more attention than a few plain words," Ryland said.

' "True." Strouse sighed. "Mrs. Grayson's address is more innocuous than the War Department's headquarters. Yes, he must have found a way to send the second telegram when he had some expectation it would reach me undetected." He waved a hand. "Go if you wish. I'll see that you get a pass on the rails to Chattanooga. If you don't find him quickly, or if for any reason it seems the town is threatened by hostile forces, come straight back here. Do you understand, Atkins?"

"I think so."

"Good. I hope to see you again soon—preferably with Jack Miller. But if you don't make contact with him, I'd still appreciate a report on the matter. Don't use his name in a telegram or a letter, whatever you do."

Ryland's mind whirled. "Perhaps you could give me a code word to use in place of Mr. Miller's name?"

At that, Strouse gave him a smile. "I'd try to recruit you if I thought it would do any good, Atkins. Say you've found the property. If all is well, you hope to purchase it. If not, it's a disappointment, and you won't buy it after all."

It made as much sense as anything. "And where shall I send such a message, sir?"

January 7, 1865

MARILLA AND JACK stuck to the main road, walking always toward Chattanooga. Whenever a wagon, a horseman, or a pedestrian came along, they got off the road. If possible, they took cover to avoid being seen, but sometimes only open fields surrounded them, so they went a few yards off the road and sat down, giving the passersby a languid wave.

They'd had to head straight north and a little westward in order to target Chattanooga. The distance to the Tennessee border was more than if they'd gone northeast from where they started, but Jack was reasonably sure they'd come into territory held firmly by Union troops sooner if they steered this way.

The air was cool, but not uncomfortably so.

"Just think," Marilla said in midafternoon. "Your family is probably shoveling snow today."

Jack smiled. "Maybe."

"How long until we reach Dalton?" Marilla had learned from Dr. Stevens that Dalton was the biggest town between them and the Chattanooga.

"I doubt we'll get there today or tomorrow."

He thought they were still in too much danger to seek a ride, and Marilla had to agree. They came to a village before sundown, and Jack scouted out an empty stable on the outskirts of town.

"You stay here," he told her. "I'll see if I can buy us something to eat and get a little news."

She gave him two dimes and huddled in the increasingly cold building, wishing she'd insisted on going with him. She ought to have taken some of her great-uncle's cash after all, to supplement what little she had. Her funds were dwindling fast. She still had her jewelry. Maybe she could sell a piece or two, though she hated to.

Jack returned an hour later with half a dozen biscuits and a rather punky apple, which he presented to her with a flourish.

"I ate one on the way, I was so hungry. This one is yours."

While they ate their meager supper, he told her earnestly, "We need to be extra careful. I'm told there's a band of irregulars hereabouts."

"What's that?" she asked.

"Like Vernon's men—not part of the army, but sort of a home guard. They're trying to keep the peace here."

"And keep out any stray Yankees?"

"Well, they are Confederates."

She ate every bit of the apple except the seeds and started on one of the biscuits.

"I'm told they're well organized," Jack said. "Much bigger than Vernon's group. Hundreds of men, maybe thousands. The governor's behind it, because of the chaos after Sherman's visit. They're called the Department of North Georgia, and they have a real army general over them."

Chewing as she considered her words, she shook her head. "But they're not part of the Confederate Army?"

"It's kind of confusing," Jack said. "I'm not really certain of their status. But I think we've been lucky so far. We might have to travel at night now and take back roads."

"We'll never get to Chattanooga that way."

Creases formed at the corners of his eyes as he gazed out the doorway of their refuge. "If we could just run into a Union force."

"Are they all gone from this area? I thought there were Union troops around here."

"Well, yeah. I think when we get to the railroad we'll find them. They have to protect the lines."

"Where will that be?"

"Dalton, I guess. But I know the 5th Tennessee Cavalry is patrolling the Nashville & Chattanooga lines to protect them from bushwhacking raiders."

She nodded. So-called bushwhackers were Southern sympathizers. "So, we keep going as we were."

"If we can get into Tennessee, I think we'll be all right. But not now. We rest until full dark. Are you going to eat that other biscuit?"

She wanted to just give it to him, but she was still hungry. "We can split it."

Jack grinned and picked it up, broke it in two, and gave her the slightly larger half.

January 8, 1865

RYLAND STEPPED off the train in Chattanooga and looked around. He was in a different world. He'd grown up in the North, and he'd survived the West. But he wasn't sure he could make his way in the South.

For one thing, he hardly understood the local lingo, and the accents baffled him. To tell the truth, he was a little bit scared of all the black men he encountered. He didn't think slavery was right, but he wasn't used to being around people so unlike him, and he found it unsettling.

"Pick up your luggage over there, suh," the conductor said, and Ryland realized he was trying to get him to move on so the passengers behind him could disembark.

He only had the bag he was carrying, so he took a few steps onto the platform.

One of the Negro men approached him with his head bowed. "Carry your bag, suh?"

"Uh, well ..." Of course, Ryland realized the man hoped he'd pay him to do so. "I'm not sure. Is there a hotel close by?"

"Yassuh, lots o' hotels an' shops. Eateries too."

A man in a Union uniform was passing and said curtly, "There's a good place on Ninth Street."

Now, that Massachusetts accent Ryland recognized.

"Hold up, sir. I'm sorry, but I'm from Maine, and I feel lost."

The soldier pivoted and grinned at him. "He's hoping you'll pay him two bits—or at least a dime—to carry your luggage, sir, or maybe call you a cab." He nodded toward a group of black men standing near the depot door. "Those are freedmen. They were slaves, but they've come here because Chattanooga is

Union occupied. They hope to earn some money and support themselves."

Ryland nodded. He would be happy to support the cause of freedom. His paid expenses were not unlimited, but surely he could do this small thing.

"Thank you," he called after the departing soldier. He turned back to the hovering man. "What is your name?"

"Mory, suh."

"Mory. Can you take me to a decent hotel, and not too far away?"

He gave a broad smile. "Ah surely can, suh."

On the way, Ryland told Mory his name and asked questions —lots of questions. He learned that one of the larger hotels had a telegraph office in its lobby.

"Take me there."

Mory eyed him with caution. "That's kinda ha priced, Mistuh Atkins."

Ryland deduced that "ha priced" did not mean laughable. It meant expensive. They soon established that the big hotel was on their path to the slightly less grand one Mory had in mind.

"Take me there first," Ryland said. "I'll visit the telegraph office, and if the rooms are too high-priced, you can take me to the other hotel."

In the lobby, he sent short telegrams to Strouse and Mr. Turner, his boss back in Maine.

ARRIVED CHATTANOOGA.

Then he turned to Mory, who was fast becoming his trusted lieutenant.

"All right, a less grand hotel, and then I need to know how to contact a commanding officer of the Union army in this town."

Mory scratched his chin through his beard. "Well, Mistuh Atkins, suh, ah don't know none of them myself, but my cousin, he joined up, and he told me about it. Ah think we can find somebody who can tell us what you wanna know."

It was good enough for Ryland, and they set off together.

January 12, 1865
Dalton, Georgia

MARILLA AND JACK crept into Dalton just after sunset, dirty and exhausted. Jack found a place for Marilla to wait unobserved with her bag while he checked on the situation at the depot. What he saw there sent him scurrying back to her hiding place.

"What is it?" she asked after one look at his face.

"There are at least half a dozen men guarding the depot."

"Yankees?"

"I don't think so. No recognizable uniforms. I didn't dare approach the ticket window."

Marilla frowned. "What if I go? I can inquire innocently about a ticket to go and visit my aunt in Tennessee."

Jack hesitated, but he couldn't think of a better plan. "All right, go." He ducked behind the shed where she'd waited and sat down in the grass. His heart wouldn't slow down, and he couldn't help imagining unpleasant things that could happen to Marilla.

She came back about ten minutes later, breathing fast, with a sheen of perspiration on her forehead.

"Those men," she declared, plopping down beside him. "They're part of what's called Wofford's Scouts. As you said, they belong to a larger outfit."

"Then the Rebs have control of the depot?"

"Yes, for now. They've wrested it from the Yankees. But the Yanks tore up the tracks a few miles north of town night before last. There's a crew working on them, but men are scarce. They've hired some blacks as laborers, and a couple of slave owners have sent what field hands they have left. They hope to have a usable track by tomorrow."

Jack sighed and looked up at the sky. Darkness was falling, and he could make out clusters of stars.

"I hoped the Union was in control here. I guess we'd better hoof it and keep clear of the tracks. We don't want to run into one of their overseers."

A flurry of hoofbeats sounded on the other side of the shed as a dozen men rode up to the depot. Shouting followed, but Jack couldn't make out the words.

"Stay here," he told Marilla. He crept to the corner of the shed. The horses circled and stamped near the platform, and several men had dismounted. One large man stayed in the saddle and carried on a conversation with the summoned stationmaster in a clarion voice.

"They must have come through here."

Jack felt movement behind him and jerked around to find Marilla at his elbow. He was about to tell her to go back when she sucked in a quick breath.

"It's him," she whispered. "It's Uncle Hamilton."

28

January 13, 1865
Chattanooga, Tennessee

"I want to go with your men, Major Kelly." Ryland said, sitting straight and trying to project confidence.

"I don't know, Atkins. I don't like my men to have to worry about civilians, and your matter doesn't sound urgent to me."

"Please, sir. It's urgent to his family. I received word this morning that his grandmother has taken ill, and she has her heart set on seeing the young man before she dies. And after all, Jack Miller is a civilian himself."

"Yes, but working under the auspices of the War Department. We sent him out there, and it's our job to bring him back."

"But if he's in trouble, sir, I'd like to help him. I did find his older brother."

Ryland thought of how he'd landed in the middle of danger in Colorado and wound up needing a bit of rescuing himself, but he wasn't about to tell that to Major Kelly. He hoped he'd learned something from his earlier excursions.

The major shook his head. Before he could speak again, Ryland rushed in.

"If Miller had reached the city, he'd have contacted the army immediately, and you'd know. He's not here yet. Sir, I won't hold your men at all responsible. If anything happens to me, it's all on my head." The major looked for a moment as though he wavered, and Ryland added, "I'm going south anyway, sir. And they're going south. Is there any reason I can't travel along with the detachment?"

"You're not armed, and I'm not going to arm you."

Ryland gulped. His experience with firearms was limited, and he hadn't planned on expanding it. But he'd been stymied too many times in his search for Elijah Cooper, and he was tired of it.

"I understand, sir, but one way or another, I'm heading for the area from which the War Department believes my man sent a telegram. If I get to that point and don't find him, I'll turn back and scour the roads between there and Chattanooga." He tried to sound brave. He wouldn't go back to Maine emptyhanded again.

"I guess I can't stop you."

"That's right. You can't."

With a sigh, the major dipped his pen in ink and reached for a sheet of paper. "Go to Fort Lytle in the morning. Ask for Captain Nason. Be there by seven o'clock, and be prepared to leave from there. Do you have a horse?"

"No, sir."

"Well, you'd better find one or be prepared for an awful lot of marching."

Mory had said he could be found at the railroad depot if Ryland had further need of him. Surely Mory would know where he could buy a horse—and, he hoped, how to tell a good horse from a poor one.

January 14, 1865
Portland, Maine

ABBY BENSON GREETED the mailman with a smile.

"A letter for Mrs. Rose and this postcard, Miss Benson."

He handed over the items, and Abby looked down at the postcard. Its front held a drawing of the White House in Washington, D.C. Her smile grew into a grin.

"Thank you!"

She ran inside and paused in the entry to flip over the postcard. It was addressed to her, not her grandmother.

> *Told you I'd get one! All well so far but no precise news on E.C.*
> *On to points South.*
> *R. Atkins.*

Abby held the card to her heart for a moment, then shoved it in a pocket and walked into the parlor.

"You've got a letter from Cousin Lila, Grandmother."

JACK AND MARILLA ran all night. Occasionally they paused for breath, but they didn't dare stop for long. They'd been cutting through fields and orchards but staying parallel to the road for an hour when a band of three horsemen charged past, headed north. The fleeing pair waited a quarter hour and set off cautiously. When Jack thought it might be safe, he angled back toward the road.

"Should we leave my bag?" Marilla asked. "We could put the jewels in our pockets."

Jack was tired of lugging the carpetbag, but he didn't think abandoning it would be wise.

"They might find it. Buckley would recognize your things."

"We could hide it."

He shook his head. "It's all right. Come on."

A creek crossed their path. He'd have waded through, but he didn't want to ask that of Marilla. The stream was at least four yards wide and could be deep.

"Let's get to the road," he said. "There'll be a bridge."

They'd nearly reached it when she grabbed his arm. "Stop. Hear that?"

Jack stood still and strained his ears. Hoofbeats, coming up from the south. "Get down!"

Both crouched in the weeds on the stream bank as several horses cantered toward them.

"Whoa!" The riders halted not ten yards from him, but still Jack heard hoofbeats. Half a minute later, more horsemen rode down from the north. He risked a quick peek. Though he couldn't be sure, he thought it was the three who had passed them earlier.

"Any sign?" called a man.

"Nothing," replied one who Jack would have sworn was Zeke Vernon.

"I'll beat that skunk to a bloody pulp." That was unmistakably Buckley.

Marilla grabbed Jack's wrist and he patted her hand.

"They must have come this way," Buckley said.

"We know he sent a telegram back there," Vernon replied. "He's going for Chattanooga."

"Agreed. The fool probably thinks this is all still in Yankee hands, like it was when he was taken."

"He won't be able to keep up the pace for long," Vernon said. "It's not like you overfed him whilst he was in the cellar."

Several of the men laughed.

"It's Marilla I'm worried about," Buckley said. "Who knows what that demon has done to her."

"Yes, suh," Vernon said gravely. "We need to defend her honor."

"Honor." Buckley spat on the ground. "She's got no honor

left now. She's gone Yankee through and through. I should've seen it earlier. After all, her mother was a Yank."

"Keep heading for the border?" Vernon asked.

"Yeah, let's ride. The others can catch up. And if I catch that boy, he'll wish he'd never crossed the line."

The horses thundered away.

"Should we go back?" Marilla hissed.

Jack thought for a minute, his heart racing. "No. If they don't find sign of us soon, they'll be back. Let's get over the bridge and then go farther off the road but keep heading north."

She glanced up at the sky. "Lead the way."

The moonlight shone on her pale face, and for a moment Jack thought she looked like one of those marble goddess statues in Europe. A beautiful statue. Instead of slowing down, his pulse kept hammering. What would happen if he kissed her?

He forced himself to look away and swallowed hard. This wasn't the time. But maybe later he would think about that.

He set out, careful to choose a path that would leave few traces of their passing. He would be able to move a little faster alone, it was true, but when it came right down to it, Marilla wasn't such a bad traveling companion. She was plucky, and she was persistent. In fact, he could think of very few people he'd rather make this journey with.

A cluster of horsemen soon went past, and he was sure they were Buckley's remaining henchmen. They walked for another hour well off the road and heard the plodding steps of one workhorse pulling a creaky wagon. A farmer headed home late, Jack surmised.

A hedgerow separated two fields. Jack followed it far out away from the byway and turned to Marilla.

"Let's rest here an hour."

"Are you sure?" He glimpsed relief in her eyes.

"Yes. I don't know about you, but I'm tuckered out. If we rest a bit, we can continue on until dawn."

"I'm tired too."

They burrowed into the hedgerow and sat side by side, their shoulders touching. After a long silence, Marilla said softly, "I shouldn't have made you bring me."

"Why do you say that?"

"You could have been in Chattanooga by now if you were alone."

He shook his head. "I don't think I'd have gotten this far without you."

They sat in silence once more. If Hamilton Buckley found them, Jack knew he would die. Probably in a painful manner. But what of Marilla? Would he drag her back to River Lea? He certainly wouldn't let her go on northward alone.

"Marilla—" As he turned toward her, she shifted to look at him, and their faces were only inches apart in the moonlight.

"What is it, Jack?"

His mouth went dry. He wanted to kiss her more than anything, but he couldn't do that. It would be taking advantage of her in this difficult situation. He swallowed hard and lifted his hand to her cheek.

"Marilla ..."

Her lips were on his. Jack wanted to take her in his arms, but he didn't dare. They lingered for a long moment in a sweet, tender kiss. He pulled back with a little sigh. She looked so lovely, and yet so vulnerable.

"Jack, if they do catch up with us, you run. Don't worry about me."

"I can't."

"But they won't hurt me, at least not too badly."

"Are you sure?"

She didn't answer.

Jack wasn't at all sure. Hamilton Buckley did not like to be crossed—by anyone. He slid his arm around Marilla. She was warm, and she leaned closer, laying her head on his shoulder.

MORY MET Ryland outside the hotel before dawn. Ryland paused and stared at the animals whose reins Mory held.

"You got two horses."

"They're mules," Mory said.

Ryland took note of the long ears, but they were big animals —as tall as respectable saddlehorses.

"Why two?"

"One for me."

"Where are you going?"

Mory looked down at the ground. "I thought maybe I'd join up with the Federals."

"Oh." Ryland was a bit chagrinned and a wee bit embarrassed, since he had no inclination to put on a uniform. "I guess they have Negro regiments."

"Yessuh." Mory's lips tightened. "Or mebbe I could come along with you. As your hired man. I could take care of the mules and see that you get meals, Mr. Atkins. Whatever you need done."

Ryland stared at him. "Did I pay for your mount?"

"Yessuh. What you gave me was enough for two. Not hosses, but good mules. And saddles."

Ryland nodded. He'd wondered when he handed that much cash over to Mory if he'd ever see him again.

"How much would I pay you?"

Mory smiled. "If I could keep this here mule when we's done ..."

"It's a deal."

Mory grinned big then.

Within twenty-four hours, Ryland knew he'd got the best end of the bargain, and he intended to give Mory a cash bonus when they were through—provided, of course, that they survived.

However, for some reason Mory's mule was content to keep up with the mounts of Captain Nason's detachment, but his own liked to drag its feet. Consequently, Ryland had to constantly prod it with his heels, which he found immensely tiring.

For the umpteenth time, he urged the mule to catch up, and Mory turned his head to look back at him, grinning. "You want I should switch with you, Mr. Atkins? I'll teach that mule what for."

Although that sounded like a lovely idea, Ryland shook his head. The fifty or so soldiers with whom they were traveling already thought he was a slacker because he hadn't joined the army. If he gave Mory the slothful mule, they'd think even less of him.

A sudden *boom* ahead caused the entire column to halt.

"Fall back," yelled their scout, who'd ridden a bit ahead.

Mory was instantly beside Ryland, reaching for his mule's bridle. "Come on, suh. He done said 'fall back.' That what we got to do."

The horsemen backtracked a couple hundred yards, then halted. The soldiers bunched up so they could hear their captain's orders. Quickly he sent two sergeants with details of four men each to go out on each side, to gain information. A few locals could be swiftly dealt with, but if a substantial force of Confederates was out there, Nason needed to know now.

"Civilians stay well in the rear," he called out at the end of his orders, and Ryland and Mory, being the only two such persons in the company, willingly complied.

Mory seemed a little excited at the prospect of action, but Ryland sat astride the stubborn mule, his heart thumping like a kettledrum and his chest aching with tension. Had he made a fatal mistake by joining Nason's outfit? Had they ridden blithely into a deathtrap?

It seemed like a year, but in actuality was probably only twenty minutes before some of the outriders returned.

"Looks like about a dozen men, Cap'n," the sergeant reported. "No uniforms, except the old guy leadin' 'em is wearin' a jacket that could be military. He's tellin' his fellers they're going to give us h—"

"We'll see about that," Captain Nason replied. He quickly

divvied up his subordinates and issued new orders but said nothing pertaining to civilians.

By brute force, Ryland sidled his mule closer to Mory's.

"Think we should stay back here?"

Mory didn't look surprised at his employer's hesitance, or that fact that he was asking a humble freedman for advice. They both knew the truth—Mory had more experience than Ryland both in the South and in matters pertaining to mules.

"Well, suh." Mory's eyes sparkled in the moonlight. "Seems to me we'd be safer if we stick close to the soldiers."

Ryland swallowed hard. The detachment was beginning to fan out, toward where the enemy lay.

"You may be right," he said, not really believing it. "Let's go."

JACK STOPPED SO SUDDENLY that Marilla almost ran into his back. For the last half hour, she'd paid no attention to where they went. She just trudged along behind him, half asleep on her aching feet.

"What is it?" she asked.

"Listen."

She did, and her pulse raced. "That's gunfire!"

"Yes."

"Should we hide?"

Jack was actually smiling. "Don't you see? That means there are Yankees nearby. If we can get to them, they'll help us."

She caught her breath. "Do you think Uncle Hamilton and his men are fighting them?"

"I don't know, but they never came back on the road we're nearest. It could be someone else altogether."

Marilla swallowed hard. "What should we do?"

"Let's advance, but cautiously. If we get close and they're still shooting, we'll circle west of the fray, then try to get close enough to see whether any of them are in uniform."

It sounded dangerous, but Marilla didn't question Jack's judgment, not after all they'd been through together. And she certainly didn't want to be left behind. No, she wouldn't let Jack out of her sight now.

Of course, if she hid and waited for him here, he could go reconnoiter and come back for her when it was safe.

But if anything happened to Jack and he didn't return, she'd be helpless. She touched her lips, remembering that magical kiss and knew she'd rather be with Jack than be safe.

RYLAND COWERED IN THE SADDLE, willing himself and his mule to shrink smaller, so that the thin copse of trees where they sheltered would better hide them. He wished he had a gun. Anything, even a derringer. He was an idiot not to have bought one in Chattanooga. Here he was, over the Georgia line into hostile territory, defenseless. He hadn't even brought along the sword cane he'd had on his trip west.

Mory, on the other hand, seemed perfectly happy to be this close to a battle. He'd surely never had the opportunity to get his hands on a gun, but that didn't make him cringe and shudder or try to run away—a course of action that kept flitting through Ryland's mind.

Two shots banged out from just on the other side of the copse, where he knew a few of Nason's men had taken cover, and his mule tossed its head and tried to turn around. Of necessity, Ryland was improving in his horsemanship, and, though it went against his own instincts, he managed to keep the jittery animal from fleeing.

"Hallooo!"

Startled, Ryland realized the voice came from behind him. Had the Rebels flanked them? Mory stared at him, his terrified eyes wide.

"Don't shoot," the voice called out. "I'm a friend."

"Wha—" Ryland jerked the mule around and stared into the dark foliage. Was this a trick? He couldn't shoot if he wanted to. But the stranger in the darkness didn't know that.

"Show yo'self, suh," Mory cried, and Ryland thought that quite brave of him.

"I'm coming out," the man shouted. "I'm a civilian and I mean you no harm. Please don't shoot."

"Awright, but put your hands up," Mory replied.

The bushes stirred, and Ryland heard footsteps—not hoofbeats. A shape took form and oozed closer. He caught his breath. There were two of them, not one. It had to be a trap!

"Hold it, mistuh," Mory called.

The shadows stopped moving. They had no horses, and Ryland couldn't see any long guns. He cleared his throat.

"State your business."

More rifle fire sounded to Ryland's left, a little farther away than before.

"I'm a civilian from Pennsylvania," the man said. "I have with me a lady who is also a northern sympathizer and is trying to leave the South. Can you help us?"

Ryland blinked and stared at them. Sure enough, he could make out the sweeping lines of a skirt on the second figure.

"Sir, you're in danger here," he said. "A detachment of Union soldiers has run into a band of local raiders, and they could tear through here at any minute."

"We're aware," the newcomer said. "In fact, there was a band of a dozen men following us, hoping to recapture me and take the lady back to a situation she does not wish to continue in."

Curious, Ryland squeezed his mule's sides, but the animal was reluctant now to move at all. The skirmish had drifted away from them, and they only heard an occasional volley of shots, perhaps half a mile away.

Ryland made a quick decision and dismounted. He was always more comfortable when he had the solid earth under his feet. Mory threw him a surprised glance and hopped down as well, reaching for the reins of Ryland's mule.

As he approached the man and woman, they walked toward him, meeting him under the trees. Dawn was still at least an hour away, and Ryland couldn't make out much, except that the woman looked young. The man was taller than he was, but gangly. He wasn't old, but he had an air of tired maturity about him.

"I'm Ryland Atkins." He held out his hand. "I'm a civilian as well. My friend and I are traveling with the military detachment."

The thin man nodded and glanced over at Mory. Even in the darkness, it was obvious that Ryland's friend was a black man. Well, what of it, he thought defensively. Mory was a good man and diligent. Under any circumstances, Ryland would be happy to call him friend. And now, in these desperate times, he didn't know anyone he'd rather have at his back, unless it was Matt Anderson.

"This is Miss Buckley, and I'm Jack Miller."

Ryland had turned a tentative smile on the lady, but he jerked his gaze back to the man.

"What did you say?"

"I said, this is Miss—"

"Not that. Your name."

After the briefest hesitation, the man said, "Jack Miller."

Ryland laughed aloud.

"Hsst," came Mory's warning, and Ryland looked around with a tinge of guilt. They might not be safe, after all.

He stepped closer to the stranger and lowered his voice. "Mr. Miller, if you're who I think you are, my work is over. I've been looking for you for almost two years."

"Why?" Miller said warily.

Unable to hold back a wide grin, Ryland asked, "Does the name Elijah Cooper mean anything to you?"

MARILLA WATCHED JACK CLOSELY. He stood perfectly still, staring at Mr. Atkins and taking short, shallow breaths.

"What do you know of the Cooper family?" he asked.

"Actually, quite a lot," Atkins replied.

"Mistuh Atkins!" The black man hurried over as quickly as he could while tugging on the reins of two mules. "Suh, they's getting' closer!"

They all turned their heads toward the sounds of random shots and galloping hooves.

"Get back," Jack cried. He seized Marilla's hand and yanked her farther into the trees.

Several horses thundered up, some halting very close to them, just outside the tree line. Shouts and staccato shots filled the air. A horse screamed, and Marilla heard the clash of a sword on metal.

"Forward, men! Don't let them get away."

Surely the speaker was a Yankee. She clung to Jack's hand as they crouched in the meager underbrush.

"You scoundrels! Don't think y'all can waltz in and ambush a detachment of Wofford's Scouts!"

She caught her breath. Those were the irregulars they'd learned about several days ago. Jack squeezed her hand and nodded in the moonlight. Glad her dress was made of dark calico, Marilla huddled lower, trying to make herself invisible.

The fighting intensified as the two forces clashed. Several shots went off, then one group retired, probably to reload their weapons, but Marilla could still hear their opponents talking among themselves nearby. This time she picked out the drawls of Georgians.

"Be ready, now. When they charge us agin, we'll git 'em. Rahht, Colonel?"

The man addressed answered in the affirmative and let out a string of oaths against the enemy.

Marilla gasped. "That's Uncle!"

"Thought I recognized Vernon's voice too," Jack whispered.

A distant shout came, and the thunder of charging horses. Jack pulled Marilla farther from the fray, taking advantage of the noise of the attack to cover their own retreat.

"What do we do now?" she asked when they stopped on the edge of a fallow field.

"Wait. If the Yankees win, we go with them. If your uncle and the Scouts win, we hide until they leave."

"What about that Atkins man?"

"I don't know."

"Jack, he knows your family."

He let out a big breath. "Sure seems like it."

"Do you think we can trust him?"

"I'm not sure. He says he's been looking for me." Jack frowned. "If we survive this, and that Atkins fella lives through it, maybe we'll get some answers. That's all we can do now."

"And pray. We can pray, Jack."

"Yeah. That too."

RYLAND RAN THROUGH THE TREES, leading his mule. As usual, Mory's mule moved faster than his, even with the noise of battle close behind.

"Mount up, Mistuh Atkins," Mory shouted when they were clear of the woods. "We best get outa heeuh."

"But—" Ryland wanted to protest. He'd spent months chasing down Jack Miller, and he'd finally found him. He couldn't run away now. And what about the girl with him? They couldn't leave the two helpless.

On the other hand, how could they assist them with no weapons?

As he swung reluctantly into the saddle, it struck Ryland that they could share their transportation with the hapless pair.

People rode double on horses and mules all the time. Of course, his mule was so cantankerous, it would probably refuse to take a step if it were loaded with the weight of two human beings.

But it would be wrong to just ride off and leave them behind. Even if he hadn't found the man he'd spent so much time and effort seeking, his conscience wouldn't let him abandon a young lady in such horrific straits.

Before he could voice a single one of his tumultuous thoughts, a heavyset man about twice his age erupted from the trees on horseback. In the gray of dawn, Ryland saw him plainly, an enraged crusader with hatred in his eyes. Another horseman came behind him, but the leader kept Ryland's attention—or perhaps it was the sword he brandished over his head as his mount wheezed heavily, clumping past Ryland toward Mory.

"You blasted—" A foul name came out of the man's mouth, and Ryland saw with sudden clarity that the man was full of battle madness and about to fall on his friend with a sword.

Mory's eyes went wild and he jerked his mule around. The madman came even with Ryland, moving straight as an arrow toward the black man and passing so close that Ryland's knee nearly brushed his.

"No!" Without another clear thought, Ryland flung himself off his mule and jumped to put his full weight on the man's sword arm. He carried them to the ground, both man and blade. At once, Ryland lit into his opponent, determined not to give the older man a chance to lift the sword again.

The hefty man's breath whooshed out of him as he hit the ground, and he lost his grip on the sword. The butt of a pistol poked Ryland in the ribs, and he saw that the attacker had it holstered under his coat. He grabbed it and drew it out.

"Colonel!" The second horseman charged toward them.

Ryland had no time to plan or regret. He swung the pistol around and fired.

The oncoming horse screamed and shied violently to his left, and the rider hung in the saddle a moment, staring open-mouthed at Ryland, then tumbled to the ground.

Shocked that he'd hit his target, Ryland ran to him and took the fallen man's carbine from his lifeless hands and whirled to find Mory tackling the big man who'd waved the sword.

He ran closer and shouted, "Mory, get off him! Mory!"

His friend looked over his shoulder with a dazed stare.

"We'll take him prisoner," Ryland said.

As Mory backed hesitantly away from the colonel, more horses burst from the trees. His heart in his throat, Ryland glanced their way and slumped his shoulders in relief when he saw blue uniforms.

"We have a prisoner, Captain," he called. "The other man said he's a colonel."

Nason rode over close and leveled a pistol at the big man. "Nice job, Atkins. Sergeant Willis, take the prisoner into custody."

At a faint hail, Nason swung around and squinted at two figures running toward them along the edge of the field.

"Is that a woman?"

Ryland's knees had begun trembling, but he managed a smile. "Yes, sir. That's a Miss Buckley and the man I was looking for—Jack Miller. They want sanctuary with you."

The young couple hurried to them and arrived gasping.

"Miller, as I live and breathe!" Nason grinned at Jack.

"Sir," Jack said between breaths. "Is the fighting done?"

"Yes, it is. We've taken half a dozen prisoners. The rest, I fear, rode off. I expect to hear quite a tale from you later."

"Yes, sir." Jack looked quickly at the disheveled young woman. "Miss Marilla Buckley, may I introduce Captain—"

He broke off. Miss Buckley was staring past him toward the soldiers and their newest prisoner.

"Sir," one of the soldiers called.

Nason pivoted in the saddle, and Ryland wheeled toward the

men surrounding the colonel. The big man clutched his chest and swayed on his feet.

"Sir, he's—"

"Uncle!" Miss Buckley held her skirts up a few inches and ran to the colonel just as he sank to his knees and sprawled prone on the ground.

29

"And so they sent me out with fifty cavalrymen to keep the rebels away from our supply line and watch out for the crews who are reconstructing the rail and telegraph lines they've ripped up. These so-called scouts have wreaked havoc along the lines." Captain Nason shook his head. "And of course the Telegraph Division asked me to sniff around for some word of you, Miller."

"I'm glad you did, sir."

Nason barked a short laugh. "Well, I'll have to admit to my commanding officer and Colonel Strouse that we didn't find you. You found us."

The campfire they sat near blazed cheerfully, and Jack watched the flames, remembering all the freezing nights he'd spent in the cellar at River Lea. "We figured we were better off trying to cross into Tennessee than South Carolina right now. Of course, our knowledge of troop movements on either side was limited. Miss Buckley and I actually thought we might find some empathy in this region."

"I suppose you would, if you looked under the right magnolia tree."

"I'm sorry about Lieutenant Peterson," Jack said.

"Well, he was the only one of my men wounded in this incident. It's a flesh wound. We'll get him to the field hospital and deliver our prisoners."

They had set up camp while the soldiers sorted things out and everyone had breakfast. Soon they would be on their way again. The captain had promised Jack a horse, and Marilla could ride in one of the wagons that followed the detachment with supplies.

Jack reached into his pocket and drew out a small leatherbound notebook. "I did manage to retrieve this, sir, but I suppose it's worthless now."

Nason arched his eyebrows. "Your cipher book? I'm sure they changed all the keys weeks ago." He eyed Jack keenly. "We all thought you were dead by now. We knew you'd been captured when the telegraph crew was attacked, but no one could get a trace of you after that. The War Department put out inquiries, hoping for a prisoner exchange, but the Confederate higher-ups seemed to have no record of your capture or incarceration. We feared the worst."

"It was Colonel Buckley. He had some grand delusion that he could use my cipher book to get secret information that would give him clout with their Congress and get him a high position in their new government. He just didn't understand how far down the chain I was."

Nason frowned. "You and your ilk are very important, Miller."

"I'm sure you're right, but it's not like we're irreplaceable." Jack shifted on the wood-and-canvas camp stool. "Thank you for giving Miss Buckley a tent, sir."

"That's nothing. I wish I could do more for her than a hot meal and some canvas. We'll take her back with us, of course, and put her on a train for Washington or wherever she likes. I'm just sorry her nearest relative died this morning."

Jack hesitated. "It's not the same as if he was shot, Captain."

"No, our medical man says it was heart failure."

"The shock of seeing his great-niece, do you think, or that of being taken prisoner by insolent Yankees?"

Nason chuckled. "We'll never know. But you said the man Atkins plugged was from his plantation?"

"His overseer, name of Zeke Vernon. A cruel man. I understand Buckley hired him to keep his slaves in line. He seemed to do all the planter's dirty work from what I could tell."

"Sounds like he's no loss to society."

Jack shrugged.

"Now tell me about this Atkins fellow," the captain persisted.

Jack huffed out a breath. "I've promised to have a confab with him when you and I are done. You probably know more about him than I do."

"He's been with us four days, since Chattanooga. Said he was on a mission to find you, but not for Washington."

"No, I take it this is a family matter." Jack didn't want to get into the details of his background, but he was very curious as to what—or who—had sent Ryland Atkins all this way to find him in the middle of a war.

"And Miss Buckley? She has other family members in the North?"

Jack sighed. "Her mother had some family in Pennsylvania, but I don't know if any are left. It's a shame she was sent to Georgia when her mother died, really. Of course, Colonel Buckley's wife was alive then. But Miss Buckley's great-aunt passed on, and the last few years have been difficult for the young lady, alone in the household with the colonel."

Nason shook his head in sympathy.

"Miss Buckley's told me things that made me shudder," Jack said. "The colonel may have been deranged, sir. At any rate, I can say that his behavior had become very erratic."

"Hmm. What will become of the estate? He has children?"

"He had a son who died early in the war, I'm told. But I believe there are daughters. Married daughters."

Captain Nason nodded. "Ah. They'll sort it out then. I see no reason not to let Miss Buckley accompany us to Chattanooga and put her on a train that will take her north, out of the war zone."

Jack hesitated. Was that what he wanted? Marilla had told him she was set on going back to Pennsylvania. Still, he couldn't ignore a pang of regret. "That's kind of you, sir. It's probably best for her."

Jack left him soon after and went in search of Atkins. He found him with his man Mory, brushing down their mules.

"I'm free to talk now," Jack told him.

"Good." Atkins patted his mule's flank and fell into step with Jack. "I have some family news for you. I need to confirm your identity, however, before I discuss details. Would you mind stating the names of your birth parents for me?"

Jack stared at him. "Who are you?"

"Just who I said. Ryland Atkins. I'm employed by a legal firm in Portland, Maine."

Jack sucked in a breath.

"I know you were adopted by Charles and Frances Miller, of Emmaus, Pennsylvania, and that you enlisted in the army with your adoptive brother Edward at the start of the war. I'm very sorry about Ned, by the way. Charles told me what happened to him."

"You've talked to my father?" Jack stopped walking.

"Yes, if you mean Mr. Miller. I met him at his new place of employment in Bridgeport, Connecticut. I've talked with Mr. Strouse at the Telegraph Department too. It's been a long journey, but I've found you at last. I have more to tell you, but not until you confirm your identity for me."

"My father was Benjamin Cooper," Jack said, still staring at him. "My mother was Catherine Rose Cooper. Born in Portland, she was."

Atkins smiled. "That's all I need, then. When we're in a better position to talk, Mr. Miller, I can give you news about the Rose side of your family."

"Tell me now." He expected bad news. Why else would a lawyer be looking for him?

RYLAND LOOKED Jack Miller in the eyes. "My employer, Mr. Turner, was hired to find you by Mrs. Edith Rose—your grandmother. She's a lovely lady."

In Jack's face, he saw a sudden hunger that made his own heart ache.

"You've actually met her, then?"

"Oh, yes. I've been to her house several times to discuss you and your siblings."

Jack reached toward Atkins's collar but drew back his hand. "What about them? Do you know anything about Zeph and Janie?"

Ryland grinned. "I'm happy to tell you, we've found Zeph. It's quite a tale, if you'd like to hear it. The end was most exciting, at least for me. Outlaws and rustlers." He remembered Abigail's face when he recounted the tale to her and her grandmother. She'd hung on his every word, her beautiful blue eyes wide with wonder and admiration, even though Ryland's own part in the tale was not the most heroic. "Your cousin enjoyed hearing it tremendously."

"Cousin?" Jack demanded.

"Oh, yes, Miss Benson."

"Abby?"

"Yes, that's her. A delightful young lady."

Jack fumbled with his shirt collar. "Do you know—" He pulled out a leather thong that hung around his neck. "Does she have one of these?"

Ryland eyed the curious coin, bending a little closer to see it more clearly. He drew back with a grin. "She most certainly does. She and Matt Anderson both—that is, your brother Zephaniah. When they were reunited, they compared them first thing."

"So Zeph went to Maine?"

"Yes. He and his new wife, Rachel."

"He's married." Jack stared at him blankly, as though this was the most astonishing news he'd heard yet.

"She's a wonderful young woman," Ryland said, "and a match for him mentally and spiritually. They plan to combine their fathers' ranches and work them together."

"Ranches."

"Yes. In Colorado."

Jack let out a long, slow breath. "Then he didn't stay in Maine."

"No. He and Mrs. Anderson—his legal name is Matthew Anderson—visited your grandmother for a few weeks in the summer of '63, not long after Gettysburg."

"That long ago. Excuse me, I think I should sit down."

"Of course." Ryland followed him to a large rock, where Jack lowered himself and took several deep breaths.

"You found my brother that long ago, but it took going on two years to find me?"

"The war," Ryland said.

"Of course. I understand the difficulty of travel." Jack shook his head. "It's chaos down here now. But what of Janie? You've looked for her as well?"

"Yes, but the family that adopted her moved, and so far I haven't been able to trace her. Their name is Weaver. I'm hoping —we all are—that when the war's over, I'll be able to get wind of them."

"So—what now?" Jack gazed up at him, those clear blue eyes that all the cousins seemed to have studying him earnestly. "I have to report back to my superiors in Washington."

"Of course." Ryland smiled. "I'd like to go with you, at least as far as Washington. If you have to stay there and go back to work, I'll return to New England." He glanced in the direction of the mules. "Mory asked me if he can go along with me. He'll see his friends in Chattanooga, but he has no living family that he knows of. He wants to go north, where he thinks he'll feel more free somehow, and find work there."

"Do you think he can?"

"Sure. There are jobs now, with so many men off to war or disabled. I think he could find work as a farmhand, or maybe as a teamster or a deliveryman. I told him he could go along with me until he finds a place where he feels comfortable."

"But you're going to Washington."

"I hope that, after they've taken your report, they'll let you go visit your family," Ryland said. "Mrs. Rose and Miss Benson, that is. And Matt said he would try to come back once you or Jane was found. He wants very much to see you."

"Yes, but ..." Jack's eyes lost their focus, and Ryland sensed that he was thinking of something else. Miss Buckley, perhaps? What would become of her when Jack reported back to the War Department and then journeyed on to Maine?

MARILLA WALKED SLOWLY beside Jack as they strolled back and forth that evening, careful to turn around each time they came within sight of a picket. They didn't want any more adventures.

She was glad the captain had agreed to see her out of Georgia and on her way to Pennsylvania. She wanted to get out of the South more than anything. Well, perhaps not quite *anything*.

"What's wrong?" Jack asked. "Aren't you pleased? It's what we wanted."

"Of course I'm pleased. It's just ..." They took a few more steps as she tried to sort out her swirling thoughts.

"Is it your great-uncle? I'm sorry it happened, but really, the way it ended may be the best outcome for you."

"Yes, I'm sure you're right."

"And Vernon," Jack persisted. "He can never bother you again."

"Yes, and I'm glad of that, Jack. But—" She stopped walking and looked up at him. "I'm still scared."

He nodded, his eyes somber. "I think once we're out of here and on our way—really out of danger—things will settle in your mind and you'll feel easier."

"Do you feel easier now about when you were in the fighting? I know you saw some terrible things."

He looked off toward the tents and campfires, and his mouth tightened. "No. I mean, there are nights when I wake up shaking and sweating. But in Washington, I was able to go about my work without thinking about it. I keep busy, and if it bothers me, I pray."

She nodded. His brother's death still weighed on him, the way her mother's haunted her. "What will become of me, Jack? What if I can't find any relatives who'll take me in?"

He didn't seem to have an answer for that. She couldn't deny her disappointment, but what had she expected? One kiss. Was that enough to bind them for life? They hardly knew each other, really. And yet in some ways, she knew him very well. They'd come through horrible times together, but Jack was too honorable to assume that gave him a right to her future.

After a pause, she said, "I suppose I can do as my mother did and find a way to earn a living."

Jack put his hands on her shoulders and turned her to face him. "Marilla, I'm sorry I ... I shouldn't have ..." His face tightened in pain. He wished he hadn't kissed her—or she hadn't kissed him. That was obvious, and her heart sank. "The Millers will always stand by you. If there's no one, you tell me."

"But you're going back to Washington, aren't you?"

"Yes, but Mr. Atkins said my grandmother in Maine wants to see me. She's old, and I haven't seen her since I was a little tyke. Captain Nason said he's sure I can get permission to go and visit her. And it's not like I'm in the army anymore."

"Of course. But I won't know how to contact you." She would be truly alone now. A bleak shadow swept over her.

Jack sighed. "I can get my grandmother's address from Atkins."

"But you probably won't be there long."

"Then write to me at Mrs. Grayson's. Or how about this? I'll give you my parents' address in Connecticut. I'll let them know where I am, wherever I go. If you need help, you let them know. And I'll give Caroline some money. If you write to her, she can send me a message."

Marilla swallowed hard. "All right." It was better than nothing, but she could tell he hadn't harbored the hopes that had sprung up in her.

"Don't worry, Marilla. I'll write to my folks the first evening I'm back in Washington. I'll tell them about you and how you helped me escape. They'll want to thank you."

"They don't need to do that." Tears welled in Marilla's eyes. She felt very small and alone, the way she had when Mrs. Steele put her on the train.

30

A week later, Jack stood with Ryland and Marilla on the platform in Chattanooga, waiting for her train. Marilla was pale, and she jumped every time they heard a whistle. Jack didn't know what to say, so he said nothing, feeling miserable at the thought of her leaving. Was he doing the right thing?

A man couldn't ask a woman to join her life to his on the basis of a brief acquaintance and one moonlit kiss. Was he insane? Yet that was what he wanted to do. How could he, though, with all the uncertainties ahead?

"I think I'll fetch a newspaper," Ryland said. "Perhaps we'll find an advertisement for a job Mory can apply for."

Jack nodded. More likely, Ryland was just making an excuse to leave them alone for a few minutes.

"Are—"

"Marill—"

They both stopped speaking as suddenly as they'd started and stood there staring at each other.

"I beg pardon," Jack said.

"No, forgive me. You go first."

"I was only going to say that I hope you find a place and things go smoothly for you." He couldn't manage to tell her what pressed on his heart. It wouldn't be right, and anyway, she'd made arrangements.

"Well, Mrs. Steele said I could stay with them until I find something."

Jack nodded, glad her telegram to her old neighbor had been answered. "I wish you'd found some kin."

Marilla shook her head. "She didn't know of anyone else, beyond Uncle Hamilton. And you know I won't go to his daughters. I only met one of them while I was in Georgia, and she didn't treat me kindly." She pulled in an anxious breath. "I think I'd die if I had to stay in the South."

"Well ..." He sighed. Watching Marilla set out so frightened and alone was the last thing he wanted. "If I didn't have to go to Washington—"

She smiled then. "Thank you. But you do, and I can't accompany you. There's no money, and Captain Nason was so kind. He got the men in his company to chip in and pay for my ticket, and I suspect most of it came out of his own pocket. I can't ask for more charity."

Jack nodded, wishing miserably that he had the means to provide for her.

She leaned closer. "Of course, I still have Grandmother Buckley's jewelry. Do you think I should sell it and repay him?"

"No, no," he said quickly. "Keep close of that, and only sell it if you absolutely have to."

Tears filled her eyes, and Jack was at a loss. He seized her hand and squeezed it.

"You saved my life, Marilla. I'll always be grateful."

She gave a jerky little laugh. "It's you who saved me. If I hadn't insisted you bring me along—" The tears spilled over, and her mouth skewed. "Oh, Jack, if I hadn't made you bring me, Uncle Hamilton might still be alive."

"And I might not."

They looked gravely into each other's eyes. How could he even have considered leaving her at River Lea?

"Marilla, I—"

The train's harsh whistle split the air, and she jumped.

"I have Mrs. Steele's address. I'll write to you there." He glanced down the track. The train was very near—too near.

"Please do."

"I will." He knew she'd never write first. It wasn't proper. Even so, he'd made sure she had his boardinghouse address and his family's in Connecticut. But he'd never quite been able to talk to her about that kiss and what it meant to him. Did she regret it? Did she feel he'd ruined her? He would never tell another soul—and yet, that kiss was possibly the sweetest moment of his life.

Ryland came from the depot with a jaunty step, a newspaper folded under his arm.

"Write to Caroline soon," Jack shouted over the roar of the approaching train.

She nodded.

"I will. Thank you, Jack. Thank you so much." She turned to shake Ryland's hand, blinking away tears.

"Miss Buckley. Such a pleasure to meet you, though the circumstances were less than ideal."

She smiled. "The same to you, Mr. Atkins."

"I wish you a pleasant journey and happiness at the end of it."

"Bless you." Marilla looked back at Jack, as the engine shrieked past them and the cars slowed with squealing brakes and much puffing of steam.

Jack grabbed her hand again. "Let's not lose touch, Marilla."

"No, let's not."

Time. That was what they needed. Time to get to know each other. But it was the one thing they didn't have.

She picked up the battered carpetbag and walked to the steps of the nearest car, holding out her ticket to the conductor like a seasoned traveler. Suddenly Jack wished he'd bought her a new carryall.

She mounted two steps and turned to look at him.

"Goodbye," he called, and her hand fluttered in a wave. Then she was gone. He shifted his gaze to the windows and searched for her in vain.

A painful lump formed in Jack's throat. What was he doing? He couldn't let her go like this. It wasn't just unkind. She was terrified. And she was taking half his heart.

He was about to stride forward and board the car, intent on pulling her off the train, when the doors closed with a thud. The whistle shrilled and, with a blast of steam, the train began to move.

"Well," Ryland said, "that's that. Let's go and find Mory."

April 10, 1865

DAVID STROUSE LOOKED over the roomful of cryptographers. "Gentlemen, I'm sure you all heard the news last night. General Lee has surrendered. The war is over."

The room was still as a crypt.

"I am told President Lincoln will give a speech tomorrow in front of the White House. Anyone who wishes to be there will be excused from duty here during the morning." Strouse eyed the roomful of men soberly. "Most of you will be released by the end of the week. A few of you will be asked to stay on and help here in the office until things have settled and we know we haven't overlooked any important messages. There will be the job of organizing our records for storage as well."

Jack hoped he wasn't one of those assigned to that boring job. He wanted to get home.

"It's voluntary, of course, but if you'd like to continue working here, please see me after we dismiss."

Jack's thoughts were already many miles to the north. As

they prepared to leave the room, one of his coworkers approached him.

"Are you staying, Miller?"

"No. My father wrote me last week that he's sure I can get a job anytime in Connecticut. They need civilian telegraphers. The lines are being repaired and expanded everywhere."

His friend nodded. "They say we're a hot commodity out West. I'm thinking of heading for California."

Jack held out his hand. "Good luck."

As the room emptied, he made his way to the front to speak to Colonel Strause.

"What can I do for you, Miller?"

"Sir, I've been happy with my position here, but I'd like to leave as soon as possible to rejoin my family."

"Of course. You've been through a lot, and we appreciate your service to the Union. If you like, I can put your resignation in for processing tonight."

"You mean—"

"I hate to see you go, but I understand. If you wish, you can consider this your last day here. Be sure to leave a forwarding address for your final pay."

"Yes, sir." Jack couldn't help grinning as he shook the colonel's hand.

After completing the paperwork, he made his way to Mrs. Grayson's house to give her the news. The landlady was already planning to go hear the President speak the next day with a group of friends.

"Here's your mail." She handed him an envelope in handwriting that must be—he hoped—Marilla's. His pulse tripped.

"Thank you. I'll be leaving you soon. I'm all done at the War Department."

"Oh dear. I shall miss you, Mr. Miller."

"Thank you. I'll miss you too."

He hurried up the stairs to his room and tore open the letter.

After reporting to the War Department in late January, they'd allowed him a brief leave to visit his grandmother in Maine. He'd traveled with Ryland and Mory, who'd found a job with a freighting company.

Since returning to the capital, Jack had written to Marilla twice and had anticipated a reply before now. But he'd promised himself he wouldn't write again until—unless—he heard from her.

Dear Jack,

I'm sorry it has taken me so long to write. You see, I have changed addresses once again. The Steeles really didn't have room for me, and I could tell Mr. Steele was upset with the idea that they had to feed me. I felt I had to sell one piece of jewelry.

As you suggested to me earlier, I took it to a reputable jeweler in Philadelphia. I decided to part with the diamond brooch, as I liked it less than the other pieces. I didn't get as much as I'd hoped, but I decided it was fair. The man apologized and said he would have given me more before the war.

Anyway, I gave the Steeles some money and told them I would move out as soon as I could find a place of my own. Through a relative of Mrs. Steele, I learned of a place at a dress shop in the city. I am learning to improve my stitching, but mostly I am cutting out patterns and pressing seams. Eventually, I'm sure I will be able to call myself a seamstress, and the owner promises my wage will increase then.

Jack, I hope all is going well for you. I cannot say I like the situation I am in, but it is paying for my meals and room in a rather depressing boardinghouse.

Things will get better, I know. I hope this finds you still in

*Washington—although part of me doesn't. I actually hope you've
been able to go north and rejoin your family. I got your first letter
before I left the Steeles, and I'm so glad you got to visit your dear
grandmother in Maine. But I hope our letters don't keep missing
each other! I do hope we can stay in touch.*

Sincerely, Marilla Buckley

At the bottom was her new address.

Jack got out pen and paper at once and sat down to reply. He
had served his last day at the War Department, and his final
wages would be sent to him at his father's house in Connecticut.
He was free to leave Washington.

He thought long and hard over his message and decided to
send a wire to his parents instead. The telegraph office would
close in an hour, so once he'd settled on his economical wording,
he hurried out.

JOB DONE. COMING HOME AFTER ONE STOP. JACK.

That would do it. He was free to leave Washington.

UP AND DOWN the pavement in front of the boardinghouse Jack
paced. The big old house sadly needed maintenance. Marilla was
right—it looked depressing. Even during the war, Mrs. Grayson
had managed to keep her house neat and inviting. Of course,
Jack and some of her other male boarders had helped out with a
bit of painting and repairs. Maybe the landlady here didn't have
nice boarders or the resources needed.

He'd been told he could wait in the parlor, but he hadn't been
able to sit still after so long on the train. After seeking out a
jeweler's establishment, he was back here, walking up and down
the block, watching for Marilla. Suppertime was near, and

dozens of people were returning home from work. The landlady had informed him that Miss Buckley always appeared promptly for supper, which was served at six o'clock sharp, and visitors would be charged fifty cents, thank you.

He'd known at once that he wouldn't eat at the boardinghouse. He'd take Marilla out for a proper dinner. In fact, he'd bought a paper from a newsboy on the corner and studied the advertisements for the name of good restaurant.

At last he spotted her, coming down the walkway along the edge of the street. She was lovely, as ever, and she wore clothes he'd never seen before. The green woolen skirt and darker green cloak covering it suited her, and he wondered if she'd stitched them herself.

The moment when she recognized him, standing there in front of the boardinghouse, sent a thrill through him. Her face lit and she quickened her steps. He marched out to meet her, extending both hands.

"Marilla!"

They met and clasped hands, gazing into each other's eyes, and pedestrians parted to go around them.

"Jack! Why are you here?"

He abandoned propriety and swept her into his arms. "I've been kicking myself ever since I let you leave Chattanooga. I shouldn't have done that."

Now she looked totally confused. "Are you finished working in Washington?"

"Yes. I'm on my way to Connecticut. Please say you'll come with me."

Her eyes widened. "But—"

Before she could protest any further, Jack sank to one knee on the dirty slates, clinging to her hands. "I love you, Marilla. Will you marry me?"

A workman passing them on his way home grinned. "Say yes!"

Marilla shot the man a startled glance, but he kept walking.

Jack grimaced. He should have gone inside with her and done this in the landlady's parlor. Would she flay his heart here in the street? Well, why shouldn't she after he'd embarrassed her in public? He pushed with his toes to rise.

"Yes."

"What?" He froze. "Do you mean it?"

"Do you?" she asked.

"Oh, yes!"

He jumped up and pulled her back into his embrace.

Two women walking past frowned at them and edged around them.

"We're getting married," Jack said, giving them a firm nod.

One of them smiled. "Congratulations."

Marilla pushed against his chest and looked up at him through her lashes.

"We'd best go inside, Jack."

He gulped. "Of course."

Hand in hand, they hurried into the boardinghouse. Jack determined to kiss her thoroughly at the first opportunity.

May 25, 1865
Portland, Maine

"ZEPH!" Jack ran across the platform in the rain and hurled himself at his brother. Laughing, Matt Anderson hugged him then pushed him away and looked him up and down.

"You're taller than I am."

Jack gulped. "I guess I am."

Matt pulled him once more into his arms. "I am *so* glad to see you. And my name is Matt."

"I knew that. Sorry." Jack stared over his brother's shoulder at the beautiful woman standing behind him. In her arms was a wriggling bundle.

"Is that—"

Matt turned and beckoned her forward. "Jack." They both grinned. "This is my wife, Rachel and our daughter, Catherine."

Jack stepped forward and gave Rachel a kiss on the cheek. "Hello, Rachel. I'm so glad to meet you. And Catherine." He gazed down at the blue-eyed baby and blinked hard, afraid his tears would get away. "You named her for Mama."

"We certainly did. Where's Marilla?" Matt asked.

"Abby thought Grandmother shouldn't come out in this weather, so they're at home, and I told Marilla to wait with them. Ryland Atkins is there too."

"Terrific!"

"Oh!" Jack opened the umbrella he'd been carrying. "Sorry. I forgot." He held it over Rachel's head as they turned toward the depot. "I've got a carriage waiting. It's not far."

Matt took the baby, and they hurried through the station and out onto the street.

"Tell us about the wedding," Rachel said once they were settled and the hired driver set the horses and carriage in motion.

"Well, as I said in my letter, we got married last month in the city hall in Philadelphia. We thought it made sense at the time, since we both knew we loved each other and we'd been through so much."

"You'll have to tell us all the details," Matt said. "When you're ready."

"Yeah. But if I'd realized how much Grandmother would have liked to see the wedding, we'd have waited and done it here."

"I'm sure she wanted to see you more than she wanted to see a ceremony," Rachel said.

Matt leaned toward him, rubbing the baby's back as though he'd been doing it all his life. "I wonder if Janie is married."

Jack smiled. "I hope we find out soon."

"You said Ryland is at the house," Matt's eyebrows rose.

"Yes. He has plans for an excursion to try to find the Weavers."

"We'll be praying it doesn't take as long as his attempts to find you," Rachel said.

Jack nodded. "And we'd better start calling her Molly, I guess."

"Do you think so, Elijah?" Matt said with a grin, and Jack laughed.

His brother was back, and God willing, their little sister would be found.

ABOUT THE AUTHOR

Susan Page Davis is the author of more than ninety novels and novellas. Her work has won several awards, including the Carol Award, two Will Rogers Medallions, and two Faith, Hope, & Love Reader's Choice Awards. A Maine native, she now lives in Western Kentucky with her husband, Jim. They are the parents of six grown children and have eleven grandchildren.

Visit her website at: https://susanpagedavis.com.

ALSO BY SUSAN PAGE DAVIS

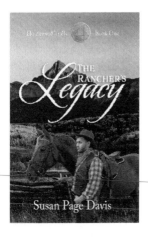

The Rancher's Legacy
Homeward Trails - Book One
Historical Romance

Matthew Anderson and his father try to help neighbor Bill Maxwell when his ranch is attacked. On the day his daughter Rachel is to return from school back East, outlaws target the Maxwell ranch. After Rachel's world is shattered, she won't even consider the plan her father and Matt's cooked up—to see their two children marry and combine the ranches.

Meanwhile in Maine, sea captain's widow Edith Rose hires a private investigator to locate her three missing grandchildren. The children were abandoned by their father nearly twenty years ago. They've been adopted into very different families, and they're scattered across the country. Can investigator Ryland Atkins find them all while the elderly woman still lives? His first attempt is to find the boy now called Matthew Anderson. Can Ryland survive his trip into the wild Colorado Territory and find Matt before the outlaws finish destroying a legacy?

Blue Plate Special

by Susan Page Davis

Book One of the True Blue Mysteries Series

Campbell McBride drives to her father's house in Murray, Kentucky, dreading telling him she's lost her job as an English professor. Her father, private investigator Bill McBride, isn't there or at his office in town. His brash young employee, Nick Emerson, says Bill hasn't come in this morning, but he did call the night before with news that he had a new case.

When her dad doesn't show up by late afternoon, Campbell and Nick decide to follow up on a phone number he'd jotted on a memo sheet. They learn who last spoke to her father, but they also find a dead body. The next day, Campbell files a missing persons report. When Bill's car is found, locked and empty in a secluded spot, she and Nick must get past their differences and work together to find him.

Ice Cold Blue

by Susan Page Davis

Book Two of the True Blue Mysteries Series

Campbell McBride is now working for her father Bill as a private
investigator in Murray, Kentucky. Xina Harrison wants them to find out
what is going on with her aunt, Katherine Taylor. Katherine is a rich,
reclusive author, and she has resisted letting Xina visit her for several
years. Xina arrived unannounced, and Katherine was upset and didn't
want to let her in. When Xina did gain entry, she learned Katherine
fired her longtime housekeeper. She noticed that a few family
heirlooms previously on display have disappeared. Xina is afraid
someone is stealing from her aunt or influencing her to give them her
money and valuables. True Blue accepts the case, and the investigators
follow a twisting path to the truth.

COMING SOON FROM SUSAN PAGE DAVIS

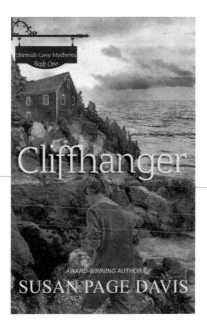

Cliffhanger

by Susan Page Davis

Book One of the Skirmish Cove Mysteries

Coming February 1, 2022

The Novel Inn's reopening goes smoothly until a guest vanishes. The new owners prepare for their first large group—a former squad of cheerleaders meeting for a reunion. Things go awry when the head cheerleader fails to show up. Sisters Kate and Jillian, the innkeepers, enlist the help of their brother Rick, a local police officer. They're confident the missing woman will be found, but they soon learn to expect the unexpected, even during a walk on the beach.

MORE HISTORICAL FICTION FROM SCRIVENINGS PRESS

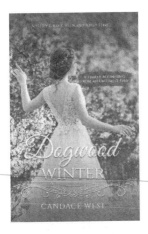

Dogwood Winter

by Candace West

Valley Creek Redemption Series

Book Three

He is walking away while she is fighting to walk.

After a springtime swim, Ella Steen is stricken with a dire illness, leaving her without the use of her legs. Meanwhile, Dr. George Curtis, the man she secretly loves, faces ruin. For over a year, the crusty New York City bachelor and vivacious spinster have exchanged dozens of letters and formed a wary friendship.

Neither are willing to open their hearts completely. Until they face each other. The past looms between them, however. Does George still love another or is his heart completely free?

A trip to Valley Creek holds the answers. Instead, when George and Ella arrive, they encounter obstacles that force other truths to the surface. Is George brave enough to confront what he fled in New York?

Can Ella confess why she hates dogwood winters? Will their hearts survive?

If only their pasts would keep out of the present.

Beyond These War-torn Lands

by Cynthia Roemer

Wounded Hearts Book One

While en route to aid Confederate soldiers injured in battle near her home, Southerner Caroline Dunbar stumbles across a wounded Union sergeant. Unable to ignore his plea for help, she tends his injuries and hides him away, only to find her attachment to him deepen with each passing day. But when her secret is discovered, Caroline incurs her father's wrath and, in turn, unlocks a dark secret from the past which she is determined to unravel.

After being forced to flee his place of refuge, Sergeant Andrew Gallagher fears he's seen the last of Caroline. Resolved not to let that happen, when the war ends, he seeks her out, only to discover she's been sent away. When word reaches him that President Lincoln has been shot, Drew is assigned the task of tracking down the assassin. A chance encounter with Caroline revives his hopes, until he learns she may be involved in a plot to aid the assassin.

Coming Home to Mercy

By Michelle De Bruin

Coming Home Series - Book One

Wealthy and sociable Margaret Millerson has always thought of her brother's Chicago mansion as her home. But when she receives the telephone call that her daughter has given birth to twins three weeks ahead of the expected due date, Margaret must leave her comfortable home, her family, and her friends to travel out of state. While she is helping her daughter care for the infants, Margaret becomes reacquainted with the town's doctor, Matthew Kaldenberg.

Dr. Matthew Kaldenberg stays busy caring for the health of the citizens of his small town. His profession offers him daily practice in defeating death, his greatest enemy. During the twenty years since losing his own wife and baby in childbirth, Matthew has saved his money for the purchase of a flying machine. But when Matthew takes Margaret for flights on his biplane, he learns that his dreams of rising above the griefs and losses of his past come with a cost. He doesn't want to lose the trust of the people he cares about most, or the chance at a relationship with Margaret.

Both Matthew and Margaret must make difficult decisions to hold on to the love they have discovered. Will Matthew's heart recover from sorrow? Will Margaret find her true home?

Scrivenings
PRESS
Quench your thirst for story.
www.ScriveningsPress.com

Stay up-to-date on your favorite books and authors with our free e-newsletters.

ScriveningsPress.com